THE CURTAIN

IT BEGINS

DAVID T. MADDOX

Made for Grace
PUBLISHING

Made for Grace Publishing
P.O. Box 1775
Issaquah, WA 98027

The Curtain: It Begins

Designed by DeeDee Heathman

Scripture taken from the New American Standard Bible, © 1960, 1963, 1968, 1971, 1972, 1973, 1975, 1977 by the Lockman Foundation. Used by permission.

Library of Congress Cataloging-in-Publication data

Maddox, David T., date,
The Curtain: It Begins / David T. Maddox.
p. cm.
ISBN-13: 9781613398654 (pbk.)
LCCN: 2016906538

To contact the publisher please email
service@MadeforSuccess.net or call +1 425 657 0300.

Made for Grace Publishing is an imprint of Made for Success, inc.

Printed in the United States of America

After a legal career in both Texas and Arizona that spanned over 40 years as a civil litigator, God called David to leave his law practice and work full time in discipleship for the ministry organization Time to Revive. That call is really the fruit of decades of prayer for revival and teaching God's word, writing discipleship materials and seeking to make disciples. David married Janet Whitehead in 1976 and they currently minister together from their Phoenix home. God has blessed them with four children and thus far seven grandchildren.

THE CURTAIN IS dedicated to four people who have had most influenced my life and ministry over these many decades. There have obviously been many others that God has used, but these people have changed my life and I want to acknowledge them and affirm how God has used them.

RICHARD OWEN ROBERTS – In my life Mr. Roberts has been like "the Bookseller" in this story – the one who opened God's word and revealed hidden truth. He taught me about revival and awakening and showed me what it means to walk without compromise at a high cost.

DR. HENRY BLACKABY – Henry (as he prefers to be called) opened my eyes to what it means to walk intimately with the Lord – to hear Him speak, to discern what He has said, to see Him working around me. He has encouraged me in the way of obedience, made me aware of the cost of my obedience to those I love, and so much more.

KYLE & LAURA MARTIN – This couple opened my eyes to what we are called to in the Great Commission, what it means to put no limits on the Holy Spirit, the importance of the Jewish people in end times, what it means to be prepared for the return of Jesus, what it means to walk in faith in total dependence on God, and so much more. Time to Revive, the ministry they began, is the only revival ministry I have encountered that doesn't' just study revival or pray for revival, but actively seeks to gather churches together in revival. I have been privileged to be a small part of this ministry for the last five years. Here God is mightily at work.

JANET WHITEHEAD MADDOX – My bride, my completion, the one God uses to keep my focus and to confront me when I get off the path. No man was ever more blessed than I have been in sharing my life with her, our kids and grandkids – sharing our relationship with God. To minister together with the same heart has been the joy of my life.

ACKNOWLEDGMENTS

Writing a book is a long journey which for me began in 2007 when the Lord inspired me to try and take the truth of Scripture about the invisible conflict that goes on around us and picture it in such a way that people could have a better understanding of this reality which affects their daily life. My attempt has in some cases been futile, but hopefully what is shared within the pages of the book is Biblically accurate and will open eyes to help answer the why questions for much of what we face today.

Many people have encouraged and helped me along the way. In 2007, Matt and Kim Clark read each chapter as the book progressed giving me valuable input and perspective as the story and characters developed. As a trial lawyer, I was used to telling stories and being sure that the stories matched the evidence, but as this book continued the characters took over the story and drove it in surprising directions. Later others including Mel Sauder and Jerry Jagoda would read revisions, there were seven in all, and similarly gave input and encouragement.

For me, the "hero" in this process has been my editor, Catherine Barrack whose insight and discernment was invaluable. Her maturity as a Believer enabled her to ask the right questions to be sure that the story did not go beyond what was Biblically possible as have others who attempted to write similar stories. Her skill and sensitivity gave new life to some of the characters at critical points in the story and gave me insight that only a third person reading the story can give. It is a much-improved story because of her partnership in the process.

Special thanks must also go to Buzz Leonard, who introduced me to Bryan Heathman and Made for Success Publishing. They quickly understood what I am trying to do and have been helpful at each stage of the process working patiently with a first-time author.

Ultimate thanks go to the Lord, who despite me having stage four cancer has enabled me to finish the book in between this past year of chemo treatments. I am hopeful that the book will bless the reader even as writing it has blessed and taught me. If it does bless you, please share it with others.

CONTENTS

About The Author. iii

Dedication v

Acknowledgments vii

Introduction. 1

Chapter 1: A Glimpse Beyond 3

Chapter 2: Conflicting Agendas .11

Chapter 3: First Impressions. 25

Chapter 4: Meetings That Matter 35

Chapter 5: The Invisible Conflict Intensifies 49

Chapter 6: Death and Breakfast .58

Chapter 7: The Bookseller Answers. 66

Chapter 8: The Forces of Light Engage 75

Chapter 9: The Power of the Right Question. 85

Chapter 10: Differing Responses. 94

Chapter 11: Masquerading as an Angel of Light 103

Chapter 12: Paul Dreams Again .113

Chapter 13: Darkness vs. Light. .122

Chapter 14: Preparations Continue. 133

Chapter 15: The Plan 142

Chapter 16: Dreams and Deception 151

Chapter 17: Events Accelerate. 162

Chapter 18: Eyes Begin to Open. 172

Chapter 19: A Grisly Mystery 181

Chapter 20: Discoveries 190

Chapter 21: Preparations for the Morrow 199

Chapter 22: Before the Storm 208

Chapter 23: Deception Succeeds Again. 218

Chapter 24: Unexpected Consequences. 228

The MD Chronicles- Book II 237

Chapter 1: The Announcement – The Response 239

Notes 249

"We look not to the things that are seen but to the things that are unseen. For the things that are seen are transient, but the things that are unseen are eternal."

—2 Corinthians 4:18

"WHY ME?" OR "why not me?" are questions which seem to pervade life for all of us. Much of what we face at times seems unfair and totally beyond our control. Often our best efforts are not enough, or we succeed when we know we should have failed. Is there some purpose at work in our lives beyond mere chance? Could there be something beyond our control, something of which we may be completely unaware that influences the decisions we make and arranges the circumstances we face? If there were, that would provide the answer to much that cannot be explained in our lives.

The Bible speaks of parallel worlds – one *visible*, the other *invisible*. They are said to exist separately, but not independently. We are told that in our lifetime we occupy the physical world, the place of flesh and blood. The other world is described as being spiritual and is inhabited by eternal beings invisible to us who are in constant conflict over control of the physical world and those who live there. The frightening thing for us who live in the physical world is that if the Bible is true, the invisible can influence us and the events that affect our lives without us even being aware of their activities. When we die, we leave the physical world and occupy our place in the spiritual world, having become one of the invisible. The answer to the question "what happens then" is beyond the subject of this book, although our story will picture some who make the transfer from one world to the next. For them, the answer will be obvious, as will the reason for their future placement.

The author asks that as you read this book, you be willing to assume that the Bible is true and that what it says about the visible and invisible is, in fact, the reality in which we live. You are invited to consider what you would see if the curtain which separates the visible from the invisible were suddenly opened, revealing the conflict, tactics and methods of the opposing forces – and how they actually impact your life.

The reader is cautioned that although this is a work of fiction, it often crosses the line to truth if what the Bible teaches is true – not in personalities or in the events described, but in how those events would be viewed if we could actually see everything that happened as it happened in both the visible and invisible worlds simultaneously. For those willing to search for the truth about what really affects their life, this book will be an adventure.

As a reader, you will also no doubt find descriptions that may be personal as your eyes are opened to the forces said to be daily contesting over you. It is the author's hope that the events detailed herein, and the characters' response to those events, will help you to better understand the biblical view of the reality of the world in which we live, so that if it is true, you can live in response to what is and not be a victim of what it only seems to be.[1]

Draw your own conclusions, but be open-minded to the reality of the invisible. It unquestionably exists and impacts everything we do.

CHAPTER 1

A GLIMPSE BEYOND

"… the god of this world has blinded the minds of the unbelievers, to keep them from seeing.…"

—*2 Corinthians 4:4*

Wednesday, January 30 – MD minus 116 days

PAUL STOOD WITH Samantha, holding her hand, drying her tears – and it was cold. It is always cold in Williams in January, depressing at times waiting for spring and signs of life. But this was not about life. This was about death, and there had been a lot of that lately.

There it was, just in front of them, only a few feet away – an expensive, overdressed metal box containing all that was left of Taylor Jones, Samantha's father, the latest in a seemingly endless stream of victims of senseless violence and terror. He was the thirty-eighth person shot at or killed by an unknown shooter. Once Pastor Holt had his say, they could get out of the open and the box would then be planted six feet down in a concrete vault that the family had been assured would protect the coffin for at least 100 years. *Get real*, thought Paul as if anyone present would be around in a hundred years to test their warranty. The foolishness of the guarantee was matched only by the seeming foolishness of what was now being said about Taylor Jones. A man of the cloth trying to comfort and make sense in a theater of the absurd.

Paul Phillips was no genius, but he also was no fool. His life had changed much over the three years he had been attending Williams College. Now with the reality that the so-called "American dream" was mostly a mirage, he had lowered his expectations and simply was looking to complete his business degree and get a decent job of some nature which would enable him to support a family and pay off student loans. Having come from small town America, his choice of Williams College was intentional. He liked the conservative reputation of the school, its academic quality and the opportunity to interface with the facility. He was serious but discouraged and recent events only added to that discouragement.

After the family shared, Pastor Holt said the usual things about Taylor Jones being "a good man" who "worked hard" and "cared for his family." His death was a "great tragedy" and no one could know why "God allowed" him to be killed by the sniper, but we could be assured "that he was now at rest in a far better place." The Bible reading was from that passage where Jesus said, "Do not let your hearts be troubled … in my Father's house are many rooms … I am going there to prepare a place for you. And if I go and prepare a place for you, I will come back and take you to be with me that you may be where I am."[2] Good words but Paul had to wonder if they really applied to the petty old man in the box.

Taylor Jones had been a church regular at First Christian Church of Williams since he moved to the city 28 years ago, but if you tried to do a business deal with him on a Monday, you had better count your fingers after you shook his hand. He was a classic example of the problems Paul was studying in his business ethics class at the Williams College MBA program. Did he really want to be in business like Taylor Jones? Was dishonesty really what it took to be successful?

Pastor Holt knew, even as he spoke, that Taylor Jones took care of one of his families, but ignored the first, and the first was Samantha's family – Samantha, her mom and two brothers. Those he had abandoned when he sought "the desires of his heart" and forgot the commitment of his youth.

The other family was also present and Paul held his tongue but hoped that God, if there was a God, had a higher standard for residence in this "Father's house" than that evidenced by Taylor Jones' life or the words of the lying preacher. In his opinion, the religious hypocrite deserved a different address, though the murder still troubled him.

Suddenly, his view began to change. It was as if a mist was falling before him and as it fell, it slowly began to reveal a view unlike anything he had seen before. Paul struggled to focus as his eyes began to take in the scene. High over the cemetery, Paul saw what appeared to be wisps of darkness, multiple figures of varying sizes with fiery orange eyes, pitch black skin and huge hands with enormously long fingers. They seemed to be gathering together in deference to one who held a pen and book. They were laughing and celebrating, although he heard no sound. The largest one handed something that looked like papers to smaller ones who immediately departed in different directions as if being sent on separate missions, each with a definite purpose.

Turning away in horror, he looked back at those standing in the crowd before the coffin. For a moment, it was as if he had been removed from the cemetery, suspended above, and was looking down on the scene. He saw large dark beings standing behind most of the people in the crowd. Their great hands rested on the heads of the people, their long fingers seemingly piercing the skulls as if they were cradling the brains of the people in their fingers. The eyes of each one of the people they touched were crusted over and the palms of their great hands covered the ears, yet the people seemed not to notice the presence of the wisps or the limits and control being exercised over what they could see or hear.[3]

Suddenly Paul saw a pair of great yellow hands reaching toward his head and his eyes began to itch. Screaming in terror, he awoke. And then the Curtain closed.

A City Under Siege

Fear is real — conscious — cutting like a knife. It is an ever-present force paralyzing its victims, and all those now living in Williams were victims. For 128 days they had lived with a reign of terror that began with the shooting of John Sample as he sought to fill his car with gas at the

Chevron on 6th and Main. The latest was last Thursday when Taylor Jones was killed as he walked from the parking garage to his office on the other side of town. Paul had attended the funeral, but it was only later that more of what had occurred there began to be revealed to him and him alone through a disquieting dream.

For over four months the city had been under furtive attack. Thirty-eight people had been killed or wounded, ranging from a five-year-old in a preschool playground to a senior citizen in a church parking lot. What made the situation so frightening was the absence of any clear pattern, just death or injury randomly inflicted by an unknown assailant or assailants, whenever and wherever they chose. Sometimes it was only one victim, sometimes more, and thankfully, on occasion, the shooter missed. To date, people had been shot at near schools, churches, homes, parks, banks, gas stations, and grocery stores. Shots had been fired at people driving their cars, walking, running, bike riding or simply sitting outside in a park. No place or activity seemed safe in Williams.

Fear was beginning to take its toll. People were now openly contemplating leaving the city. Among those who remained, there was a developing bunker mentality. Outside activities of any nature were minimized. Businesses were hurting as both customers and employees increasingly stayed away from any public place. Some parents were now keeping their children home from school.

The only businesses that were not suffering were those who sold firearms. The level of anger and outrage was rising. There had already been shootings of innocents as frightened residents fired at sounds in the night or early morning. The situation was getting out of hand. Something had to change – fast. The violence had to end, and the people had to believe they were safe.

Headquartered in room 107 at 1632 Washington Avenue was a group of four men and one woman who were charged with this task. There, throughout the ordeal, they had pored over files and notes, interviews, pictures and forensic evidence looking for anything which would provide a clue that could lead to the capture of the sniper(s) and end the reign of terror. They had used computer models and experts, other law enforcement agencies, and even mediums, all to no avail. They had sought national help including requests for the use of spy satellite imagery and photographs to help find the sniper or his means of transportation after an attack. They had sought security camera videos following attacks seeking to identify anything that would lead to the sniper. It was almost as if a phantom force motivated, protected and controlled this human killing machine, inflicted for some unknown reason on this small Midwest American college town.

The appointed team leader was Detective Pete Samson, an organization man. He left no stone unturned, using task forces and division of labor to cover all the bases. It sounded trite, but it worked by forcing accountability on each member of the team who had a single responsibility, leaving him in control, able to look at the big picture and plan, rather than simply react to the shooter's next move.

"Listen up. I just got back from a meeting with the mayor, and we have to change our focus. This thing has gotten crazy. The governor is threatening to call up the National Guard for additional manpower and institute a curfew. We are going to lose control of this investigation if we cannot find the sniper quickly or calm the public and buy some time. The politicians seem to be more concerned about their survival in office than they are about dead people in the streets. We have become the target. Expect more public criticism. It's coming. They are looking for someone to blame and that someone is us!"

"Whatever happened to a simple police investigation," Troy Dallas asked in frustration and disgust.

"There is nothing simple about this investigation," answered Inspector Todd Wilson, the old man on the team. "We've followed procedure and worked through all the logical means to identify the killer, and we are no closer today than when we began. People are afraid with good reason. This sniper seems to kill simply for the pleasure of killing. He doesn't care who he kills. How can we stop someone like that? He's inhumane. He kills indiscriminately. He even targets children. What kind of monster does that?"

The marker board was out, and Officer Sally Johnson wrote two words in capital letters – WHAT NEXT. "Enough already," she said. "Let's go to work and stop this killer."

Located less than a half a mile from room 107, the shooter was considering how to proceed and how she wanted this all to end. She felt safe, protected and concealed in her garage apartment close to the campus. The key for her was the garage. It provided a place where she could do in secret everything necessary to prepare for her next move. She waited for inspiration. The specific target didn't matter. What she was looking for was surprise – effect – then escape. Hit hard and be smart. It was a game, like the video games she had grown so accustomed to over the past few years. She liked that the games had become more realistic as technology developed. It made what she was doing more fun.

Beyond the sight of human eyes, inspiration arrived in the form of one of the messengers sent from Taylor Jones' funeral. There was a smile on the dark wisp's bright yellow face as the message was delivered to another whose huge hands and long fingers dug deep into the shooter's head. Message delivered. His master would be pleased. Soon another of these human creatures would perish.

The Target of Darkness

Argon waited for each of the dark wisps to return from their assignment. His thoughts were interrupted by one such excited being who asked carefully, "Sir, what is the greater plan? Why did you send those messages?"

"And who gave you permission to ask?" he responded in anger at being interrupted. "Have you suddenly become one with authority?"

"No, Sir," came the answer deferentially.

"What is your name, little one?" Argon asked.

"I am called Zaccur."

"A noble name with history I know," Argon replied and paused for effect. "I will answer you although you have no right to know. The messages are for those who hold influence over human instruments we can use to advance the Dark Master's plan. Consider the shooter. We protect and guide her; we confuse those who seek her, and we create fear and anger in the hearts of the masses. That you should have expected. The goal hasn't changed. The Dark Master hates all made in the image of the Enemy, the one they call God."

"Yes, but there is more here than that. I have seen others and have heard them talking," Zaccur continued pushing for information despite the danger.

"What makes you think I know the Dark Master's plan? I merely rule a city under other authority. The Dark Master rules the earth."

"You had to know something to direct the messages," Zaccur probed.

This one is both smart and ambitious. A dangerous combination, Argon thought.

"The Dark Master's target is not simply this city and those the shooter may be persuaded to kill before she is ultimately killed. It is what we have been waiting for two hundred years, the end of arrogant America – the so-called "land of the free and home of the brave," the nation that proclaims "in God we trust" on its money and "one nation under God" in its pledge. America, the "Christian nation." It's all a lie, but many people in the world believe it. America will be humbled and then destroyed. They will crawl and beg for the end. And Williams has a special place in the Dark Master's plan – we will not fail."

"Come and I will show you some of what I have been entrusted with," Argon said arrogantly as he led and Zaccur followed, flying through the sky unseen by human eyes.

"Look now," Argon said as they descended through a wall to enter a building where a meeting was in progress. "The one talking is called Sam Will. He is a retired truck driver with a high opinion of himself. He thinks he is the inspiration behind an organization they named the Citizens' Militia, a name they took from some old document. This bunch wants to organize the gun owners in Williams to act as a private law enforcement group to stop the shooter. They have given up on the police. The possibilities for mischief are enormous."

"Let me show you another," and they moved toward an old rent house off of Bell and 17th which they entered with equal ease. "Those you see here were trained along the Afghan and Pakistan border in the fine art of killing masses of people. They will be most useful. They are but a test of a strategy which will be inflicted on the whole country as part of a larger plan. There are other groups forming in other cities, and even now many corresponding trained Jihadists are crossing the Mexican border to advance the Dark Master's plan. It is not clear to me what the others are to do, but I know the intent is that together they will deal the United States a blow from which it can never fully recover," Argon spoke with joy and passion.

"Respectfully, Sir, wasn't that what September 11th was supposed to do?" Zaccur asked.

"September 11th was to humble America by destroying national symbols, killing masses as well as some of its elected leaders. It ended up embarrassing America, but only 3,000 died, and our instruments missed the targeted leaders. This is nothing like that. That was for show; this is to finish what we have been trying to do since the beginning. Just wait and watch. We won't fail this time."

Argon smiled, anticipating what was coming, excited at his part and loving the attention of the little one. His instructions had been obeyed fully. The messages, when delivered, had resulted in multiple long fingers digging deeper into skulls, the brain of each target being cradled as direction was planted in their consciousness so that they believed it was inspiration from their own thoughts and ideas. The scales over the eyes kept them from seeing anything their Keeper did not want them to see while the great hands covering their ears kept them from hearing anything other than what their Keeper wanted them to hear. As long as the Curtain remained closed, no one was the wiser and nothing in the physical would appear out of the ordinary.

CHAPTER 2

CONFLICTING AGENDAS

"For the desires of the flesh are against the Spirit, and the desires of the Spirit are against the flesh, for these are opposed to each other...."

—*Galatians 5:17*

Thursday, January 31 — MD Minus 115 days

THE CURTAIN HAD not been fully opened for Paul Phillips as he slept. He had seen much in his dream which had not been apparent when he attended the funeral. Much of forces of darkness present at the funeral had been revealed in the dream, but he had drawn a wrong conclusion. He cried out in fear at what he saw because to him, it appeared that he was in great danger when in fact he was being delivered and shielded from the influence of his Keeper, who had influenced his thoughts and controlled how he saw things for many years. Reality is rarely as it seems.

Had Paul been able to see the complete scene of which he was apart, he would have witnessed the forces of light also present, but in reduced numbers, for there were few servants of the light present that day at Taylor

Jones' funeral. As he viewed the crowd looking back from the coffin, he would have seen some who radiated light from within as if they were inhabited by light[4] – a fact which he would not have understood, even as he did not understand the dark beings he could see. Those few, although in the presence of all the mass of Keepers, had no huge yellow hands resting on their heads or long fingers piercing their skulls with direction from the Dark Master. They received their direction from the light inside, from the Holy Spirit[5], who obtains the messages He transmits directly from the Father, another name for God whom the forces of darkness call the "Enemy." What had actually occurred was that a Keeper's great hands and long fingers were removed from Paul's skull by Simeon, a Guardian with the forces of light. It was Simeon's strong arms that forced the Keeper away. Paul's momentary and partial view behind the Curtain revealed the conflict between Simeon and the Keeper as the Keeper's hands were forcibly removed from Paul's head. Paul also didn't realize that something like scales had fallen from his eyes and that his ears were now opened because the Keeper's hands no longer covered them. He could now see, hear and seek to understand, rather than simply accept the Dark Master's steady diet of deception. The Father had chosen him to be a searcher and had placed within him a passion for understanding what he had seen and experienced, and that made him a very dangerous human being to the forces of darkness – and search he did.

Argon had not missed the events following the funeral. The Keeper assigned to Paul had blazed across the sky to report Simeon's actions. Some of the messages which had been sent were intended to deal with this new threat directly. The Dark Master had made it clear that a searcher was not to be feared unless the search could not be directed to those living under their influence. The most logical possibilities had been sent detailed messages on the "truth" the Dark Master wanted Paul to find. Since Paul's chest did not reveal the light inside, there was still great hope that he would continue to be a useful instrument for advancing the Dark Master's agenda for Williams and ultimately for America. The coming days would determine much.

Argon had been promoted to head the Dark Master's forces in Williams for a reason. He had studied the human creatures since the rebellion and knew what to expect from one without the light inside. Paul's first inquiry would be to his girlfriend, Samantha. She had been prepared by her Keeper. Paul was unknowingly walking into a trap – the first of what Argon hoped would be many leading him back to the camp from which he had been momentarily freed. His Keeper stayed close, waiting for the opportunity to again seize the place of influence, but for now, Simeon, his Guardian barred the way. Unknowingly Paul had been freed at the funeral, but freed for what?

The plan for the conversation with Samantha was simple and followed what the Dark Master had worked from the start in that garden of the Enemy's long ago. It was easy then to cause the first two human creatures to respond to emotion. They reacted to their perceived needs, and in reality, planted desires. It was all a lie, but that didn't matter because their feelings told them it was true, and when feelings rule, anything is possible. Without much effort, the Dark Master had turned that first woman called Eve to believe that the Enemy had lied to her and that she needed knowledge to be free of dependence on the Enemy. In those moments, she actually came to believe that she could replace the Enemy and become like Him. The man, Adam, stood there in silence doing nothing because of his feelings for the woman and ultimately joined her in her rebellion.[6] He didn't want to offend her. Peace with the woman was more important to him than the fact he was offending the Enemy.

The human creatures had not changed over the centuries. If anything, it had gotten easier. Samantha would be offended, hurt and ultimately lash out at her boyfriend. The target would feel guilt and desire to change to please the object of his affections and lust. The search would end quickly with influence reestablished. At least, that was the plan, and most of the time the plan worked.

Samantha was hurting. She was possessed by feelings of guilt and anger. Anger at her now-dead father who had not been there for her and guilt for the anger she felt. She felt a desperate need to be held and reassured by Paul for he, unlike her dad, had always been there for her since they began dating at the end of the fall semester of their sophomore year. Their friendship, which had blossomed into much more over the years, was her anchor.

What she saw was not what she expected. Paul was obviously agitated, troubled and tired. Was it reality or was it just a dream – a nightmare? He didn't know. It seemed real. He knew what he had seen and was afraid to close his eyes. He didn't want to see the dark creatures again. He was afraid they were coming for him. Samantha saw it even in the midst of all she was feeling. "Paul, what's wrong? You look terrible," was all she knew to say. Her great need within was being replaced by a desire to meet Paul's.

He trembled and reached out for her. Samantha held him close and waited for him to speak. She wanted to reassure him but had no way of knowing how because she didn't know what was wrong. She had never seen him this way. It was disarming for she truly cared for him.

In a few moments, the trembling ceased and Paul spoke in an almost hushed voice, timidly, "Samantha, did you see anything unusual at your Dad's funeral? Did you see something standing behind the people or near me?"

"Like what, Paul? Did I see what?" Samantha responded.

It was as if a dam broke as the dream poured out of Paul. He trembled again as he described the great yellow hands with the large fingers reaching out for him to surround his head and pierce his skull. His description and obvious fear convinced Samantha that he had seen something.

Argon was alarmed. How could this human creature have seen the Keepers? They are spirit, nothing about them is physical. They should be invisible to this human. He thought he knew what was going to happen, at least, he knew the plan, but something was wrong. Already Samantha's reactions were not as had been inspired. Then he saw it, another Guardian from the forces of light had been pushing a Keeper's hands away from Samantha's head. Influence had been lost, at least temporarily. Why did the Enemy care about these two? They were totally unchurched and had never expressed any interest in religion except to criticize those who claimed to be religious.

"Did you see anything around me?" she asked, now concerned about herself.

"I was not looking at you when I saw the dark things," Paul responded. "I don't know if they were after you. It all happened so fast. I was so frightened that I awoke screaming almost as quickly as I saw them."

"Look, I have no clue what you saw or what the dream means, but if it were me, I would try to dismiss the whole thing as a bad dream and just forget it. It can't be true."

"But it isn't that simple," Paul explained. "It was real. I know it was real."

"If that is what you really believe then you better find someone who can help you work through this and find some answers."

"Who can I ask that won't think I am nuts?"

"Perhaps Professor Thompson could help. He seems to be someone who would listen and who knows history well enough to give some perspective to this. If it is real, you can't be the first. If it isn't, then maybe he can put your mind at rest. Listen, Paul, I need you. You have to get beyond this."

Argon smiled in agreement. "Professor Thompson has been very helpful over the years, and he has already been well prepared for this conversation. I wonder if Chaplain Forest will be next," Argon said to the seemingly ever-present Zaccur. "Watch this. The answers Professor Thompson will give won't be enough to end the search, but they will put doubt in the human's mind. Forest is nothing. He won't have answers either, and even if he did, he would be afraid to say. Forest is a people pleaser — no danger to the Dark Master's agenda. We don't even need the inspiration of a Keeper. He is of little use to either side," he said.

Argon was still surprised by the action of the Enemy. Why had this human creature's spiritual eyes been partially opened in a dream? What possible purpose could the Enemy have for these two? The Dark Master must be advised immediately. They cannot be allowed to obstruct his greater plan. He would suggest that perhaps they should inspire the shooter to remove these two. He quickly wrote another note, which he entrusted to Zaccur, who immediately sped away to carry the message.

Paul hugged Samantha one more time and then left for the campus to find Professor Thompson.

Others at Work

There were meetings all across the city that afternoon and evening with very different agendas and varying participants. At 1632 Washington Avenue, Officer Sally Johnson had completed her work on the marker board summarizing the investigators' answer to her "WHAT NEXT" question. There were five entries which would guide the five task forces in leading the effort to stop the shooter and restore some level of peace and confidence to the city. They were:

1. Change the public perception of safety
2. Public involvement – real and perceived
3. Expand the investigation – draw on other law enforcement resources
4. Rapid response to future attacks
5. Damage control – contain the problem

It was a good list – a challenging agenda, thought Detective Samson. He liked that it attacked the entire problem, not simply focusing on catching the shooter. This problem had gone well beyond a single criminal spree and must be addressed as such. The order of priority was realistic. The most significant problem was public panic and fear; but they had to keep in mind the potential for expansion as others sought to join in, copy or use the opportunity to advance another even more violent agenda. And they still had to do whatever it takes to catch this killer.

In dividing up the responsibilities, Samson assigned himself number 3, the actual investigation. This was where he belonged by experience and where he wanted to work. He assigned Sally Johnson to number 1, change the public perception because she had a take charge personality that engendered confidence and was good before people. The other responsibilities were divided among Troy Dallas, Greg Petersen and Todd Wilson, the remaining team members.

Dallas was assigned number 2, public involvement, and was directed to organize an effort to use the public to both help with the investigation and prevent future attacks. The goal was to shift the public's focus from fear of the shooter to working together to catch the shooter. Petersen, a former Army ranger, was assigned number 4, the rapid response team, and was directed to organize swat teams to respond immediately 24/7 with all possible force to any additional attacks. If they could kill the shooter, it would send a message to the public and to those who might be considering a similar reign of terror. Samson had no interest in catching the shooter and having to have to deal for years with lawyers, courts and the press who would victimize and excuse the shooter's conduct. He had seen enough of that over the years. This time, he wanted a graphic example of immediate justice – an eye for an eye. They needed a body.

Wilson, the old man, was assigned number 5, containment, and was directed to utilize all available sources of intelligence, informants, wiretaps, warrantless searches, profiling, preventive arrests, detention, liberal interrogation techniques, etc. to address potential future threats now. The last thing the public would tolerate was more violence. If individual rights had to suffer for a time, that was a small price to pay to prevent future violence and protect the public. They would buy into it. To live with a sense of safety was more important than to be free.

The five agreed to put together their own teams, to flesh out what would be required for each functional area and to gather again tomorrow afternoon to share their plans. They were encouraged. Although they had been working furiously for months now, the political intervention of the mayor and governor provided the backdrop on which to base a total "whatever it takes" effort. The gloves were off. This had to end, and they had just been given the freedom to bring it to an end whatever the cost.

Keeping this investigation under his control was important to the future of the Dark Master's plans, so Argon took the time to unknowingly join the five. Already present were four Keepers and numerous Tempters on assignment. The Tempters were another of the dark wisps who were able to attach themselves to the human creatures by their invitation. As silly as it seemed, Argon thought, the human creatures' fleshly desires and wants provided the opportunity to influence them in ways that could ultimately lead to their destruction.[7] For those under the influence of a Keeper, there was no limitation on what could be done once temptation was accepted, and Tempters were not limited to those under the influence of a Keeper. When a temptation was accepted by a servant of the Enemy, at a minimum the Tempter would be able to limit their usefulness and cause them to have difficulty hearing the voice inside.[8]

Tempters went by the names of their temptations, and there were multiple millions of them with the same name, for the Dark Master simultaneously attacked multiple targets in different geographic locations with the same temptations at the same time. Names such as Doubt, Fear, Lust, Impurity, Liar, Hatred, Anger, Discord, Envy, Jealously, Pride, Riches, Pleasures, Worry, Tolerance, Activity, Ease, Excess and Glutton to name a few.[9] They were an interesting, diverse and sometimes inconsistent group, but useful to advance the Dark Master's agenda of chaos, deception and death.

The Tempters were seemingly a great advantage to the forces of darkness. Even a Guardian was prohibited from obstructing the work of a Tempter once the temptation had been accepted. Unless a target actively opposed the temptation or admitted they had succumbed and cried out for help, the Guardian could only watch and await a changed heart.[10] What was really frustrating to the Guardian was the knowledge that the Tempter's purpose was to attach himself to the target and create an insatiable appetite for the particular fleshly desire. Worse yet, a victory over a Tempter was often short-lived. Tempters were free to return with their temptations at what they viewed to be a more opportune time, and they could, and did, target the most holy and pure of all the Enemy's servants. No one was immune from attack. The Dark Master had himself tempted Jesus continually.[11]

"The really wonderful thing about temptation as an offensive weapon," Argon said to Zaccur, who had just returned, "is that the Enemy really is holy and just and must respond to one who accepts temptation in a way that is consistent with who He is. When the Son, Jesus, became one of the human creatures, He revealed that the Enemy considers even accepting thoughts of committing an action the same as having fully succumbed to the temptation and committed the act. Jesus said lust equals adultery and anger equals murder.[12] Can you believe that? He made it almost too easy. Throw in a little "righteous" confusion and these human creatures ignore what Jesus said and convince themselves that the act is all that matters. When that happens, they can be led into almost any thought as long as you stop short of trying to make them do it. They think they are perfectly fine, but the Enemy sees their thoughts as evil and thus their usefulness to advance His purposes is limited. Those without the light inside are easily drawn into acts following temptation. We actually rule the world through temptation. It's fun – a game which these fools are too stupid to see."

"And you, as the ruler of a city, can order Tempters to attack humans so they can be used for our purposes?" Zaccur asked enviously, wanting to have this authority himself someday.

"Absolutely," Argon responded, again his pride causing him to ignore any possible future threat by Zaccur. "Look at this crowd trying to find the shooter. See the one that Lust has? Lust has been all over this human for years. He is so into pornography that it is beyond addiction. He can't look at a woman – any woman – including Sally Johnson without a sexually explicit fantasy going off in his mind. Think about what interesting possibilities that offers," he said smiling.

"Yes, but don't you see that she is not alone and she has the light inside," Zaccur observed. "Can that be overcome?"

"We will see what the strength of her faith is,[13]" Argon responded. "She must be the focus of the fight to control this group. She is a bad influence and will be a bad example. Perhaps we can motivate a rape. After all, she is only a woman."

Zaccur was right again to consider her a threat. The forces of light were not entirely unrepresented that afternoon. A Guardian was present, standing over Sally Johnson as she received her direction from the light within. Sally was also blessed to be under the influence of several Providers, members of the forces of light, who under the direction of the Holy Spirit both negate the Tempters and enable the servants of the light to accomplish His purposes by providing them with specific abilities. Like the Tempters, they took their names from what they were intended to accomplish in and through those to whom they had been given. Their names included Faith, Boldness, Wisdom, Discernment, Truth, Joy, Peace, Patience, Kindness, Goodness, Faithfulness, Gentleness, Self-Control, Purity, Contentment, Perseverance, Humility, Servant and Love.[14]

The specific lineup at 1632 Washington Avenue that afternoon included several Tempters, named Doubt, Fear, Anger, Envy, Jealously, Lust and Pride, who had four targets to work with. But, also present were Providers for Sally Johnson named Wisdom, Peace, Faithfulness, Humility and Love. The Tempters tried to attach themselves to Sally Johnson but failed. Her faith was strong. Like Jesus had, she rejected their advances. The battle was on.

"Johnson is the concern," Argon continued, "but fortunately she is only one and she is a woman. She is not in charge of the investigation. Even so, the Dark Master must know" so Zaccur was off again to carry the news.

Public events would be required to accomplish the investigators' agenda, and thus, the teams headed by Sally Johnson and Troy Dallas would need to work together to some extent. It was agreed, as a goal, to set a press conference for next Tuesday to announce the new efforts, and a community forum for next Friday to initiate public involvement, hoping to begin to change public perception. Much would be out of their control between now and then, but they had to move forward and they couldn't announce what wasn't yet decided. Tomorrow's meeting would be important – more important than they knew. They left to gather their new teams and to flesh out the details of their areas of responsibility.

The Greater Threat

In an old rent house off of Bell and 17th, a group of eleven committed and trained Jihadists prepared for action. They were part of a much larger effort intending to bring America to its knees, but their charge was not to cripple the economy or kill millions. That assignment had been given to others. Their job was to create terror by removing any remaining sense of peace and safety, while targeting those among the infidels who were declared enemies of the faith, the Christians and Jews, and others whose death would so traumatize the masses that they would be paralyzed with fear for the safety of those they loved – and would demand their government bow to the requirements of the Jihad. It would be a glorious victory over America – the Great Satan.

The house was rented by three college students who had been sent to enter the United States legally on student visas. This was all part of a new strategy intended to make discovery more difficult and to protect the greater plan if a portion failed or an individual was captured. The three students' sole contribution to the effort was to provide a safe place for ten of the eleven warriors to sleep, plan and prepare their attacks. The three would never be told anything about the plans. They were not allowed to attend any of the planning meetings or to discuss operations with any of the eleven. They had been directed to attend classes, work hard, do well in school and stay out of trouble. They were to keep their Jihadists views to themselves. They were to socialize and seek to make non-Arab friends. They were to be Americanize in dress, language and custom. The goal was to present themselves as secular Muslims to break the American stereotype of young Arab males being dangerous religious fanatics. They would be forgiven what they did against the purity of the faith for it was only being done to facilitate killing infidels.

Of the eleven, one had remained in the country after finishing graduate school and now was teaching history in a local junior high. The ten had come into the country through America's soft underbelly – the Mexican border. They were in Williams illegally but possessed of ample identification, including multiple social security cards, drivers' licenses, passports, credit cards, etc. and lots of cash. With multiple identities, they had the security of movement and protection from a mistake using any particular ID. The credit card accounts were addressed to post office boxes in multiple cities other than Williams, but the bills were picked up online and paid by bank transfers.

There were many such groups that had been sent in over the past two years as part of the greater plan. The goal was that no state containing a major city would be without such groups, each operating independently, but contemporaneously. Williams had been chosen as the place to test the operational concept and work through the bugs before it went national. For now, the others must wait.

Of the eleven, only Abdul Farsi understood the outline of the greater plan, but few of the operational details. Those were known only to an elite council, meeting at that very moment far beneath the earth in a safe room constructed in a cave on the Pakistani/Afghan border. After the death of Osama bin Laden, the leadership had returned to the safety of the caves where the drones could not see or go. What Farsi knew was that cells were being established in college towns throughout the United States. Mosques were being constructed near all major college campuses by friendly Arab governments. Teachers were being sent to either convert young infidels or change opinions. Eyes were always to remain open, searching for recruitment possibilities.

The other major effort Farsi knew of was in American prisons. This was the place to find angry, experienced men and women of violence who could be used almost immediately. Teaching hate and revenge would not be a problem, and it could be done under the flag of religion. Chaplains were recruited and trained to advance the cause of the faith and the agenda of the Jihad.

The outline of the greater plan, as Farsi understood, was to establish two kinds of operational units in the United States. Others would target Americans and American interests outside. The first was a tactical terror unit, which was what Farsi headed in Williams. The second was an economic destruction unit which would use the selected domestically available weapon of choice to inflict significant damage on the economic infrastructure of America. Again, not a single attack, but a coordinated campaign. It would take patience, persistence, and much blood to bring America to its knees – but it could be done, and quickly.

Farsi liked teaching school because it gave him a priority work permit, allowing him to remain in the United States and eventually become a citizen. He could travel in and out of the country without suspicion, as long as he chose his destinations carefully and used other ID for travels to meet with the Jihad leadership in countries that would raise concerns. It was really not that difficult. He would fly from the US to either an adjoining country or to a Western European nation and from there, use false ID to travel to his real destination. He would return the same way leaving no record of suspicious activity.

Much thought had been put into this new approach, and he had been privileged to be part of developing the initial concept. He had been in that cave as part of the meeting when the domestically available weapon of choice had been selected. It had been his recommendation. Having been educated in America and having lived among the infidels for all these years, he understood their vulnerabilities and weaknesses. He knew what would work and what was readily available.

As the teams prepared to meet separately, Farsi left on a walk to pass by the selected sites for the initial attacks to gather additional operational details and to think through escape scenarios. He drew no attention, appearing to be a graduate student walking between classes on campus. The team leaders had already been briefed, and his presence was no longer necessary for the moment. His physical contact with the group would be minimal. He had become a most valuable asset to the Jihad and must be protected in the event of discovery or failure. He would not be involved in the actual field operations and lived elsewhere in the city.

The leader of the first team was Kalb Sawori. His team met downstairs. Sawori understood from Farsi that his team's mission was to begin a concentrated effort to attack the enemies of the faith by striking selected churches and synagogues, killing some of the infidels indiscriminately while striking terror in the hearts of others who worshiped this enemy of the faith. They needed to be shown that their god could not protect them. For now, the cover would be to be sure to kill people of color if they had the opportunity. This, they hoped, would create confusion and misdirect the investigation into who was responsible for the killings. In the Williams' test, they would not publicly take responsibility for their acts. Ensuring proper tactics and learning how people and the authorities would respond was what leadership was seeking to confirm before releasing a much larger national effort. When the effort went national, they would go public and claim responsibility.

The leader of the second team meeting upstairs was Allahabad Doeg, a hardened veteran of the fight in Afghanistan and Iraq. He knew how to kill Americans from experience and hated all Americans of any age with an unholy passion. His view of how to deal with Americans was how the 'Jewish God' told their first king to deal with the Amalekites who had opposed them on their exodus from Egypt. The whole exodus thing was just fiction in his eyes, but the instruction was what he liked. The command was to go and attack and completely destroy everything they had – to kill men and women, children and infants, oxen and sheep, camels and donkeys.[15] Doeg joyfully accepted his current assignment to kill children and infants. That would send a message that these infidels needed to hear – convert or die – surrender to the Jihad or be destroyed by its power. Nothing would be able to stop them. America must pay for its interference in the homeland and its opposition to the faith.

Had the Curtain been parted for even a moment, darkness would have been revealed so complete that it would have appeared impenetrable. Present for the meetings were Keepers and Tempters galore including those named Liar, Anger, Hatred, Jealously and Pride. Also present was the one called Death, a direct report to the Dark Master. He was here because of the importance of Jihad to the overall plan that the human creatures perish. Success would require much blood, but it also required a one world government and religion. Both were in play through the Jihad.

There were no Guardians and no Providers present, for none in attendance at the meetings sought guidance from a light within. There was no light in any of them. That did not mean, however, that the forces of light were unrepresented. Present, but uninvited was Barnabas, the leader of the forces of light in Williams. He was parallel in authority to Argon with whom he was well acquainted, having opposed him all the years there had been a Williams.

Also present was the light itself, for God the Holy Spirit is present everywhere. [16] The agenda of the light at that moment focused on those who were planning to kill. There was no anxiety in Heaven over the intentions of the eleven for they could not proceed unless the Father allowed[17] and the future had not yet been revealed. The concern was that those under the influence and temptation of the darkness needed an opportunity to understand the evil they were seeking to do and be drawn to make another choice. None of those made in the image of God were unimportant to Him, including those now meeting and planning death and destruction.[18] Even the most evil, like Saul, who became Paul, [19]or David, who murdered Uriah in seeking to cover up his adultery,[20] could be changed if they were willing. It was here that the invisible battle was also being fought, and there was already some success as doubts began to arise in the hearts of some of those chosen to kill children.

CHAPTER 3

First Impressions

Thursday, January 31 – MD Minus 115 days

AS PAUL WALKED across the campus toward the Chadwick History Center, Professor Thompson was just completing a lecture in his class entitled, "A Historic Perspective on Biblical Israel." With his mind on the burning question of what had he seen in his dream, Paul walked quickly passed Abdul Farsi, who was headed to College Church on the corner and then to Kingdom Day Care a couple of blocks over on the other side of the railroad tracks. Coming toward him was a rather non-descript woman who Paul vaguely remembered seeing in some of his classes last year. He didn't know her name and was unaware that she had just come from an inquiry at Kingdom Day Care. Looking for a part time job is what she had told the workers. The looking part was true.

On the other side of town, some of the armed citizens of Williams gathered as the Citizen's Militia to organize a campaign to save their city from what they saw as the incompetence of local authorities and the threat of the shooter. Most considered the authorities to be as much of a threat to the citizens as the shooter.

Sam Will was angry. His level of anger surprised even him. Almost overnight he had become passionately determined to stand and fight for the safety of the city. It was becoming even more than a passion; it was a compulsion. He wanted just one clean shot at the shooter and the crisis would be over. He was prepared to fight with anyone who got in his way. He was a little frightened by what he felt but knew he had to finish this and that he was right.

Fortunately, the Citizen's Militia had their own version of Officer Sally Johnson. It was Tom Campy, a no-nonsense, but no less passionate leader. Tom didn't have Sam Will's compulsion; rather, he had a steadfast dedication to labor together until the job was done. He was both persistent and patient, and he was a thinker. The contrast between Sam and Tom was the classic distinction between one who reacts in response to a situation and one who acts in the reality of the situation. At its simplest comparison it was intentional conduct vs. emotional response – thoughts vs. feelings.

Tom had already invested the time to think through a plan to establish the equivalent of a citizen's army. "We've got to take advantage of the state firearms laws to bring the public into this before we have mass panic," he argued. "People have to see that they are safe, to feel safe, and the law allows us to be in public with guns visible. We need to do that in a way where the public and law enforcement know we are the Citizen's Militia and not the shooter. If we are successful, we will be invited to provide visible protection in parks, schools, and businesses – just about anywhere in the city. Once we are physically present, the people will feel safe and the shooter will be afraid to show himself. If he does, he dies. We shoot back."

All agreed that was the answer, but how could it be done quickly and effectively. There were massive organization problems and coordination issues. Fortunately, money would not be a problem, for one of the city's wealthiest citizen was a gun enthusiast. That ensured access to paid media, the ability to obtain some distinctive clothing as identification for members of the militia, transportation, additional guns and ammunition. Maybe even life and medical insurance. After all, there was a killer out there that would be targeting them even as they targeted him.

Suggestions came from all parts of the room. Although Sam stood up front as the head of the group, Tom drove the discussion because he already knew where he wanted it to go. It was as if he had been directed how to lead, which he had, even as Sam had been directed how to feel. It was light versus darkness, the classic confrontation continued.

"We need to hold a press conference and announce what we are going to do," said one.

"Yes," another responded, "but also hold a public meeting of some sort to answer questions and recruit members. We don't have enough members to carry this out citywide."

Others expressed their concerns – their questions – some practical, some emotional; they just kept pouring out. "We need an office, some way to organize our people."

"We need to coordinate with law enforcement and have some kind of uniforms, so we don't shoot each other."

"We need to know when to shoot."

"Can we use automatic weapons?"

"Can we shoot to kill?"

"Won't we just be making ourselves targets for the shooter by being out there identified as ones who intend to kill him?"

"How do we know where to be to defend against an attack?"

"This shooter has been totally random. What do we protect?"

"How can we identify the shooter?"

"Can we be present on private property?"

Several hours later there was a consensus and a plan. Tom summarized for the group. "We will order red jackets, hats and shirts with *'Citizen's Militia'* on them so that members on duty can be readily identifiable to all." Tom went on, "I will contact the authorities to explain what we are going to do and see if there is a way to coordinate our efforts. We don't want the police working against us if it can be avoided."

One businessman piped up, "If we need to we can line up some NRA lawyers to be ready to file suit and protect our right to defend ourselves if we are challenged. We have to organize. The authorities haven't been able to stop the killing. There won't be any businesses left in Williams if this shooter isn't stopped."

"We will schedule a press conference for early next week," Tom read from his notes, "where Sam can introduce the Citizens Militia to the public, seek recruits and lay out the plan to defend the city. That will also be an opportunity to promote the Security Fair."

One of the really exciting ideas to involve the public had come from Josh Douglas, the high school football coach. He had said, "If you want the public's support, you have to give them something to get excited about. We need something like a pep rally with speeches, a band, contests, bumper stickers, food, something where people can have fun and get their fluids running."

"Great idea," another had added. "We can have guns and ammunition available for sale by local businesses, booths to sign up for gun training and to join the Citizen's Militia. We can have the whole area patrolled by armed Citizen's Militia in their red shirts and hats. Everyone will want to join."

"Yes!" shouted Sam and with glee, pumped his fist high into the air. "A visual feast to announce that there is a new sheriff in town. Like that line from that old news movie, 'I'm mad as hell and won't take it anymore.' People will love that." Josh volunteered to organize the fair.

"We need someone to handle public relations," Tom had asked. Diane Conway, a writer for the local newspaper, volunteered. "It will be important to get as much positive coverage as possible. You will have to help us know what to do to get free press and how to use advertising to push our message and recruit help." Diane had recently been the local campaign manager for a state Senate candidate and she knew how it was done. A very good choice thought Tom.

That left the boring part – organization. John Tremble volunteered office space and a computer. His receptionists would answer a separate line for the Citizen's Militia and it would be set up to receive messages in her absence. "Just in case," John said, "I will have a security camera installed and the receptionist will be armed. You never can be too careful when confronting violence."

Tom would coordinate the teams in the field and the requests for protection. All Sam wanted to do was be the face of the organization and be in the field where he could get a shot at the shooter. He wanted blood. "We need our own hit team. We need to figure out where he will strike next and be waiting for him." Two very different agendas motivated by two very different influences in the same organization.

Tom put in a call to the local police and was referred to Officer Sally Johnson. They agreed to meet tomorrow. Sally was concerned, but something about Tom gave her a sense of peace. Actually, it was something in Tom, for Tom, like Sally, was guided by the light inside. Argon was not pleased with this development and again, the ever present Zaccur was dispatched with the news. He wondered how long he would survive continued bad news. The Dark Master was without mercy and accepted no excuse for failure. Argon was afraid.

Professor Thompson Weighs In

Dr. Daniel P. Thompson was a Bible history professor extraordinary. His classes filled quickly, for they were interesting, timely, and often controversial – but not religious. The focus was to take the history expressed in the Bible as compared to other writings and traditions that were now generally accepted as fact. He saw it as a search for truth with the Bible simply being another opinion – an often wrongly interpreted opinion, he thought. A case in point was the class he was just wrapping up.

"A Historical Perspective on Biblical Israel" was a fascinating study, if you could take the mysticism away from political Israel. He used the class as an opportunity for an examination of the history of the whole Middle East as a stage upon which a nation called Israel has appeared for several extended performances, the most recent of which began in 1948. The class looked briefly at the history of all the peoples of the Middle East with a focus on Israel as discussed in the Bible. He really planted himself in the study of modern political Israel in comparison with biblical Israel and the land promised to Abram[21] (later Abraham).[22] Were the citizens of Israel today God's so-called chosen people[23] as spoken of in the Bible? What about the other people in the Middle East and their view of Israel? What about end times mythology?

To say the class was controversial would be to put it very mildly. He made people mad but didn't really care as long as it made them think. His agenda was transparent. He believed that the nation of Israel was nothing more than another nation that has little connection to the Israel of the Bible, beyond the name and general geographic location. He concluded that others in the Middle East had as good a claim to the dirt as did the citizens of Israel. As he saw it, Israel had no special right to take the land from others.

His class attracted a lot of foreign students. The current class had three Palestinians who, he learned, lived together. They really invested in the class with passion and added a lot to the discussion by putting a face to the people who were suffering at the hands of political Israel. He saw them as clear evidence in the flesh that he was right in his conviction, that terrorism was a response to violence, not an inherent part of a belief system. These young men were Muslims; but in language, dress and practice they were as Western as the kids born here. They had American friends, went to American movies and acted like American with few exceptions. "Assimilation does work," he thought. "Reaching out in friendship was the way to deal with terrorism, not violence. Violence would only spawn more violence. The world was certainly big enough for many belief systems. Too bad the current crop of politicians in Washington and London were so stupid. At least, I have a podium from which to teach the next generation of American leaders. They won't be so blind."

By contrast, most of the American-born church-going students were angry with him from the first day of the class. To him, they were closed-minded idiots. They actually believed the Bible taught that to mess with modern Israel was to mess with God because they were His people and He had given them that land. "These children of the crusades are not interested in considering the results of violence," he thought. "They're as good as Pharisees, as wrong as that crowd of religious leaders who thought they were serving God by killing Jesus.[24] It was merely violence to preserve their place in the social and political order. Not much different from today."

He was thankful for Faith Church of Joy, the place he attended. The leadership was more realistic and modern in their views. They were not the prisoner of tradition and Bible myths. They understood that the Bible was a collection of the thoughts of many men written over hundreds of years. Men could always be wrong. Beyond that, he understood that things change over time and what might have been true two thousand years ago for a society living under the Roman boot was hardly true for America, where values and standards evolve as society matures. The Bible had to be kept in its rightful place – useful but not authoritative.

What really pleased him about his church was that Roy Elkhorn, the

Senior Pastor, had asked him to teach what had become the largest class in the church on Sunday mornings. He was given a free hand on what to teach. The class had become a second golden opportunity to debunk Christian fanaticism on a horde of political and social issues.

The students with a Jewish heritage avoided the class. As he saw it, they obviously feared truth, choosing rather to live in their imaginary world of black and white where they were always right regardless of how it impacted others. It was in the blood. There were Jews and then everyone else. They were totally unrealistic. He believed that America had to come to the place where it dealt with political Israel no differently than with Syria or Iran. They were simply three countries from the same part of the world with differing political agendas.

He was exhilarated from the day's discussion as he left the class and encountered Paul Phillips in the hall. "Professor Thompson, I desperately need a few moments of your time – privately." Thompson knew Paul Phillips as a serious student and his demeanor indicated that he believed whatever was going on was serious.

"Sure, let's go to my office," he responded. "What's happening? You look like you haven't slept in a week." No response.

As they entered his office, Professor Thompson noted that Paul's hands were shaking and he was as pale as the dead. Something was obviously terrifying him. He was short of breath, having rushed from somewhere to get here. Professor Thompson's voice rose as he questioned, "Paul, what in the hell is going on?"

"Look Professor, you are a man who knows the Bible and you know history. I'm not crazy, but I saw something in a dream – a nightmare – that I don't understand and it has me living in absolute terror and fear. Please, just promise me you will hear me out and give me any perspective you have on what happened – on what I saw. I have to know, please."

Paul's desperation got his attention and he responded kindly, "I'm listening, but slow down. Take your time and tell me everything you can about whatever happened."

His Keeper's large hands grasp more tightly around Professor Thompson's head to control what was heard and to influence his response. This was an opportunity not to be missed, a chance to end Paul's search and with it, end any danger of a search by Samantha. But there was the issue of Paul's Guardian, which put the Keeper ill at ease. Influence was never easy when the forces of light were even in the vicinity. He would have to be careful.

Paul trembled as he spoke, trying hard to miss no detail. His look revealed that he was reliving the moment. Professor Thompson could only wonder at what could cause such a reaction.

"It was after Samantha's dad's funeral. He was another of the sniper's victims. I saw nothing unusual at the funeral, but later in a dream I was back in the cemetery and I saw in the air some kind of creatures, which I can only describe as being like wisps of darkness. There were many different sizes. All had fiery orange eyes, bright yellow skin and huge hands with enormously long fingers. They seemed to be everywhere. Their hands encircled the heads of most of the people. Their long fingers seemed to pierce the skulls as if they held the brains of the people in their hands. The eyes of the people were crusted over. I awoke screaming when I saw hands reaching for me. What did I see? They were real. They were there; only I couldn't see them. Why are they after me?"

"I have to ask," said Professor Thompson, "are you on anything?"

"No nothing," was the response. "I wished it was that simple."

"Did anyone else tell you they had seen anything?"

"No," Paul answered, "and I asked Samantha, she saw nothing."

"You only saw this in a dream? It was not real."

"It sure seemed real to me," Paul replied, "but it was only in the dream."

Sitting up in his chair and assuming his professorial demeanor, Thompson began his analysis. "OK, let's take the emotion out of this and get logical. First, it was a dream, a nightmare, probably nothing more. You are afraid because whatever it was seemed to be coming for you, but is that any different from when you saw a horror film as a child? After watching such a movie, did you ever have nightmares? Were you ever afraid to be alone?"

"Sure," was the answer, "but this wasn't like that. I actually could smell sulfur and sensed physical danger."

Honing in for the kill, Professor Thompson began, "Think about what you are imagining – dark wisps who, by your description, are ghost-like, controlling humans by literally holding their brains, blinding them to the outside world and, by implication, using them for whatever they want. Religion, folklore and mythology would all tell you that the creatures you imagined in your dream are demons. They are described as supernatural beings considered to be malicious hurtful spirits. The Bible says they are fallen angels if you take the Bible literally.[25]

"The rest of what you saw would be a classic portrayal of demonic activity in humans, most often described as demonic possession. Historically, the view regarding demon possession is that one possessed is under the absolute control of the demon. You probably saw the movie *The Exorcist*. That was Hollywood's view of demon possession. Sells tickets, but pretty thin. What you dreamed would make a better movie.

"The Bible says a lot about people possessed by demons and what that does to them. A lot of the healings credited to Jesus were really exorcisms, which had the result of freeing the victim from some disease or disability.[26] There is not much science to support that, but then how would you be able to test and observe the invisible?

"Here is my problem with what you describe. It simply doesn't work by any historical measure and is inconsistent with all studies of demonic activity I have seen, even including what is discussed in the Bible. In your dream, virtually everyone is pictured as possessed by demons. That is not the teaching of anyone at any time in history. It is certainly not your experience or mine. I am not demon possessed and I don't believe you are either. You may be mixed up, but not possessed. I can't say I have ever been around anyone who is demon possessed. Demons may somehow cause disease or disabilities, but even those demons would not be completely in control of the person. What you dreamed was a dream and nothing more. You are not in danger and need to simply let go of this as nothing more than a nightmare, which is all it is."

Professor Thompson's Keeper smiled as the forces of darkness literally danced with joy, leaping in the air and howling the praises of the Dark Master. Paul's former Keeper once again reached out to surround Paul's head and dig deeply into his skull to grasp his brain, to initiate influence and end the search. This Keeper had a lot of years of experience with Paul and he was anxious to get back on the job, but that was not to be for Paul's Guardian stood as a hedge of protection around Paul blocking every attempt to reach him.

Paul response was not as expected. "Professor, all you say is logical and fits with what I have heard, but I know what I saw and I cannot simply walk away from it. It was too real."

Professor Thompson responded in frustration and a bit condescendingly, "If you want to live with fear that some demon is reaching for your brain, that is your choice, but be realistic. Everyone you encounter is not demon possessed. You cannot get around that truth. I don't know what you saw, but I know you didn't see a world of demon possessed people because it does not exist anywhere except in the movies. Go find yourself a Catholic priest or Chaplain Forrest or some other religious person and they will tell you the same thing I am telling you. If you want to be afraid of something, get real and be afraid of that crazed killer out there who shot your girlfriend's Dad. That is who you should fear, not some imagined evil force seeking to control all mankind. You are far too intelligent to be that stupid."

Paul left somehow strangely encouraged. "I don't know a Catholic priest or any other religious person I respect enough to listen to, he thought, so Chaplain Forrest it is." At least he now had some direction and some new questions.

Also unseen, but now present with Paul, was a Provider named Peace, exactly what Paul needed at that moment to continue his search.

CHAPTER 4

MEETINGS THAT MATTER

Thursday, January 31 – MD minus 115 days

AS PAUL PHILLIPS sought to find Chaplain Forrest's office, meetings were being held as groups of leaders and planners gathered at various places around the world to advance the two very different agendas that were at work. One sought to act while the other sought to prevent, but neither could predict or control the future, for they had little actual knowledge of the other. Simultaneously unseen gatherings of rulers, powers and authorities of both the forces of light and darkness gathered to forge the different futures desired by their very different rulers.[27] One to force his will, the other to act as necessary to make possible the future He desired to provide, but would not force on an unwilling people.

In human thought, the two meetings that appeared to matter most were one occurring in that room far beneath the earth on the Pakistani/Afghan border and another in the Washington office of the director of Homeland Security. The events of 9/11 and the military action which followed had changed everything. The underground room had become the unofficial headquarters of the man they called the Sheik, because the one was now dead who had originally declared jihad against America. Before

9/11, there had not even been a Department of Homeland Security. Homeland America had not seen the threat coming and was unprepared when it arrived. They hoped not to repeat that mistake and thus far had been successful – actually lucky – or maybe even blessed and protected.

"What report, El-Ahab," asked the Sheik, "are we nearing readiness?"

"Yes," he responded, "but patience is still required. Remember please, mighty one, we worked on a comprehensive plan for over four years and have been seeking since then to put in place all that is required to make it operational. We are close, but not yet ready. We will get only one chance to use the weapons of choice to bring the infidel nation to its knees. The strike must be coordinated and fatal. We can't forget that 9/11. As successful as it was, it only made the infidels mad and they launched another crusade. We did not really hurt them. We just embarrassed them. This time, it must be a fatal blow."

"Most of our brother Arabs have shown themselves to be cowards and traitors," the Sheik answered angrily. "They have not risen in mass to expel the occupation in Iraq and Afghanistan. We must do it ourselves while preparing the attack on the American homeland. Later we will deal with all the Arab cowards. They too must die so the land will be purified. There is no place for any but those faithful to jihad."

The Sheik paused, wondering how there could be any who claimed adherence to the faith but were without the passion for fighting. They were becoming soft, like the Americans who do not understand that if there is nothing worth dying for, there is nothing worth living for. "The Americans have no stomach for a real fight against a dedicated foe willing to battle for decades and committed to spilling their blood at any cost," the Sheik continued. "Vietnam and Beirut showed that, and there is every reason to believe that Iraq and Afghanistan will be a repeat performance. Look at what ISIS has accomplished. This so called Christian faith of the infidels is powerless to stand against the Jihad. I despise the weakness of these cowards, with their technological weapons to kill at a distance without dirtying their hands. They will taste their own blood soon enough," and then he was silent, looking down in obvious thought.

Ahem El-Ahab never spoke in these moments, waiting respectfully, almost worshipfully until the Sheik looked at him, signaling that his moment of meditation had ended and he was ready to proceed. It was in those moments of silence that he knew the Sheik sought inspiration, which he was unaware, was received from his Keeper and also from Legion, the ruler of the spiritual forces of darkness in the Middle East.

Legion was a direct report to the Dark Master, a member of the inner circle known as the Counsel of Darkness. He was one who actually encountered the Son in the flesh; a story included in the Enemy's Book. He was cast out of a man and sent into a large herd of several thousand pigs, which immediately rushed down a steep bank into a lake and were drowned.[28] The Dark Master took note of his inspired ability to promote suicide, which was what he knew would be needed to advance his agenda from the Middle East. Because of that, Legion had been promoted over many others and had served the Dark Master well. He would continue to be needed to raise an army of those desiring death so they might indiscriminately kill many others considered enemies of the faith. It is a unique talent to be able to deceive a healthy young man into killing himself so that others might die, simply for the hope that he would be rewarded for his service in the afterlife by having all his sexual fantasies met eternally.

Obviously, they had to keep the Enemy's Book away from that crowd. The truth was that Legion had barely escaped being sent to the pit by the Son. Fortunately, few read the Enemy's Book and most of those who did could easily be convinced it contained nothing more than myths and fables.

When El-Ahab's eyes again met the Sheik's, he continued, "Let me go through the basics of the plan and update you on where we are and what's next. We have established research centers at Universities in Tehran, Mexico City, and Madrid to independently conduct an investigation using the internet. The centers have been useful in determining what firms to acquire to obtain control over the weapons of choice. They have also been helpful in identifying and targeting vulnerable installations so we will know where to strike. With internet access to satellite photographs, we do not have to send people to physically investigate a target and thus avoid attracting suspicion."

"Yes," said the Sheik, "but what have we done with what we have learned?"

"Mighty one, we have refined the plan. We now believe we need a minimum of a 1,000 weapons and an equal number of trained warriors dispersed across the infidels' land for a coordinated attack at night. Since the target of this part of the effort is economic destruction, and not killing people, a night attack offers a better opportunity for operational success and for mass terror as they will awake to the destruction of industries necessary for their continued economic survival. We are going to put Americans on foot, living in the dark. It will be a great victory."

"The warriors have been recruited. That was the easy part. Training has been ongoing in our camp located in the Kerman Province of our brothers in Iran. Once trained, the warriors are being transported to a gathering point in Oaxaca, Mexico where they are equipped, assigned a location for their mission and prepared for the border crossing. We have a coordination unit located in Carmen, Arizona, a small town down Interstate 19 not far from the border. Thus far we have been able to get warriors across without detection by sending them in groups of one or two. Patience is the key to success as discovery with equipment could be disastrous. We have tried to limit the possible damage by not telling the warriors anything about their targets or timing."

"Our brothers in Saudi Arabia have provided richly the resources need to purchase the businesses that own and operate the weapons. We will not have to commandeer a single unit. They will be owned by operatives through American or Mexican shells. We will employ Americans and pay American taxes until the warriors are in position and ready to use the units for our purposes. We will give the American workers a paid holiday, substitute operators and complete our mission of destruction. How glorious it is to take the money the foreign infidels spend to purchase our oil and use it to finance their destruction."

"Yes, but what of the plans to kill millions of these infidels," ask the Sheik. "I will not rest until they beg to sit at my feet and cry out for peace. Then we will drive them from Muslim land and prepare for the final assault that will demand they convert or die."

"Mighty one, we continue to work with our Iranian brothers hoping to develop and obtain atomic weapons to clean from the earth the Jewish curse and bomb parts of America into the stone age, killing millions. We have tested new chemical weapons and are directing our efforts on a way to attack their food supplies and to poison the water supplies of major cities. This is the focus of their investigation, which makes it more difficult and dangerous. It is also harder because of the technology we don't yet fully understand. We will not be ready for this before we launch the economic strike."

"What about the execution units? We cannot let these Americans send their troops to kill our brothers and not feel pain," the Sheik cried in a loud and passionate voice, pounding the table in front of him. "I have had to endure years of threats and all the attempts to hunt me down like an animal and kill me. They killed bin Laden in his own home, but they have failed to kill me because I was protected and wise enough to retreat to the caves. They too must be driven by fear to seek safety deep within the earth."

"We continue to guide our people across the border," El Ahab responded, "and they are being housed with college students around the country. A test is being prepared in Williams, Illinois. We have two teams there in the final planning stages for their first strikes. One will hit open enemies of the faith and the other will strike at the heart of fear so prevalent in these Americans. We are using this test to confirm tactics and gage response. We want this to be a continuing effort over a long period of time, so we need to be sure what works before we unleash the total assault."

"If you have followed Williams recently, mighty one, you can see the fear our teams will be able to inflict. A single shooter has had the whole town living in terror for months now. They cannot catch him and the people are a step away from rebellion. Many are leaving the city. What a great model. When we unleash our assault across the country, there will be no safe place for them to hide. Eventually, the people will force the American president to beg you for peace on his knees."

"What a great day that will be," the Sheik said with joy and expectancy. "It will happen. What the Russians learned in Afghanistan, the Americans will learn in their hometowns. We cannot be defeated and we will not surrender. Kill us and we only multiply. Victory will be ours."

The discussion closed by El-Ahab advising the Sheik, "Messengers have been sent throughout the Muslim world to gather selected Jihad leaders together to finalize plans. It won't be long now."

"Good. It cannot happen too soon," was the Sheik's only response.

A Discovery, But of What

On the other side of the world, in the Washington office of the director of Homeland Security, the head of the CIA, the head of Military Intelligence, the director of the FBI and the president's National Security advisor had gathered at the urgent request of Director Hollister. "Something is definitely afoot. We not only have detected increased chatter out of the Middle East, but numerous messengers have been sent to known operatives which would indicate that a centralized plan of some nature is nearing the operational stage. We have no clue regarding the details of the plan but believe that it is directed at a major assault on the nation as a whole based on some of the intercepts. They are frankly terrifying, and if true, indicate that whatever is planned has been being put in place over a period of years and is almost ready to be launched. The enemy is among us preparing to strike. The information is credible and cannot be ignored. Somehow we have to ascertain the details and prepare a defense."

As the group struggled with how to respond to the limited information they now had, the forces of light and darkness gathered to advance their competing agendas through those who were now players on what had unknowingly become an eternal stage.

Contrasting Consultations

Two other meetings of significance were being held in Williams. They were different in that only one person was visibly attending each. In a garage apartment close to the campus, a young woman shut down her computer, having gathered the bus schedule for the park and ride in a neighboring city. She was ready to continue the game tomorrow, but it was getting a little boring. It was too easy now. She was searching for something more challenging and dealing for the first time with an internal conflict. She was troubled and didn't know why. Beyond her sight, in the invisible, a Keeper and a Guardian were in conflict. The Holy Spirit had begun to open her eyes so that she may see herself what she was doing.[29] She would have choices to make.

The other meeting was being held in a room in a converted warehouse beside the railroad tracks, down a couple of blocks from College Church, and within two blocks of Kingdom Day Care. There, the Bookseller prayed alone – or so it appeared. In reality, the forces of light in Williams were centered there. Argon feared this old man more than any other in the City of Williams. The Dark Master had told him that the Bookseller was one of the five most dangerous people in America. They had been trying to inspire the shooter to kill him, but this man lived under the protection of the Enemy. Argon sent Zaccur back to the Dark Master. This time, he sought instructions. The message was simple, "How can I neutralize the Bookseller before he interferes with your plan?"

Samantha is Stirred

Samantha had not been able to shake Paul's dream from her consciousness. It was as if someone or something had burned a desire deep within her to know what the dream meant.[30] What were these creatures? Were they after her too? Did they already have her?

The dream was real to Paul and it was increasingly becoming real to her. She was glad that they would be going out in a few hours. Perhaps he would have some answers after his discussion with Professor Thompson. She had to know. It was important, although she didn't know why. It seemed as if the search was drawing her closer to Paul.

Paul Continues His Search

The discussion with Professor Thompson had helped some. Clearly these creatures were demons and what they appeared to be doing would fall under the broad category of demonic activity against humans. But what was it exactly that they were doing and what was their effect on the humans? He agreed with Professor Thompson that the people he saw in the dream were not demon possessed. The argument that not everyone is demon possessed was convincing. Beyond that, however, as he understood demon possession, a demon inhabited the body of a human so that the human effectively ceased to exist other than in the flesh, and the demon lived as it wished through the body of the one possessed. It was kind of like putting on someone else's suit of clothes. Contrasted with his dream, where the demons were pictured as being outside the human's body except for the fingers reaching into the skull, what he saw was not demon posses-sion, but it certainly was demonic and it appeared to be forced unknow-ingly upon humans.

Paul couldn't get the picture of the huge hands reaching for him out of his mind. He had a strange conflicting sense of peace in the midst of fear of what he did not yet understand. Professor Thompson was a begin-ning, thought Paul, but he apparently didn't know much about demons and was obviously uncomfortable with the subject. Hopefully, Chaplain Forrest could provide some additional illumination to all this darkness. It seemed that the answer must lie somewhere in an understanding of things religious. The search continued.

Chaplain Forrest

Chaplain Forrest was guided by the light within, but it did not burn brightly within him, for he chose to listen to other voices as well. What made Argon so comfortable with him speaking to Paul Phillips was that Forrest had become a victim of his own fears. Having embraced the temp-tations of fear, doubt and worry, Chaplain Forrest had opened himself to the continued attacks of Tempters by the same names. Though the forces of darkness did not have a Keeper to place the Dark Master's influ-ence into his head and heart, the Tempters he had accepted gave them the opportunity to control or negate Chaplin Forrest's service of the Enemy, and when necessary, to protect the Dark Master's agenda. They had done well over the years. He was not considered a threat.

For eighteen years Derrick Forrest had been the Chaplain of Williams College. He had five years until retirement and surviving until then had become his real motivation. Things had changed over the years. The stu-dents were different with different values; their parents demanded more and would put up with less. Large donors to the college had their own agendas on social issues which they enforced by the power of the purse. Professors openly ridiculed the teachings of scripture and the president of the school, although a professed believer, was using his position to advance a political agenda. He felt naked and unprotected, no longer free to teach or preach as led.

Worse yet, Chaplain Forrest had come to doubt his own faith. When his adult kids rebelled against what they had been taught and openly renounced their faith, he was not only crushed, he began to wonder what was true and what was nothing but the teachings of man. There were no simple answers and simple is all anyone wanted to hear. He felt dry and burned out. People were unwilling to listen, so he had stopped saying what he had always believed. The gospel of this generation was spelled "t-o-l-e-r-a-n-c-e" and so rather than boldly proclaiming what scripture taught and create conflict, he turned away so he would not see and have to confront what he knew in his heart was wrong.

There had been a time some ten years ago when he thought that he was part of a great movement of God. A group of college students from Texas had come and spoken at a regular chapel. Something happened that could not be explained. Suddenly, kids were in tears rushing down to the stage to take a microphone and confess what in the old days was considered sin (lust, fortification, pornography, cheating, stealing, lying, homosexuality, etc.).[31] They asked for forgiveness and prayed together. This went on day after day for a week with breaks, only late at night to allow for some sleep. More people came and emotions were high. Everyone wanted the microphone. It began to be a contest for who could "confess" the worse sin. Fellow students began to excuse the sin with a blanket, "Don't feel so bad, everyone does that." He hadn't known what to do, so he did nothing. It ended. The school term ended, and the students left. It did not appear to have made any long-term change in any of the student's hearts. How could that be? How had he failed?

His doubt and confusion were real. It had been carefully crafted and encouraged by the servants of darkness over many years. Having embraced it, he allowed it to control him and to negate his usefulness to the Father. He now looked to his own fears and had ceased listening to the light within. As a result, Chaplain Forrest had become blind to the activities of the forces of light. "Wrong choices with negative consequences," thought Barnabas. Fortunately, wrong choices were not necessarily permanent choices. It was time to seek to retrieve this man to usefulness, and so another battle in the invisible began.

Paul entered his office and introduced himself. "How may I help you," asked Chaplain Forrest. "You can tell me what my dream means," and with that, Paul went through the same description he had given Professor

Thompson. He had seen wisps of darkness with fiery orange eyes, bright yellow skin and huge hands with enormously long fingers, the hands encircling the heads of most all of the people, the long fingers seeming to pierce the skulls as if they held the brains of the people in their hands. The eyes of the people became crusted over. He had awoken screaming when he saw hands reaching for him. His questions had not changed. "What did I see? Why are they after me?"

"What did Professor Thompson tell you?" asked Chaplain Forrest. He knew that Paul has just left Professor Thompson's office because Thompson had called to tell him that Paul was probably on the way to see him.

"Professor Thompson concluded I had a nightmare and should forget it, but before he came to that conclusion, he convinced me that what I saw was a picture of some kind of demonic activity, but not demon possession. Beyond that, he did not know and seemed irritated that I wouldn't drop the subject. Look, I know this has something to do with the spiritual world. Please, Chaplain. I have to know what I saw. They seemed to be coming for me. What was it, and what were they doing? Can you help me or direct me to someone who can?"

Chaplain Forrest paused to phrase his answer carefully. He was immediately filled with a sense of conflict. He did not want to say something that would get back to Professor Thompson and offend him, and at the same time, he had a sincere desire within to help this young man if he could. This student was obviously searching for truth. It had been a long time since he really felt like a chaplain dealing with serious spiritual issues, and something deep inside told him this was important. He felt a strange sense of boldness as he prayed silently for wisdom, something he hadn't done in a long time – and reached for his Bible – that too was something he hadn't done while counseling in a long time.

Unseen, there had been a change in influence within the chaplain. The three Tempters had been vanquished by his Guardian as Chaplain Forrest chose to shift his focus from self to the searcher before him and how he could help him. The prayer was the turning point as he had asked for wisdom.[32] The response of the forces of light had been immediate. The void created when the Tempters departed was filled by Providers named Wisdom, Discernment and Boldness, because that is what Chaplain

Forrest needed most at that moment. His light within now glowed brighter. Argon looked on in horror, considering how to respond and retrieve what had been lost with no control or influence over what was playing out before him.

"Paul, I have to start by admitting that there is little I can do for you, but I do believe I know a man who can help you if anyone can. I have years of education and experience as a pastor. I have studied and preached the Bible for over 30 years, but what you experienced is something that is way over my head. I have avoided growing in understanding of the invisible world, choosing rather to focus on the physical world I can see and touch and feel. I have chosen that as my escape because I fear what I don't understand – and that is wrong. The Bible teaches that what is real includes the invisible.[33] You cannot know what is real without understanding the invisible. They cannot be separated. The invisible world drives and often controls the visible world. The saying, 'Things are not always as they seem' is a universal truth," he said pausing for the moment to gather his thoughts.

"I agree with Professor Thompson that what you saw was demonic activity against humans. There is nothing else it could have been. I don't agree with him saying it was simply a nightmare. In my heart, I have an assurance that what you saw was real and that you were chosen to see it, but you were not shown everything that was occurring at the funeral in the invisible world.

"The Bible teaches that there is a great on-going struggle for humans in the invisible world. Another Paul, this one a first-century follower of Jesus wrote, 'Our struggle is not against flesh and blood, but against the rulers, against the authorities, against the powers of this dark world and against the spiritual forces of evil in the heavenly realms.'[34] What you saw in your dream is some of that which Paul the Apostle warned about. Apparently you did not see the forces of light, but they were there, for that is the conflict – light versus darkness.[35] It is a conflict over every man, woman and child on the face of the earth. When you saw what appeared to be a demon reaching for you, I believe that it was a clear warning that there is a fight going on right now in the invisible world for you because you have been chosen by God for some greater purpose."

Paul gasped and asked, "How can that be? I am not religious. I don't even go to church. I despise the religious hypocrites I see every day. I have no respect for their so-called religion. Look at the world today, how many people die every day, killed in the name of some religion? People kill innocent men, women and children by blowing themselves up in the name of service to their god because they have been taught that their god will reward them for eternity. The history of religion is a history of the shedding of innocent blood. Where is this God you speak of who allows all of that innocent death in his name and the killer loose here in Williams inflicting death and injury seemingly at will? I want nothing to do with that kind of religion or that kind of god. I am only here today because I don't want to become like the others I saw. This is about self-defense for me and for Samantha, my girlfriend – protection from those dark things that are after us."

Chaplain Forrest paused and again prayed silently for guidance. In the invisible Argon screamed as if in pain. "Perhaps," Chaplain Forrest continued, "it is because of your unwillingness to become a religious hypocrite or to accept a god of violence and hate that you have been chosen to be shown something of truth in the invisible world and how that affects the visible world. God is reaching out to you to reveal Himself as He truly is, not as He has been portrayed in the name of man-made religions. The Bible reveals a God, who has the same opinion you have expressed about what many call religion. He hates religious hypocrites and those who kill and destroy in the name of religion more than you can imagine.[36] I told you there was one who I believe could help you if you are serious in your search. Are you serious?"

Paul was filled with conflicting emotions – anger, fear, passion, and desire all flooding through him at once. It was again decision time as the forces of light and darkness sought to influence the future of this young man and their conflicting agendas, but Paul chose wisely. "I must know more. I know I will never have real peace until this search ends. It is strange, but right now the only peace I have is in the search."

"Good," responded Chaplain Forrest. "You know the old warehouse just inside the railroad tracks down from College Church?"

"Yes," Paul responded, "I drive by it nearly every day."

"The old man who lives there is named Samuel Evans White. He is known around here simply as the Bookseller. He converted that warehouse into a rare and old bookstore years ago. He and his wife live upstairs in an apartment and mind the store. If anyone can help you, he can."

"How can this Bookseller help me?" Paul asked incredulously.

"Oh, this man is so much more than a simple book salesman," Chaplain Forrest answered. "He is an iterant preacher who for decades has gone anywhere he is invited to speak to anyone willing to listen. He looks and talks like one of the Old Testament prophets, with flowing white hair and beard. He is slight in body, but when he speaks he can burn the paint off the walls with his force and power. He knows the Bible better than any living man I know and speaks carefully to be sure what he says is absolutely consistent with all its teachings. But I have to be honest with you. Some of his teachings frighten me, not because they are wrong, but because I fear he is right. I have been afraid to allow him to speak in chapels because of the reaction he would generate. I only wish I had followed my heart and not my fears. He has things to say that the students needed to have heard.

"The Bookseller believes that 9/11 was a judgment of God, clear evidence that God's hedge of protection around America is being taken away, making us increasingly vulnerable to the attacks of our enemies within and without. It was, however, a judgment with mercy, he would say, for only 3,000 were killed. Had those attacks come at the noon hour, the numbers could have easily exceeded 50,000.

"What frightens me most is that the Bookseller doesn't seek to blame the nation or any group advocating what the Bible would describe as sin for this judgment. I know some have sought to blame 9/11 on homosexuality or abortion etc. He would not agree. He would take you through scripture and show you that God's judgment falls on his own people first, the Christians of America, for the way they live and for what they are willing to tolerate.[37] We proclaim one thing but live another – hypocrites just as you said. He would agree with everything you have said about religion, but disagree with your conclusion. He is the one you should go see if you really want to know what you saw in your dream."

"Please, yes, I want to meet this man," Paul answered. "How can I get an introduction?"

"I know him and will call him for you," Chaplain Forrest offered. "If the Bookseller is in town, I am sure he will give you all the time you want. He will understand the importance of your search," and with that, a phone call was made and time set aside to meet at the bookstore tomorrow at 10:00 AM.

"When you have your answer," Chaplain Forrest asked, "please come back and let me know for I too must search before it is too late."

Paul left to go and spend time with Samantha, wondering what all he had been told meant, but more committed than ever to stay with the search. All that could stop him now, he thought, was if the shooter made him a target – a possibility Argon intended to explore further before it was too late. In a panic, he sent off another of the dark wisps, this one to Molech, the leader of the forces of darkness over America. Molech had been chosen by the Dark Master because of his service as a god who required children be burned in the fire as a sacrifice.[38] In America his success in the destruction of children through abortion, drugs, sex, rebellion and divorce was unparalleled. He would know how to deal with this young searcher.

CHAPTER 5

THE INVISIBLE CONFLICT INTENSIFIES

Thursday, January 31 – MD Minus 115 days

MOLECH CAME QUICKLY with the leaders of other cities in response to Argon's plea. He had been following developments in Williams closely and he was not pleased. How was it possible to lose influence over this searcher and his girlfriend? How could Argon allow that worm of a chaplain to fall away from their influence after all these years of living in fear, doubt and worry? Worst of all, how could he allow the Bookseller to become involved? He was angry and puzzled, but not discouraged. The Dark Master still had many advantages in this conflict.

Argon bowed before his superior, not in respect, but out of fear. A word from Molech to the Dark Master and he would instantly be nothing more than a mere messenger. Failure was not an option. He must somehow overcome the forces of light and regain influence so that the Dark Master's efforts against these human creatures might advance in Williams, and he be allowed to retain his position of authority.

As he began to explain the situation, Molech cut him off sharply, "Shut up, little one, and listen. You have failed, but fortunately your incompetence can be overcome by the Dark Master's deception. Remember, the searcher does not have the light within. He may be protected and encouraged; he is even surrounded by some of those slaves of light, but he is still nothing but a human creature. Even the Enemy's Book acknowledges that 'The man without the Spirit does not accept the things that come from the Spirit of God, for they are foolishness to him, and he cannot understand them because they are spiritually discerned.'[39] There is our advantage. Even when the Bookseller speaks truth, the searcher will not understand and will be easily confused, diverted to our version of truth. Fortunately, our 'truth' is not limited in any way; it can be whatever is required at the moment to accomplish the Dark Master's purpose. The Son understood this and was right when He said of the Dark Master, 'When he lies, he speaks his native language, for he is a liar and the father of lies.'[40] Quite a compliment when you think about it. Whatever it takes to convince the target of whatever is necessary to accomplish our purposes. Without the light inside, the searcher will be completely open to our deception, which is how we will overcome and return him to the fold. It should not be difficult.

"Keep in mind though, the searcher is not your only issue. The Enemy has been working on the shooter and on some of the Jihadists. We know He is at work in the Bookseller and now in the chaplain. I also have a concern about some of the leaders of the investigators and this new group called the Citizens Militia. I must get to Washington to deal with developments there. You, go back to work. There is much to do here before tomorrow."

The Forces of Light Gather

In another unseen gathering, the forces of light met to consider how to proceed in Williams. At the request of Barnabas, Lucius, the commander of the forces of light in North America, came to offer counsel and encouragement. "Be at peace, Barnabas," he began. "Remember who sits on the throne and what you see Him doing.[41] The movement in the searcher, in Samantha, the Chaplain, even the shooter and Jihadists is the activity of the Father and of the Holy Spirit. Changes are at work in hearts as God does what only He can do. What the people will receive or allow is still at issue. The Father has not yet set boundaries, so we don't know what is possible for the evil one. The Father has not revealed the future so we must walk carefully in the present. Our problem is the absence of human warriors to stand with us. There is little prayer which evidences little faith. We are severely limited in the absence of faith.[42] Instruct the Guardians to stir God's people to pray. I will be back but must leave now for Washington. For the Light."

Barnabas echoed, "For the Light." And with that exchange, Lucius was gone.

A Relationship Healed

Chaplain Forrest made a second phone call to the Bookseller soon after Paul left and they agreed to meet later that afternoon. The Bookseller came to Chaplain Forrest's office where a relationship was healed and a partnership established. Both men sensed the importance of continuing what God had begun in Paul's life. Chaplain Forrest had shared their earlier conversation; all Paul had said about his dream and the absence of any religion in his life. He shared what he had told Paul about the invisible world and the battle constantly being fought there over what will happen in the physical world.

Because they knew and had studied the Bible, they were both acutely aware of what the Dark Master would seek to do with tomorrow's conversation. Jesus had used a parable to warn how Satan is able to keep people away from the truth. He pictured a farmer sowing good seed along a path where the birds came and ate it. Jesus later explained to His closest followers that the illustration meant "when anyone hears the message about the Kingdom and does not understand it, the evil one comes and snatches away what was sown in his heart,"[43] That was what Chaplain Forrest and the Bookseller knew must be protected against. They must be sure that even though he does not have the light inside, Paul would understand.

Then there was the unspoken reality of the shooter and all the hurting people – the injured victims and the families of those who had been killed. The city seemed to be under a dark cloud of fear. It must end, but they both knew that the heart of God also had room for the shooter, desiring that he might come to see the evil of what he was doing and turn to seek forgiveness.[44] That would not excuse what he had done or eliminate the need for justice, but like the thief on the cross, [45] they knew God remained with arms outstretched wanting to see even the shooter with the light inside.

They knew that there was really only one answer, and that was to pray. They had no other power or ability to affect what would happen but knew that God was sovereign and possessed that power[46]. They felt a compulsion within to pray, and so they did. The Bookseller's prayer was spoken as to a friend.

"Well Father," he began, "You have healed a relationship long broken and reestablished a friendship for which I am thankful. You have again done what only You can do. Tomorrow when Paul comes, please give me the words to say that Your will might be accomplished in his life. I don't know what You are doing in opening his eyes to see something of the invisible world, but I know it is for Your purposes, and I don't want to in any way divert him from those purposes. Please give me wisdom and discernment to know what You would have me say. Open Paul's eyes and ears to see, hear and receive Your truth. Protect him from the evil one and do not allow the seed You have planted to be taken from him.

"Lord, You know there is a shooter out there who has wounded or killed many people in this town. Your Word tells us that You want none to perish, but want everyone to come to repentance.[47] I pray within Your will for this killer, that like the thief on the cross his eyes may be open to his sin and he may be drawn to seek forgiveness.[48] End the violence Lord, in a way that You are honored and glorified and the eyes of those who do not know You might be opened to You. We pray too for all those who are survivors of the attacks; relatives and friends of those killed, that You be present to comfort and provide for them. Particularly Lord, for the children. In Jesus' name, Amen."

In the invisible world, a blood-chilling scream was heard as a strong blow had been struck for the forces of light. Through pain and curses, the voice of the Dark Master could be heard screaming, "The Enemy is a fool, and none who dare defy me will heed what he says. Kill the Bookseller. Now! Find a way." Argon panicked in fear, not knowing how to obey.

The Survival Commission

At the White House, President Joshua Strong gathered a group of trusted friends and advisors to meet with him and his National Security advisor Troy Steed. This was his version of a "kitchen cabinet," men and women who were present not solely because of their positions in government, but because of their relationship with him over many years. He had often thought to himself that he would trust anyone in that room with his life. Now he would trust them with the country. Most, but not all, carried the light within, as did the president, which explained the invisible presence of both Molech and Lucius and the involvement of others above them.

"You have heard Troy's report on the meeting at Secretary Hollister's office earlier today," he began. "I want you to form a working group to coordinate our response and preparation to this unknown, but obviously imminent, threat. Model yourselves after the group President Kennedy put together to deal with the Cuban Missile Crisis. I want real options totally independent of any political considerations. I believe that the very survival of the country is at risk and nothing else matters. All agencies will funnel intelligence to you. You will act with my full authority but in complete secrecy. I want nothing released publicly until we have determined the extent of the threat and our response. We are not going to scare the American public with what we do not know.

"I have asked Tom Knight, the White House press secretary to serve as chairman of this working group which I am calling the Survival Commission. I understand that it is both unprecedented and seemingly inconsistent to appoint an official who must daily work with the press to this position, but I believe deep within that he is to be the leader. He has agreed to accept the assignment for which I am grateful.

"The commission's first assignment is to work with the appropriate agencies to coordinate law enforcement and military preparation. For now, stay completely away from mayors, governors and other political people who might have different agendas unless threats appear to be specific to a particular state or city. This is mandated now because, as you know, we are approaching an election cycle. We will bring them in later, but not now. I don't want strategy to be played out in public. The longer the Jihadists believe we are in ignorance, the better chance we have to discover their specific plan and stop it."

Without taking questions or inviting comments, the president dismissed the members of the Survival Commission to begin their work.

Together Tomorrow

Down the street in the majority leader's capital office, a group of senators and representatives met to address issues forced on them for the upcoming campaign. Syria, ISIS, Russia, and the economy were expected issues, along with the usual group of social issues, but now they were faced with immigration issues, foreign business acquisition questions and North American economic union questions. They had little interest in addressing any of these, beyond the immigration issue as a way to garner millions of new voters likely to support their party's candidates. But since politics was money-driven, they could not ignore the agenda of this new group, which went by the name Together Tomorrow. The Together Tomorrow. group was the moving force behind issues tied to immigration, foreign businesses and an economic union of Mexico, the US and Canada. Their legislative agenda seemed harmless enough on the surface, and they had a seemingly unending source of funds for candidates who supported their agenda.

The public face of this new group was former President Leonard Cox. Cox was on retainer for $2 million annually. Because of the generous pay, and since this group gave a massive quantity of funds to his party's candidates, he embraced the opportunity to advance their agenda with enthusiasm. What neither Cox nor the group who were gathered in the majority leader's office realized was that the agenda they were seeking to advance had been the same one approved in that room far, far beneath the earth in the cave on the Pakistani/Afghan border.

"I love politics," Molech told Chemosh, the leader of the forces of darkness in Washington DC. "It offers us so many opportunities for our Tempters – particularly Greed, Pride, Envy, Jealously and Riches, to work in these so-called American leaders, driving the agenda of the Dark Master. Remember when Benjamin Franklin walked out of the Constitutional Convention in Philadelphia those many years ago and was approached by the woman asking, "What kind of government have you given us?' Do you remember his response? He said, "A republic, ma'am, if you can keep it." It has taken some time, but America is no longer a republic. By acting carefully and gradually, we have been able to turn the American government into what they call a democracy, which in reality means mob rule. The opinion of the masses at any particular moment mandates policy. It is no longer what is right or principled or even historic, but what do the polls say the people want this minute. Using the appearance of reality to create what the people want is what we are all about. It is a wonderful system to work with – a government led by the fear of loss of position. Watch these fools as they engineer their own destruction."

Paul and Samantha Prepare

Back in Williams, Paul embraced Samantha and the events of the day poured out of him. He told her of his conversations with Professor Thompson and Chaplain Forrest, and of the meeting tomorrow with the Bookseller. He left nothing out. He wanted her to know all that he had learned, his feelings, and the still unresolved questions.

"I don't know what to expect from this Bookseller. When Chaplain Forrest spoke of him, there was an obvious respect and even sadness for the way he had treated him over the years. It seemed for a moment that I was sitting in a confessional, listening to him. I don't get it. I have never had an experience like that. I am not looking for religion, but it almost seems the answers are not available apart from it."

Paul was both surprised and pleased as she told him how she had spent her day researching demons. The support encouraged him, making him feel not so small – he wasn't in this alone. She seemed changed. She was engaged. She had joined him as a searcher who had to have answers. "While you were gone," she shared, "I also called a local Catholic church and spoke briefly to a priest describing your dream. I asked about possession and exorcism and he affirmed what you were apparently told. The dream didn't picture possession. Beyond that, it got formal when he started talking about church doctrine and an invitation to some introductory classes about the Catholic faith. I felt uncomfortable, excused myself and hung up. Why do these religious people always end up trying to get you to join their church or give them money?"

"I don't know," Paul responded. "It almost seems as if most churches don't have much to do with God beyond using His name to advance their particular church in competition with other churches – if there even is a God. I am not convinced on that one yet. There is plenty of evidence in the world that argues against the existence of God."

"Paul, if this Bookseller is so smart and knows a lot about God, this is our chance to ask questions that are never addressed. Let's put a list together for you to ask him. If he truly knows God, and there is a God, he will be able to answer. If not, then you won't have to waste your time with him and we can dismiss the dream as a nightmare and the demon stories as myths. We have to be sure about the dream, but like you, I feel a real need to know something about this God. Looking at those who claim to be His followers would lead me to believe it's all a lie, but I want to know the truth if I can."

So they made their list on a single sheet of white paper. There were six questions which read as follows:

1. Is everyone who is a member of a church and claims to be a Christian really a Christian? If not, how can you know for sure?
2. Why all the killing now and throughout history in the name of religion?
3. Is the God of the Old Testament, who instructed the nation of Israel to completely wipe out whole peoples, the same God as the one in the New Testament as seen in the life and teachings of Jesus? If they are the same, how do you explain the differences? One seems to be a God of anger and wrath that is always mad, the other a man of wisdom and kindness and love.

Neither had read much from the Bible, but they had heard the stories enough to raise the obvious questions about the seeming differences: Moses calling for people to be stoned to death for what is now accepted behavior, and Jesus, who stopped a woman from being stoned for what Moses said she should be stoned.[49] It was confusing at best, but important because it seemed to define who God is.

4. If God controls everything and is a God of love, why all the natural disasters, disease, crime and cruelty in the world today?

5. Why doesn't God simply strike the shooter and the terrorists dead and protect the innocent?
6. If there is one God, why so much confusion and contradiction among different religions?

"This list is more accusatory of God than anything else, but they will learn that God loves a sincere searcher," Barnabas thought. He rejoiced at the list because they were asking what they honestly wanted to know about God, and Paul had been directed to a man who would listen for the answers within to tell them when they were able to hear. Their search had broadened beyond simply understanding the dream. What they didn't yet understand was that their search had been the intended purposes for the dream.

*

Argon sent Zaccur to find Molech in Washington DC. It was time to get his specific direction on how to deal with Paul and Samantha and on how to obey the Dark Master's order to kill the Bookseller. What he was trying simply wasn't working and time was short. There was much in play and this needed to be resolved. If there was going to be another failure in Williams, he wanted to be sure that the wrath of the Dark Master was directed at Molech and not at him.

Paul and Samantha kissed and parted for the evening. Paul needed sleep before his meeting with the Bookseller.

The shooter had long before gone to bed. It would be an early day for her as the game continued.

In Washington, Argon's message had been received. Molech raced back to Williams followed closely by Lucius. Elsewhere in secret throughout Europe, South America, and the Middle East, men began to travel to Tehran to continue planning for the Sheik's big event. Tomorrow would be important for both agendas.

CHAPTER 6

DEATH AND BREAKFAST

Friday, February 1 – MD Minus 114 days

THE DAY DAWNED early for the shooter. The bus schedule said the first bus would arrive at 4:45 a.m. Her plan was to greet the first arrival at the park and ride on the outskirts of Greenville on Knox Road. Like the other occasions, it didn't matter to her who it was – race, age, sex, etc. All that matter was that they were the first. One shot and she would be gone – kill, injure or miss. That was the game.

Greenville was a community adjoining Williams. Until today, she had intentionally limited the game to Williams proper, but it was time for a change. She continued to contemplate an end game to this so she could get on with her life. For the first time, she experienced a twinge of guilt rising up in her chest and was beginning to be troubled by the whole exercise, but was committed to it until the end – and she intended to dictate how it would end.

As she got behind the wheel and prepared to leave her garage apartment, she felt a moment of pride for what she had been able to do and how it had been accomplished. She had come up with the game, modified her car to serve as the shooting platform, provided for any unexpected emergency, and had thus far avoided suspicion or capture. It had really been simple to cut through the trunk behind the license plate and hinge the license plate so that, when lowered, she had a portal for firing. She had adjusted and modified the back seat so she could lie on it and into the trunk to fire. The windows were tinted so dark that no one could see inside.

The trunk was equipped with emergency gear so that if after shooting she had a problem, she could pull the seat back in place and stay in the trunk for as long as necessary. From inside the trunk, she could fold the license plate up and it looked like any other parked vehicle. Since she could fire with the car alarm on, no one would suspect anything unless they actually saw the muzzle blast when she fired. The rifle was inherited from her dad, so there was no sale to trace, and since she only fired one shot, she didn't need to purchase a lot of ammunition. She had actually caused all the havoc with a single box of shells that came with the gun. It was a common hunting rifle, so there was nothing special there to trace either.

The car helped too. It was one of those new hybrids which meant it could be started silently and with the lights off, was nearly impossible to detect. She had tried to think of everything, which is what made the game fun for her. She was outsmarting all those that sought to catch her.

The other reason for picking Greenville was that it was on the way out of town where she wanted to go for a long weekend to rest and plan for the future. She intended to drive to a cabin by a lake that she had also inherited when her dad died. It was a beautiful retreat, even in the winter, and her presence would not arouse any suspicion.

It was a short drive to the park and ride. She found a place near the entrance where she parked, adjusted the back seat, set up in the trunk, lowered the license plate and waited for the "lucky" first arrival. She did not have to wait long, for Dwain Robinson, a middle-aged lawyer, was almost there. He always caught the first bus so that he could work during the ride to his downtown office. Lots of billable hours had been generated in those early morning rides on the bus.

Robinson arrived and parked near the pick-up site for the bus. He was earlier than usual this morning. As he stepped out of his car, he noted one other car in the parking lot. That was his final observation, for from the trunk of the car a single shot fired that hit him in the chest. He fell and was dead before he hit the pavement, his car door still open.

She watched him as he fell, but before she could turn to adjust the back seat and depart in silence, the Curtain opened and what she saw terrified her. Suddenly she was in a new place, different from anything she had seen before, where she saw a great white throne with someone seated on it. The man she had just killed stood before the throne as books were opened and a search was done for his name in a book entitled *The Book of Life*. When his name was not found, fearful glorious beings grasp him and he was thrown alive into what appeared to be a lake of fire and brimstone.[50] The screams, cries, gnashing of teeth and the smell of burning sulfur terrified her.

The shooter gasped in horror and for the first time sped from a crime scene, not to escape the police who were as yet totally unaware of the murder, but to escape the scene that had just been played out before her. What had she just seen? What had she just done? She was not troubled by having killed Dwain Robinson; it was what happened after the shooting for which she began to cry – another first – and speak out loud to herself.

"I just sent a man I don't even know into some kind of awful pain and suffering. Forgive me, forgive me," she cried out to the body left behind. "I did not mean to do that. I did not know. Is that what I have been doing all this time? I thought since I killed them they all went to a better place. That's what they always say at funerals. What have I done?"

She drove on, lost in the reality of what the Bible calls the second death.[51] A Guardian accompanied her along with Providers, ready to join with her if she opened herself to the light. Her Keeper fought to maintain his hold on her and to pour the Dark Master's influence into her, but the battle had been joined, and after what she had seen, she no longer accepted his guidance without question.

Back now from Washington, Molech saw what had happened and knew just what had to be done. The Dark Master had prepared him for a time such as this. If the forces of the light were going to open the Curtain, they would respond with their version of a different curtain. It was all about appearance anyway and they could counterfeit almost everything the Enemy could do. Argon was shocked that Molech seemed so calm and wondered what method he knew to reclaim influence and control over the shooter. She was still needed to silence the searcher or the Bookseller, or both. He departed quickly, leaving the shooter to Molech, for he had business in Williams to again mislead and misdirect the police.

Police Response

It was another ten minutes before the call came in reporting the murder. Dwain Robinson had arrived at the park and ride early to be sure to get his regular seat on the bus. His unopened coffee and McDonald's breakfast lay with him in a pool of blood. As calls were made to scramble the swat team and gather the Williams investigation team, two men were preparing to pray in the converted warehouse near the railroad tracks.

Argon had moved quickly through various Keepers to create confusion and conflict. "The murder is under our jurisdiction," said Greenville Chief Gary Monroe to Detective Pete Samson. "We can handle this. No one knows whether this has anything to do with the Williams' shooter. I have dispatched a team to investigate. We don't need your interference."

"How can you be so hard-headed?" Samson's angrily responded. "Everything about this screams the Williams' shooter!"

"Look Samson," Chief Monroe answered, "you people in Williams have nothing to brag about and little to offer. The Williams' shooter has had his way for months and you haven't a clue to this day. We are not going to allow you to turn our city into another shooting gallery. We will deal with this ourselves and pass on what we learn. Stay home. You are not welcome here in this investigation. We will catch your shooter."

Samson clenched his fist as he hung up, wishing he could express what he felt. Argon smiled for the dispute had cost precious time, allowing the shooter to be far from the scene of the crime, safe and on her way to an encounter with Molech. Barnabas, who was present in the warehouse, was also pleased, for the forces of light had not abandoned the shooter to the ultimate end Dwain Robinson suffered. "Sometimes the agenda of the Father required allowing the forces of darkness to seem to have their way," Barnabas thought. "Fortunately, they have never understood and thus can be used purposefully to advance an agenda totally opposed to their own."

The List

Even as the investigation team gathered at 1632 Washington Avenue and a forensic team from Greenville scoured the crime scene, there was a serious discussion going on at a CIA workstation in the Directorate of Intelligence section in Washington. Having spent the night reviewing intercepts, web postings and emails from known Jihadists sources, David Barnes was tired and ready to go home when he stumbled across a strange posting on a website that was initiated from Pakistan. It was a list, perhaps an agenda for a meeting, he thought. It read:

Purpose

Weapons

Targets

Personnel

Coordination & Communication

Timing

"I have never seen anything like this," David reported to his section chief. "With all the reports on the movement of people and increased chatter, I find this alarming. If this is the agenda for a Jihadists leaders meeting, there is a level of sophistication in planning I haven't encountered before. This is more than a 'how can we kill masses of people' or destroy symbols of America event like 9/11. This indicates to me a carefully considered plan to strike a death blow at the country. It is that first entry, 'Purpose' that evidences the difference. Someone has been thinking and planning for a long time on what to do and how to do it. The 'Coordination & Communications' entry indicates a large scale event. 'Timing' may mean it is close. This needs to be circulated urgently."

"You are reading a lot into a list," was the section chief's response. "I frankly think if we are not careful, we are going to get back to the days of the red scare – a communist under every bed. I know that was before your time, but the nation got crazy over a threat that never really materialized, and a lot of people got hurt unnecessarily."

"There is absolutely no comparison between a perceived domestic communist threat and the Jihadists," David answered getting frustrated now. "Remember 9/11? The communists never struck on American soil."

"OK, David. No lectures. We haven't had an attack since 9/11, and most of what we have encountered as threats to America proper has been almost comical in their lack of sophistication. I'll give you that with the Iranian's help, they have developed technology and weapons that are killing Americans in Iraq and Afghanistan, but not here. Write it up and send it on. We will let someone up the line make the decision whether this is relevant information to go in the morning White House briefing."

Unknown to the CIA, the posting of the list had been made by El-Ahab before he began his clandestine journey to Teheran. It was indeed the agenda for the leadership meeting. Lucius, who was aware of the plan, had been careful to direct David's attention to the website. Lucius' instructions had been to keep the possibility of discovery open. He always obeyed immediately and completely but wondered why it mattered. All the efforts of the Guardians to get God's people to pray had been unable to produce more than a token prayer from God's people. There was more talk about prayer, but little actual prayer. He knew that God's people were no threat to the Dark Master's agenda in the absence of prayer. He wished they understood.

A Possible Partnership

Officer Sally Johnson didn't wait for the meeting to begin. As soon as she heard that there had been another shooting, she put in a call to Tom Campy with the Citizens Militia. "Tom, this is Sally Johnson. There has been another shooting. This time in Greenville, but everything about it points to the Williams' shooter. We need to meet. Can you get your press relations person and meet later this morning?"

"Sure," was the response, "but what exactly is it that you want to discuss?" Tom responded, not yet ready to fully trust the police.

"In light of this new shooting, I believe that it is absolutely essential we present the public with a unified front to show them we are addressing this threat in a new way that they will believe will protect them. If not, God help us. They can't take much more and the investigation is going nowhere right now. I have some ideas on how we can work together starting with a joint press conference tomorrow. I am going to get approval from Detective Samson and the others at a meeting that's starting in a few minutes and then I will call you with a suggested time and place. I am going to bring along Troy Dallas, who heads our public involvement team. In the meantime, can you get approval from whoever you must?"

"Absolutely," Tom answered, his attitude having been changed. "Most on our side of the gun issue expected to have to act independently of the police. This should be a welcomed change. We have to protect the public and stop this killer together." He knew that was not a view shared by all, but it was what he firmly believed.

Hanging up, Sally entered the meeting of the investigators already in progress. The tone was negative and loud with Detective Samson leading the way. "Nice of you to show up, Johnson," was his opening barrage. "You want to start over with your 'WHAT NEXT' discussion? I'll tell you what's next! We have another body and a hard-headed chief of police who won't even let us investigate. That's what's next."

Joining in the frustration, Greg Petersen blurted out, "This investigation is going nowhere. I can tell you what the Greenville people will find. We all know – one shot fired – same gun as before – no witnesses – no physical evidence – no nothing! I can't stand it. Why can't we find anything? It is as if we are facing a stealth killer – invisible, shielded, protected – a machine."

"Hold on before you make a superhero out of this killer," said Todd Wilson. "I'm the old man of this crowd who has been through hundreds of murder investigations. There is a logical answer. Let's start over and go back to the drawing board and review all 39 shootings. There has to be a pattern, something that either will enable us to identify this killer or predict his next move."

"Before you go there," Johnson inserted, "hear me out. I have a more immediate concern. We have to address the public's fears and lack of confidence in this investigation. We have to do something new and different to make the people believe they are safe going through the regular events of their daily lives. The reality is we can't do that alone. We don't have enough police officers and we don't want the National Guard in here."

"No one disputes that," Samson's responded, "but how is it possible? What can we do beyond another press conference to tell a bunch of people who don't believe us that they are somehow magically safe now?"

This was Johnson's chance and she took it. "These are perilous and unusual times which call for unusual actions. I want authority to partner with the Citizens Militia and help them recruit a massive force of armed volunteers who we will coordinate as a presence on the streets, in parks, schools, etc. I don't expect them to do anything beyond deterring the killer from striking where they are, but their presence may be enough to give the people a new sense of confidence that they are safe. It also gives the relatives and victims an opportunity to do something to stop this killer. That will help them deal with the anger and grief over their loss. It will give the people an opportunity to do something and not feel helpless."

Petersen's reaction was as expected from a former Army ranger. "You want to turn loose a bunch of untrained, undisciplined, red-necked civilians with guns? You can't be serious."

"I am, if you pardon the expression, 'dead' serious. Our real enemy now is not the killer; it is fear of the killer. That must be overcome, or he has won and we might as well surrender the city."

"Sally, do you honestly believe we can control these people once they get on the streets?" It was a thoughtful question by the old man who was deep in contemplation.

"No, not completely" was Sally's honest answer. "But we can work with them and support them and we will know what they are doing. Remember, they don't have to get our permission in this state to openly carry a firearm in most public places and they are going to do something. We are better off doing it together and the reality is we need them to be with us and not against us. We have enough criticism already. They will either lead the people to believe in what we are doing or lead a revolution against us."

"Sounds like there may be an ounce of brain behind this after all," concluded Samson. "Take your best shot, but keep us in the loop with details on how this is going to work."

"Troy, this overlaps your team's area and I need help. Can you come with me," Sally asked. "I am going to meet with some of their leadership now."

"Troy, go with her," Samson instructed. "But remember, don't go beyond encouraging visible patrols. We don't need a bunch of vigilantes on the loose."

CHAPTER 7

THE BOOKSELLER ANSWERS

Friday, February 1 – MD Minus 114 days

AS PAUL APPROACHED the warehouse, there was a war going on within him. All his anger and frustration at religious phonies welled up inside, as did his doubts about the existence of God based on the evidence of what was going on around them. He had heard a radio report of the Greenville shooting on his way over and began to wonder why he should bother listening to an old man who's only real credentials, according to Chaplain Forrest, was that he knows the Bible better than any living man he knew. Paul wasn't sure he even believed the Bible was true.

What Paul did not know or appreciate was that the Bible was written under the inspiration of the Holy Spirit, the light inside, and that the Holy Spirit, who was God, could cause the men whom He called to write what was revealed to them without error.[52] That was knowledge Argon intended to keep from Paul if possible. The forces of light sought to advance the opposite agenda. That conflict was the war Paul experienced as he stood at the door to the warehouse. It was a war over his soul. Both sides wanted control of his life, his heart, his desires and affections – all that he was.

Paul's agenda was much simpler. All he cared about was "old number one" – himself and Samantha, who he was coming to understand he really cared for in a way he had never cared for anyone else. The dream had frightened him, but he could have easily disregarded it as simply a bad dream, except for the end when the huge hands of the dark creature seemed to reach to grasp his head and pierce his skull. That was too real, and the reality of that moment simply would not go away. If this old man could help him understand what he had seen or enable him to disregard it as nothing but a bad dream, he would listen to whatever the Bookseller had to say. It was a chance worth taking.

The Bookseller was predictable if you understood his history and the basis of his faith. The light within glowed brightly for his walk with God was his life. He had been raised a Congregationalist. That denomination was almost dead now and in practice, had been deceived into beliefs that conflicted with most everything in its history. This denomination had been that of many of the founders of America, but they would not know it today, a fact in which the Dark Master took great pleasure. Perverting the work of the Enemy was what gave the Dark Master his greatest joy, and it was so easy to deceive these human creatures – with a few exceptions. Unfortunately for the forces of darkness, the Bookseller was one such exception.

The Bookseller, Samuel Evans White, hung onto the original teachings of the Congregationalists, which mandated evidence of the activity of God in a person's life or they would not be accepted as a Christian. Before the American Revolution, it would often be two years before someone who expressed an interest in joining a church was allowed to join. They had to prove by their life that God had changed them. Like John the Baptist's declaration to the Pharisees and Sadducees, they had to visibly "produce fruit in keeping with repentance."[53] That made religious deception much more difficult. Fortunately for the forces of darkness, few today were either willing to wait or willing to make someone wait for confirmation from God.

Along with a fundamental belief that God had to change a person's heart if they were to be changed, was his absolute belief in the truth of the Bible. He believed that the Bible was God's revelation to those created in His image and that it formed the foundation of a faith that would not change – because God would not change. He wasn't arrogant about it. He did not claim to understand it all, but he knew the Bible because he was constantly studying it, seeking to understand what he didn't know. Studying it was a source of great joy as the light inside would take a passage he had read 100 times and open something new about it. He loved that. For him, the Bible was alive.

The Bookseller was a man of many miles and many battles, a writer whose works were, for the most part, ignored, a teacher and preacher rejected by religious leadership and many local churches where he had been invited to speak. The efforts of the forces of darkness to destroy this man and his message had been intense and constant. They were in many ways like the "thorn in his flesh" which Paul the Apostle suffered as Satan sought to destroy him.[54] They had the same result, however, as he was driven to a deeper reliance on God – exactly the opposite of what the attacks intended.

The attacks had not been limited to him alone; they had fallen on his family and business, his wife and friends. He had been discouraged, disappointed, hurt, cheated, lied to, insulted and sometimes confused by what he saw and experienced. But in spite of it all, he remained faithful. That is why he was considered so dangerous to the forces of darkness. He could not be moved or made to compromise. Even now, the plan for his death advanced as Molech sent a messenger to Legend, advising that when the planning session was over in Teheran, he would be needed in Williams.

On this day, the Bookseller was as yet unaware of the Greenville shooting. His early morning hours had been spent in conversation and prayer with Chaplain Forrest. He was ready to hear Paul out and knew that he would be given the words to respond. "What a peace there is in complete reliance on God," he thought as the door opened and Paul entered.

"Good morning, I'm Paul Phillips. I have an appointment with the Bookseller."

"Yes, please come in. I have been waiting for you. I am sometimes called the Bookseller."

Paul was shown to a table in the front of the store surrounded on all sides by old books. They were everywhere – on shelves, in boxes, stacked in piles. It seemed as if there were miles and miles of books. Even the air was filled with a unique musty scent of old books. It was as if he had entered some hidden ancient center of learning and before him came the smiling Samuel Evans White covered in his usual working apron.

He seemed frail but strangely powerful, Paul thought. His voice was rich and heavy, spoken with a distinctive care for every word. He sounded like someone from the East Coast except that he spoke so slowly. All of that discerned from a greeting. Paul was surprised at how intently he was already listening to this little old man.

"Why have you come?" the Bookseller asked, opening the door for Paul to pour out the dream and all his questions and concerns. The Bookseller listened intently as Paul repeated the things he had told Professor Thompson and Chaplain Forrest. He ended with the still unanswered questions, "What did I see and what does it mean?"

No answers were given, only more questions. "What did they tell you?" The Bookseller was praying for discernment even as he listened to the words coming out of Paul's mouth. He already knew something of the conversations from what Chaplain Forrest had told him. He was listening for something different than what he had already been told, something more, but he didn't know what. He knew he would know it when he heard it. Thus far there was nothing new, so he dug deeper, seeking to draw everything possible out of this young man God had sent to him.

"Now Paul, think carefully, have you told me everything you saw in your dream?" The question set Paul back. He paused. He hadn't thought beyond what he considered to be the threat to himself and Samantha. As he reviewed the dream in his mind, he remembered other details.

"No, there was more. Not a lot, but I also saw a great number of the dark wisps gathered together in deference to one who held a pen and book. They seemed to be laughing and celebrating. The one they deferred to was larger physically than the others and he was giving what appeared to be papers to smaller ones who departed in a rush in different directions. It was only then that I saw the dark beings with their great hands resting on the heads of the vast majority, but not all of the people. I had forgotten the beginning of the dream."

"Every detail is important to comprehend the message," the Bookseller replied. "Let's start with the ground rules, so you will understand what I am about to tell you. I understand you are not a believer, so some of this may be confusing to you, but you asked for an answer and I am going to give you as clear an answer as I can. To do that I am going to take your experience – the dream – and lay it along side the Bible to judge whether it is real, and if so, whether it was from God. I know you doubt that the Bible is true. I don't. I believe that it all came from God and thus is all true. It is from that perspective that I draw my answers. You can accept them, ignore them or reject them as you please. That determination will be part of your search."

"Look, Mr. White, I didn't come here to argue about your religion. I came here to listen and ask questions because the chaplain said you could help. This is not a game for me. I don't understand what is going on in me. It's like I have a war inside, seeking to draw me this way and that. My emotions are silly crazy going everywhere. I want your honest opinion and I want to know how you support it. I have to get beyond this."

In his heart, the Bookseller rejoiced. That is what he had been looking for. Here was clear evidence that Paul was truly a searcher. The hunger in Paul to find truth was only possible because God had placed it there by His Holy Spirit.[55] God was reaching out to him to reveal Himself and to call Paul to Himself. Paul retained free will. He could reject God's call, but in these times he had been freed to hear truth and now was the time to start.

Barnabas and others in the forces of light rejoiced too. Paul's Guardian blocked the Keeper seeking to influence him while others of the light surrounded him to protect him from Tempters sent by Argon. This was Paul's time to hear and the forces of darkness would not be allowed to interfere.

"We need to begin with hard reality if you really want to get beyond this. Start out considering what this scripture means in light of what you saw, 'The god of this age has blinded the minds of unbelievers, so that they cannot see the light of the gospel of the glory of Christ, the image of God.'[56] Paul the Apostle wrote those words to a church in Corinth. Think about what you saw – the vast majority of the people had lost control of their minds to the darkness. Their eyes were crusted over so they could not see truth. Their ears covered by the huge hands so that they could not hear truth. That is the condition of all unbelievers – you included until God moved to free you so you could seek truth for yourself."

"Wait a minute," said Paul. "You mean to tell me that everyone who is not a believer is blind and their mind is under the control of the dark creatures I saw."

"Not control, but influence, which can be the same thing," the Bookseller responded.

"How, then, can you explain that I can see, hear and understand," Paul asked.

"Like I said, God moved, and you are capable of understanding truth," the Bookseller answered. "That is why you are searching for truth and that is why the huge hands you saw were not wrapped around your head. They had been, but that changed because God enabled you to search. Jesus made that clear. He said that 'No one can come to Me unless the Father has enabled him.'[57] You have been enabled."

"Why me?" asked Paul.

"Ask God," the Bookseller responded, "He obviously loves you and has a desire to use you somehow in His service, but let's back up for a minute. The first question you should have asked is whether there is a biblical basis for a vision of spiritual forces such as you saw. I can tell you there is, which is why I agreed to meet with you when Chaplain Forrest told me about your dream. There is both Old and New Testament authority for such a vision. I know that is confusing to you now, but you will understand if you continue in your search."

Opening his Bible, the Bookseller showed Paul passages in 2nd Kings, Daniel, Matthew and the Revelation where eyes were opened to see into the invisible, eternal, spiritual world.[58] Paul quickly seized on 2 Kings where the story was told of the prophet Elisha and his servant who was afraid because of all the enemies he could see with his eyes. The prophet told him not to fear and then prayed, "Oh Lord, open his eyes so he may see.' Then the Lord opened his eyes, and he looked and saw the hills full of horses and chariots of fire all around Elisha."[59] Paul's own experience had been just the opposite; his eyes had been opened to see the forces of darkness, but not the forces of light.

"Why did I see only the forces of darkness and not the forces of light?" Paul asked.

"I believe you had an incomplete dream because you woke up in fear before it was finished," the Bookseller sought to explain carefully. "There is obviously much you did not see since you missed the activity of the forces of light. But let's come back to that. For now, consider the meaning of what you saw beyond the blindness and influence over the mind. What do you think the celebration by the forces of darkness at a funeral meant? What about the book? What about the papers and the small ones going off in different directions? What do you think that all meant, Paul?"

"Obviously, I don't know. Help me please, Mr. White."

"I will try, but please listen closely with your now opened ears," the Bookseller answered. "I believe that each of the things you saw is significant, although the picture remains incomplete. The celebration by the forces of evil at a funeral can mean only one thing, the second death. The forces of darkness are celebrating because they won. The person whose funeral was being observed has experienced the second death, which is Satan's goal for all humans.[60] That is why he blinds eyes and ears and seeks to use influence to control minds regarding spiritual truth. Jesus said that what Satan comes to do is 'only to steal and kill and destroy.'[61] Unfortunately, the second death is not simply physical death, which we all experience; it is an eternal death. I didn't write it, but what Scripture says is the second death is 'the lake of fire' – eternal punishment. Satan rejoices because another is experiencing what he knows he will someday experience. It is clear in the Bible.[62] That is how it will end for him."

"That is hard to swallow," was Paul's immediate response. "If God is love, how can he allow that?"

"A better question might be how can He not allow that. What kind of God would He be if He left evil unaddressed? But because of His love, God gave man a choice. I am sure you have at least heard John 3:16 quoted somewhere."

"I think so, but I'm not sure."

"Well, it says that 'God so loved the world, that He gave His only begotten Son that whoever believes in Him shall not perish, but have eternal life.' Samantha's dad didn't believe, so he perished. I hope you will come to understand that having the choice evidences God's love, for God paid an unbelievably high price to give us that choice."

"Believe what? What choice? I still don't get it."

"Paul, don't be concerned that everything is not immediately made clear. I believe that all of this is a part of that process and the time will come when it will be made clear to you, but for now, focus with me on every detail of what you saw in your dream. All of it is important if we are to understand what you were shown."

"All right. Let's start with the book, what could that mean?"

"I believe that it is within Satan's character to review every 'victory' to determine what worked so he can use that against the remaining humans still living. The meeting you saw was most likely a group of the forces of darkness reviewing the life of the deceased and how they had been successful in keeping him away from the knowledge of God. They wrote it down to pass it on to others of their kind. I am sorry. I know that the deceased was your girlfriend's dad, but what you saw did not indicate a man who will spend eternity with God.

"Consider the differing sizes of the dark beings," said the Bookseller, seeking to direct Paul's thoughts away from the deceased and back to the living, "that represents rank and authority among the forces of darkness. They are not all the same. Remember, you said they deferred to the keeper of the book. Scripture teaches that there are hierarchies of authority leading to Satan. The leaders appear to be assigned geographic or territorial 'kingdoms' for which they are responsible.[63] What you probably saw in your dream was the leader of the forces of darkness in Williams.

"Now, you saw the leader writing what appeared to be notes. That is significant. When you study scripture, you will learn that there are many differences between the forces of darkness and the forces of light. There are major differences in power and in abilities as well as in purpose and direction. Satan and his forces can only be in one place at one time. Accordingly, they must send messages to each other. By contrast, scripture teaches that God is everywhere and that nothing can be hidden from Him.[64] He doesn't need a messenger. He already knows the past, present and future. The Holy Spirit is at the same time present in all believers. Accordingly, the sending of an external messenger to a believer is not necessary. The Holy Spirit can communicate with all or any believer at any time.[65] External messengers are used, on occasion, for emphasis, but they are not required."[66]

"Wow, that is a lot to take in," was Paul's only response.

The Bookseller was silent, knowing that an unbeliever would never be able to understand all of this unless God opened his mind, which might take a while. He remembered that scripture says, "The man without the

Spirit does not accept the things that come from the Spirit of God, for they are foolishness to him, and he cannot understand them for they are spiritually discerned."[67] Without the light inside, understanding is impossible.

"If only he will continue to search," he thought. At that exact moment, the Bookseller was given wisdom for what he needed to complete, what God wanted him to do at the moment. He knew what to say.

"Paul," he began, "I want to ask you to consider doing one more thing." Paul waited to hear. "Remember the prayer we read earlier by the prophet Elisha for his servant who was afraid in the face of the enemy? I want to ask you if you will pray that prayer for yourself – personalize it. Pray this, 'O Lord, open my eyes so I may see the forces of light at the funeral.' If you are allowed to see the dream finished, come back and let's discuss what the dream as a whole means."

His face became somber and the Bookseller cautioned Paul, "With that request goes a warning. I told you that Satan counterfeits everything God does to draw people away. Scripture tells us that when necessary, he even 'masquerades as an angel of light.' His servants masquerade as 'servants of righteousness.'[68] That is why I told you to measure everything by the Bible. If he is seeking to restore you to his influence, he may appear to you in a dream or otherwise to draw you away. Be very careful to consider what happens in response to your prayer in the context of what we have read from the Bible and the first part of your dream. Don't allow yourself to be deceived."

As Paul was preparing to leave, he remembered his list of questions and handed them to the Bookseller. "I need answers to these too," he said. The Bookseller read each slowly and smiled. "Great questions but they must be saved for another day. I am going to put them here in my Bible and when it is time, come back and we will work through them together one at a time until you have your answers."

"Can I come back Monday?" Paul asked.

"I should be here," was the response, "and will look forward to it. Perhaps by Monday, our prayer will have been answered and your dream will have been completed."

CHAPTER 8

THE FORCES OF LIGHT ENGAGE

Friday, February 1 – MD minus 114 days

DAVID BARNES WENT home tired but happy. His report on the agenda intercept had been forward to the White House as part of the president's daily security briefing. He was relieved that this piece of intelligence and his analysis on its possible significance had not been disregarded. He felt stronger about its possible importance than anything he had previously encountered in his service at the CIA. Something inside was telling him not to ignore this. He intended to make a search for more information on the detail behind this list his daily priority.

As Troy Steed, the National Security advisor went through the daily briefing; it was as if President Strong experienced an electric shock when the part about the list was discussed. He lurched forward in his chair, grabbed the phone, "Troy, wait a minute." On the phone now to his chief of staff, the president said, "Get Tom Knight in here right now." The tone and bluntness of the instruction were unusual. This president didn't usually act that way. Something was definitely up.

Hanging up and turning back to the meeting at hand, the president said, "Troy I don't know what there is about this list, but I feel deep within that this is significant. It is a gift, a warning, some direction about what is being planned. The Survival Commission has got to get to work fleshing out the meaning of each of these categories. While they are doing that, get your group of department heads together and push further intelligence on this. We have to have operatives somewhere who have picked up information. Run all the traps, full time, we cannot allow ourselves to be surprised again. We have to identify this threat and end it before they can execute whatever their plan is – and have someone find this David Barnes. I want to hear his views on this."

"Mr. President, you have a special commission and all the security agencies who will flesh this out for you. Don't get too hands-on or you may actually impede the investigation."

"Easy for you to say, but I have to live with any attacks that are launched on my watch. I won't interfere unless I think it is necessary, but I am going to be on top of this one and you tell the directors that. If any of them does not share my concern, ask for their resignations. I want people as serious about this threat as I am."

Troy was shocked. America had lived under the declared threat of additional terrorist attacks every day since the president took the oath of office. What had built such a fire under him over a simple list?

The answer to that question was not of this world. America would be given its chance, but would America accept the gift? Lucius wondered and waited additional instructions. On the opposing side, Chemosh considered how best to divert attention away from the reality of the threat.

Survival Commission Chairman Tom Knight entered the oval office breathless, having literally run through the White House in response to the president's directive. The whole place knew something was up. When the meeting ended, he ran again to get to his office to set up a commission meeting after telling the assistant press secretary to handle the press briefing today. Another kind of search had begun. This one correctly described as one for survival.

Target: College Church

Back in Williams, Abdul Farsi gathered his two team leaders, Kalb Sawori and Allahabad Doeg in an upstairs room to review what he had learned from his recent walk to the selected target sites. This operation would be much more difficult than others he had organized because it would require an escape plan. Their normal operation had been to use either a remotely detonated explosive device, such as were widely used in Iraq and Afghanistan or suicide attacks. Since they could not smuggle in an unlimited number of operatives willing to die or the quantity of explosives necessary for multiple IEDs, their people had to survive the attacks and prepare for the next. It was a whole different mindset. They were soldiers in an extended war which would involve many battles. It would be continuing guerrilla warfare even after the big attack that was coming.

"Listen closely. This college church is huge with multiple meetings and many people. Timing will be everything. We have to determine the exact time to hit during a service when there will not be masses of people leaving or arriving in cars. We need to target specific individuals by location. There is a large gathering area before you get to the big meeting room. We need to decide now who to shoot so we can get access to the meeting room, shoot the leader and then others randomly. Terror is the goal, not masses of deaths, so you will hit hard, quickly and get out. I already have an idea for the next target. We will strike at the ultimate occupiers – the Jews. I have found one of their meeting places called Temple Shalom. That will be next."

Sawori asked, "Do you have a drawing of the site so we can plan our moves and kills?"

"Better than that Kalb, you are going to church on Sunday," Farsi replied, a hint of humor in his tone. "Pick one other from your team who appears the most like the Americans and go separately to the earliest service. It has to be one who reads and speaks English well. Sit separately in the back and observe what is happening. Pick the time when most of the people have arrived and the meeting has started. Pick your targets coming in and once you are in the meeting room. Identify the leaders, where they sit or stand, so you know who to be sure to shoot. See if you can find any black people to target. That will help with our cover as you escape."

"How do we escape and how do we hide our identification with Jihad?" was Sawori's next question.

"Relax for now. I have a plan for both which we can discuss later. The date for the first attack is one week from Sunday, so pay close attention to detail when you go this week. You will not have another opportunity. Be careful to act like the rest of the infidels. Sing when they sing, stand when they stand, repeat what they say in their public readings. Be careful to do nothing to draw attention. Act like you are interested in what is happening. Be friendly if someone talks to you, but leave quickly when the meeting is over."

"Doeg, I am still thinking though the timing and method of the Kingdom Day Care attack. All I know right now is that it will be soon after the college church attack. We need to see how the authorities respond to the first attack before we complete the plan to kill the children. Be patient for a while longer."

Patience was not something Doeg was known for. He would be looking for a way to strike a blow soon if Farsi didn't need him. He hadn't given up the chance to kill Americans in Iraq and Afghanistan just to sit in a rented house in America. He came here to kill Americans and if Farsi couldn't figure out how, he would. His anger and hatred would be impossible to control.

"Good," thought Argon, "a weapon that can be used. Maybe he is the one to kill the Bookseller. I will suggest that to Molech. Perhaps a promotion will be forthcoming."

Going downstairs, Farsi took the three Palestinian students providing the safe house aside and told them, "Over the next ten days, on alternate days I need for a different one of you to go to different stores and purchase a king sized set of white cotton sheets and pillow cases and bring them back to the house. Start today. I want five full sets. Be careful not to do anything to arouse suspicion."

Escape to the Lake House

The shooter was normally a very careful person, calculating every move to provide an alibi to protect her from discovery. This morning before leaving the apartment for the park and ride, she had remotely activated the telephone message machine at the lake front cabin and recorded a new message. "Hello. This is Susan. Today is Friday, February 1st and the time is 5:00 am – really! If you get this message, I am either out for a walk in the woods or on the lake fishing. Please leave a message and I will get back to you as soon as I return. Have a great day." If anyone had checked on her, she would appear to have been at the cabin when the shooting took place.

All that careful planning was in the trash now as she finally arrived at the cabin. She was a total mess, physically and emotionally. Fortunately, her neighbors were also absent owners, so no one was around to see her as she stumbled into the cabin, still shaken by what she had seen. Molech let her stew for a time, but through her Keeper began to instill in her the idea that perhaps there was a purpose in what she saw and in what she had been doing. There was a conflict drawing her toward the reality of the horror of what she had done. Obviously, there was no one she could talk to about what she had seen after murdering someone, so she fretted and began to drink. She had to somehow escape the memory of the man she shot being thrown into a lake of fire, the sound of his screams and the smell of burning sulfur. Soon the alcohol and fatigue caught up with her and she fell asleep.

Partnership Established

Greg Petersen had been right. The Greenville investigation had turned up nothing new and there were no witnesses. The bullet matched the gun used in all the other shootings. No dispute, the Williams shooter had expanded his field of operations.

Down the hall in a conference room, Officer Sally Johnson and Troy Dallas met with Tom Campy and Diane Conway to work through how the police and the Citizens Militia could work together to restore some sense of safety among the citizens. It was unnatural the way these leaders of two groups with such different backgrounds and focus became one in intent and purpose. It was as if they were reading from the same agenda, which they, in fact, were, for the light within burned brightly in Sally Johnson and Tom Campy, so the guidance they had been receiving was the same.

When the initial round of discussion had ended, Sally Johnson's "WHAT NEXT" board contained the following five objectives:

1. Primary purpose and mission – visibility and presence to encourage the public and discourage the shooter

2. Begin with the most public and vulnerable sites – parks, schools, major public gatherings and expand as broadly as possible and as quickly as possible

3. Immediate major public recruitment drive – police check of all applicants for membership

4. Joint training in use of firearms and rules of engagement

5. Immediate deployment with police – shift in police to visibility

Diane Conway was excited. "As a writer for *The Sentinel*, I can jump on this with an article in the morning edition on our plans and should be able to get something on local TV news and radio almost immediately. We can get this out as 'good news' to be reported along with the Greenville shooting even before tomorrow's press conference. Finally, the public will have a way to join together and strike back at this killer. It should really help the families of victims by giving them an outlet for their anger and grief."

"The red jackets, shirts and hats labeled 'Citizens Militia' are in, so we can wear those tomorrow at the press conference and select areas to begin highly visible patrols with those who have already signed up," added Campy.

"Tom, I need your current membership list so we can run a quick police check on them," added Johnson. "No insult intended, but we have to be sure that we are not empowering someone who could be a danger to the public. We need to be able to tell the public we have checked these people out and they can be trusted. You understand that it is unprecedented to encourage a group of armed civilians in public other than in a time of war when the nation is physically at risk."

"I do, but this is war," was Tom's response as he provided the list. He knew that request would be made and had brought the list with him. He intended to be a team player on this one. It was too important. The killer had to be stopped and he knew somehow that time was short.

Paul Reports Back to Samantha

Samantha had waited expectantly for Paul to return. She wanted to know everything he had learned about what the dream meant, the answers to their list of questions and something about this mysterious Bookseller.

Paul didn't know how to begin. He wanted her to know everything, but how do you tell someone that your dream was confirmation that their dad had suffered what Mr. White called the "second death," eternal punishment because he had never repented and allowed God to change him? This was a lot to swallow, particularly in a single sitting, and he was still working his way through what he had heard.

"Samantha, you have to meet the Bookseller. I have never met anyone like him. He listens so intently and pauses before he speaks as if taking time to ask an invisible force for the words. When he speaks, he talks slowly and deliberately with every word chosen poised like a work of art. You cannot help but feel compelled to struggle, to be sure you understand what he is saying.

"So much of what he said was foreign to me. He read from the Bible, a verse that would seem to say that the creatures I saw are demonic beings that blind people to the things of God. If that is true, it would mean that we have been blind and that nearly everyone is. According to the Bookseller, we can search now because God has freed us from the blindness. I don't know whether I believe that, but that is what he read, and we are searching. One thing for sure is that he believes it. He speaks with a quiet confidence that is disarming. What should make me mad or want to ridicule him only makes me want to think about whether what he says is true. It is very strange to me.

"About having the dream, he told me that in the Bible there were times when God opened eyes of someone to allow them to see the invisible world. He read about a prophet who prayed that his servant's eyes be opened to see into the invisible and they were. He said that is what happened to me and made me tell him all I dreamed, saying every detail was important. At that moment, I remembered details I had forgotten, some of which I wished I hadn't remembered."

Paul paused, "This is hard, but I have to tell you what he said about the celebration at the funeral." As he continued, Samantha cried and Paul held her. The reality hurt, but in her heart, she knew it was true and frankly justified.

After a time Paul continued, now whispering in her ear as he held her close, "He said I had only seen half the dream. That I must have awakened before I could see it all, and we agreed to pray that God would open my eyes so I can see the forces of light at the funeral. I am going to pray that. If this is real and he is right, the prayer should be answered."

Samantha asked quietly while wiping her eyes, "How do you pray? No one ever taught me. I wouldn't know how to begin."

"I don't know," was the response. "I guess I am going to talk with God like I talk to you, only maybe with more respect because, well, He's God." And so he did, right there, right then.

"God, I don't even know for sure you are real, but if you are and if as the Bookseller has said you are, then you are the only one with the answers. I'm afraid. I don't understand the dream. I don't know what this choice means that the Bookseller spoke of. All I know is that I have to understand the dream, what it means, what you are trying to say to me. The Bookseller says I did not see all that was going on at the funeral. He says that your forces of light had to be there and active as well. But he warned me that dreams can also come from Satan, who counterfeits what you do. I need your help. I want to know everything that was going on at the funeral and I need to know that the message is from you and not from others. Please, however you can do it, if you can do it, open my eyes to know and understand everything that was going on at the funeral and to be sure that what is revealed is from you and is true. I have to know. We have to know. Show me so I can believe in you. Amen."

Samantha closed her eyes in agreement and prayed for open eyes to see and understand as well. She wanted to know. It was becoming a passion for her as well. "I guess that makes me a searcher too," she thought, which brought her some peace.

"What about our questions," Samantha remembered. Paul's answer was the last thing she expected. "He put them in his Bible for a later time. He said I wasn't ready for the answers. I am going to meet with him again on Monday. I want to know more."

"Listen, Samantha, this may sound a little strange but how would you like to get your mom's Bible down and let's find where it talks about what Jesus said and did? Everyone I talked to told me that the Bible says Jesus encountered demons and dealt with them. I want to know what it says about that."

"Sure, I'll find the Bible and let's read for a while. Maybe we can find some answers." And so they did. Samantha got the Bible and they looked through and found where the red letters were and started there.

There was a silent scream in the darkness even before Paul and Samantha started to pray. The power of the prayer was released when they set their minds to pray, as was the answer to the prayer.[69] There was a crowd of the forces of light gathered over Samantha's apartment that night. It included Barnabas and Lucius, but they had been joined by Niger and Manaen, who had been called in by Lucius. These four and others formed a protective shield around the apartment until God's business there was completed.

Lucius turned to Niger and said, "Do you remember the great battle that was fought when Daniel sought understanding of one of the visions given to him? This seems a lot like that."

"How well I remember," was the response. "The battle fought over that prayer was monumental. Before it ended, there had been 21 days of conflict and the intervention of Michael, one of the Lord's two Archangels, was required to defeat the massive power of darkness thrown to obstruct that prayer and discourage Daniel. Had he given up before the fight was won, he would have lost the answer to his prayer forever."[70]

"Yes, persistence is often required," Barnabas added. "Jesus taught about that when he told the parable of the persistent widow. Dr. Luke got it right, 'Jesus told His disciples a parable to show them that they should always pray and not give up.'[71] I hope these two don't give up."

"Well let's help them with that," was Lucius' response and he assigned Providers named Faith and Perseverance to help Paul and Samantha continue to ask and wait for the answer to their prayer.

As they continued to read, Paul began to take notes of what was said about demons and about incidents involving demons. He felt that it might be important to be able to find what it said again and to be able to look at it all together at one time in one place. To help with that effort, Barnabas assigned Providers named Wisdom, Discernment and Truth to open the Bible to them as they read.

Barnabas loved it when the Bible was read out loud like Paul was doing. The Apostle Paul has written that in the invisible war, the Bible, like prayer, was a weapon against the forces of darkness. The Apostle called it "the sword of the Spirit." It certainly was proving its effectiveness here.[72] The forces of darkness had fled from the sound of the reading of the Bible and were all out of hearing range of Paul's voice as he continued to read aloud from the Book of Matthew.

The battle raged in the invisible world over the delivery of an answer to the prayer of Paul and Samantha, which had been joined in at other times and in other places by the Bookseller and Chaplain Forrest. The Dark Master was determined to keep the Curtain closed on their activities and on those of the forces of light. "The answer to the prayer must be stopped or delayed," he thought. "Surely what the Enemy had begun in this human He would complete unless the humans could be made to reject what the Enemy offered. Accordingly, an all-out effort should be made to delay the answer, while discouraging their prayers in the hope that they will lose heart and cease praying before the answer arrives. It has worked so often before. If only the Enemy does not use one of the Archangels to speed delivery. These human creatures have no idea of the power of their prayers. That truth must be kept from them."

Instructions were also issued to Molech for delivery of an alternate message to the praying searchers. Perhaps the delay would be long enough for deception to once again succeed.

CHAPTER 9

THE POWER OF THE RIGHT QUESTION

Saturday, February 2 – MD minus 113 days

MORNING BROKE CRISP and cold, but then it is always cold in Williams in February. Paul awakened having had no dream. Discouragement came to him immediately as did doubt, but they were quickly offset by a reminder to continue to pray and by excitement at the possibility of reading more of the red letters with Samantha. He stopped right then and again prayed for God to open his eyes to see the remainder of the dream. He was not giving up after only one night. He had made a promise to the Bookseller.

The morning paper, *The Sentinel*, carried two front page articles on the shooting. One, a review contained the standard report described the Greenville shooting, but also chronicled the other 38 shootings, including pictures of the victims. It was heart-wrenching and would create more fear and anger looking into the eyes of those who had suffered at the hands of this killer. The other was different. It was upbeat and positive, regarding a new citizen's organization cosponsored by the Williams police which would provide armed security around the city in public locations and elsewhere as requested. It was a call for volunteers, a chance to get in the game and help stop the killer. The group, known as the Citizens Militia, would be introduced at a press conference this afternoon. Paul's initial response was to consider signing up.

North and west of the city, the shooter awoke at her cabin on the lake but wished she hadn't. She was suffering from one of those sick hangovers that make you wish you weren't going to live. That thought lasted about one second as she slapped herself into the reality that her death would be followed by a scene just like that of the lawyer. "Help, someone!" she screamed at no one. She didn't want to live but was afraid to die. Her cry was heard by both sides in the invisible battle and they both prepared a response.

In Southern Arizona, a young man named Juan Martinez rode his bike toward the school gym to play basketball with friends. As he rode past the old Craig place, he wondered why in a little town like Carmen, Arizona there were so many different off-road trucks stopping at the same house. It seemed as if they were there several times most weeks. It didn't make any sense to him. "I wonder who lives there," he thought to himself as he rode on. His stare had been noted by one of the foreign occupants.

In Teheran, Jihadists continued to arrive in preparation for Monday's meeting. The agenda had been distributed and even now, work was ongoing on the details of the plan. They knew they had to be careful, for although the Iranian government supported their efforts, they knew they would be monitored.

At President Strong's direction, the combined intelligence services of the United States had "run the traps" and discovered unusual movement throughout the Mideast and elsewhere to Iran by persons of interest in terror investigations. "Do we have any resources in Iran?" asked Tom Knight. "Perhaps," was Troy Steed's response as he left the Oval Office to contact the department heads and find out.

"Mr. President, this is getting too real," Tom Knight continued. "We may need to start thinking about going public to find out what the people know or have observed that is unusual."

"Not yet, Tom," was the president's answer. "We need to see if we can isolate where in Iran they are meeting and what can be done to get details on the meeting. We know that everything of significance in Iran is monitored. It is not much different than the old Soviet Union in that respect.

There has to be a way. I do want the commission to put some thought on how and when to go public, but before we go public, we need to have a better idea of what to look for and when to expect them to move."

The Conspiracy of Darkness

Above the city, Molech had gathered Argon and others to coordinate their efforts and strategies to advance the Dark Master's agenda. Present also were Baal, Asherah and Ashtoreth who had been called in because of their unique abilities to manipulate the human creatures. All three, like Molech and Chemosh, had been worshiped as gods. Baal had been seen as a storm-god pictured with a club and grasping a thunderbolt. Asherah was worshiped as a fertility goddess with a horned hat. Ashtoreth was worshiped as a mother goddess of fertility, love and war. Together they had often been able to draw the nation of Israel away from worship of the Enemy, outside His protection and into His righteous judgment. Their services now would hopefully have the same effect — turning those who claim to serve the Enemy into their allies against the Enemy. The intended targets of their efforts were obvious.

Molech began, "I come from the Dark Master's presence. The Enemy has struck and we must respond. The Dark Master has suffered another of those humiliating blows when he was called before the Enemy to give an account of his activities. It was apparently like the times when he was called before the Enemy and the subject of the human creature Job arose. Remember the result of those encounters? The Enemy set limits – first, we could take or destroy everything he had, but not him – then freedom to attack his physical body, but not take his life.[73] What fun to attack what Job loved and then to seek to destroy his body, but we failed to destroy him and the Enemy restored everything Job lost twice over. That was only because Job remained faithful throughout the attack.[74] Had he not, he would have been totally destroyed. It was a great effort and almost worked except for the direct intervention of the Enemy Himself. I don't believe He will do that here."

"The Enemy's subjects, this time, were that cursed one they call the Bookseller, the kid, Paul Phillips, and his girlfriend, Samantha. The Enemy's limitations regarding the Bookseller are that we cannot touch him; specifically, the Dark Master was told we cannot now kill him. The limits on the other two are the same. The Enemy declared that they would be given the chance to choose. The issue for us is how to respond. We will not surrender either to the Enemy's purposes. We will not bow our knees to His desires."

"Didn't we learn anything from the Job fiasco?" responded Baal. "These human creatures are always vulnerable despite what the Enemy declares because He has allowed them free will. They get to choose and we get to throw all kinds of temptations at them until they fall out of the Enemy's protection. We tried with Job's 'friends' to do that and only succeeded in drawing the friends into the Enemy's judgment, but it could have worked and we ought to try again."[75]

"You're right, for a change," Ashtoreth replied condescendingly. "We are not powerless here. The earth is the domain of the Dark Master.[76] He controls it and all the human creatures here except those few in whom the light glows. We battle for each soul and we have the advantage. If we are careful, we can at least draw them out of the Enemy's service."

"Not enough!" screamed Asherah. "The Bookseller must die and this kid cannot be allowed to end up with the light within. He frightens me because the Enemy has such an interest in him. There is something we haven't figured out about him. He is dangerous and must die before he has the light within. We cannot risk leaving him here for the Enemy to use."

"Agreed," chimed in Argon, who was way out of his league in this crowd. "I already have identified one who will kill them both. It's the terrorist Doeg. He is already in Williams and wants to kill."

"You fool," was the cold reception from Molech. "Doeg has already been selected to kill the children. Would you dare to sacrifice the Dark Master's purposes for him?"

Smitten and angry, but afraid that he would soon be reduced to nothing but a messenger, Argon shrank to the back of the crowd to listen and not be seen.

"You both have the right idea," Molech answered Baal and Ashtoreth. "We learned in the great rebellion that the Enemy cannot be overcome by direct force. Don't forget that when the Dark Master was known as Lucifer, one of the three Archangels, and we were all angels, the plot was launched to depose the Enemy. We failed though the fighting was fierce.

A third of the forces of the angels had joined us and now we are all known as demons on the earth with the Dark Master still our leader.[77] We have to learn from our failures. Although we cannot defeat the Enemy directly, we don't have to. All we have to do is defeat the human creatures."

"Here is the Dark Master's plan. Ignore the Enemy's dictates and attack the three targets. Throw everything possible at them to keep the kids from gaining the light inside, deceive them into wrong choices, make them lust for one another and draw them away from the search by getting them involved in other things that seem important."

"The Bookseller is more of a challenge, but we have to draw him into doubt and discouragement such that he doesn't have the faith to be used by the Enemy. If Paul and Samantha fall, he may be discouraged enough to become disobedient and fall outside the Enemy's protection. If that occurs, we can kill him. Simple summary, we will ignore the Enemy's arrogant commands, provide Paul a 'religious' experience and move forward with an effort to kill them all."

Details and specific assignments were discussed and they rushed to their immediate places of service to begin. This plan had to be accomplished within the other work before them here, in Washington and in Teheran. "Much to do," thought Molech, "glad we have so many demons to work with and such exceptional leadership. I know Legion will control and advance the terrorist agenda against America and Chemosh will control the fools in Washington. It won't be long now. We will overcome the Enemy using those made in His image. It's almost humorous. They're so stupid. I hate them all."

The Williams Press Conference

As it neared 2:00 PM, the press gathered to hear this bold new plan for uniting citizens and the police to stand together against the shooter. With the 39th victim, the cable news channels had determined this made "good nightly news" and had directed their evening news shows to cover the Williams shooter. As a result, the networks determined to follow the announcement, and what had been intended as a simple press conference for the local media had gone national – even international on some of the cable networks. That complicated the politics surrounding the event.

Suddenly, fear of failure took center stage as the concern of those with political futures at risk and the politicians maneuvered to protect themselves. They didn't even know the details of the plan, only the concept.

Officer Sally Johnson knew if this failed, she would be looking for new employment, but didn't really care because she believed it was the right thing to do. She and Tom Campy had thought through the details carefully and believed that what was proposed was workable and capable of accomplishing its purpose. Nothing else had been able to meet the public's need to feel secure, and this could work.

The politicians went first, but before walking out to do the introductions together, the mayor had turn to the chief of police and said, "I hope you understand if this doesn't work, you are toast." And with that "kind" word of encouragement, the mayor put on his best public smile and walked out to portray brilliance and confidence and togetherness. The police chief would really have liked to deck him on the spot. He was rude, arrogant and a jerk, but he was the mayor, and the mayor was needed to make this work if it could work. "How did I ever let myself get talked into this" the chief thought as they approached the microphones and television lights together?

Once the politicos had their moment, they introduced Detective Pete Samson as head of the investigation and Sam Will as head of the Citizens Militia. Sam was first to be seen publicly in the red uniform of the Citizens Militia, and he was obviously armed. After their moment in the sun, Sally and Tom were introduced and immediately got down to business.

As the police representative, Sally led off. "I want to thank you for coming this afternoon. Tom and I are coordinating this joint effort of the police department and the Citizens Militia. We want to outline for the people of Williams our plan to provide greater security by working together to end this threat. We want to let you know how you can be part of this effort and how you can call upon us to provide security patrols for an event or at a location." And with that, out came the latest of her "WHAT NEXT" boards and a handout for the press providing some additional detail on each topic. There were five topics.

1. Security Together – Protection and Deterrence
2. Operations
3. Command and Control

4. Involvement and Opportunity
   a. Want to Join – 1-800- helpnow
   b. Need Security Patrol 1-800-safenow
5. Security Fair

"The concept is simple," continued Officer Johnson, "we are inviting the people of Williams to join together to end this threat by putting trained armed men and women visible throughout the city working under the direction of the police to provide additional security and deterrence. Those who would become members of the Citizens Militia will be required to pass a police check for prior criminal activity and a psychological evaluation; they must complete training in the proper use of their firearms and in the rules of engagement. Once these steps are completed, they will receive tamper proof picture identification cards which are to be worn on the distinctive red Citizens Militia jackets. These partners with the police will be easily identified by their ID badges and uniforms."

"They will be sent out two by two to patrol the areas believed to be most at risk and those where requests are received for a patrol," Tom added. "The police will direct deployment and will command the operation. All members will stay in contact with the police command center by cell phone. They will be given a special priority number for immediate access to report any unusual activity and the police will have their numbers by location."

"The current membership of the Citizens Militia has already gone through the evaluation process and training," Sally continued. "Beginning Monday you will see patrols at all public schools throughout the day and at public events. We begin here to protect our children, but want to significantly expand the effort. To do that, we will need your help. We need both additional members and suggestions on where to deploy the patrols. Employers, we need you to either give your member workers one day off a week with pay or allow them to work four ten hour days so they can patrol for a day. Tom?"

"We have obtained two toll-free numbers to give you the citizens the opportunity to join in the effort. If you want to join the Citizens Militia, call 1-800-helpnow. If you know of a need for a patrol, call 1-800-safenow. The first number will reach the offices of the Citizens Militia where you can get your questions answered and start the application process. The second number will reach police dispatch where the decisions will be made on where patrols are to be sent."

"Before we take your questions, we have one additional announcement. Next Saturday in the Memorial High School gym we will hold a Security Fair where the public will have the opportunity to get information on the Citizen's Militia and join or request patrols. There will be other activities including a time for a special memorial remembering the victims of the shooter. We will seek to honor them and will be conducting fundraising efforts for medical expenses to assist the injured and survivors. The event will be patrolled, so do not fear for your safety. Things are going to change in this town from this day forward."

The questions were as expected from a press crowd that did not favor armed citizens. They were handled with grace and patience, ignoring the insults directed at the failure of the police to resolve the case and the hysterical expressions of fear of shootings by members of the patrols. Tom and Sally did not care what the media thought. Their audience was the common people of the city. If they would feel more secure, the effort had already been successful.

As the press conference neared its end, a cable news reporter asked the obvious question everyone seemed to ignore, "Look, won't the red jackets simply offer the shooter an easy target?"

"Perhaps," Tom answered, "but then that is a risk worth taking to secure our city and keep our children safe. It is a risk that the police take every day with no fanfare."

"They are being sent out two by two for many reasons," Sally added, "but one obvious reason is so that if one member becomes the shooter's target, the other member will return fire. No more free shots at citizens. That is the goal. This must end."

Suddenly at the floor microphone, which had been installed to facilitate the asking of questions, an old man appeared with temporary press credentials that looked like he didn't belong. It was the Bookseller and he was there because Tom had felt led to call and invite him, and he had felt led to accept and attend. Tom knew him from an earlier time when the Bookseller had served as his church's interim pastor. He didn't know why he had invited him, only that he should.

The Bookseller began, "I wonder if we could add another dimension to this effort and call on believers everywhere to covenant to pray for God's deliverance and for the wisdom to understand why God has allowed this to happen. Allowing 9/11 and its progeny are, after all, His judgment on His people. We must understand why He is angry and change."

It was as if a nuclear device had been set off in the building. The news reporters mobbed the Bookseller, throwing questions at him, most insulting him for daring to bring God into the discussion and asserting that 9/11 and all this was somehow a judgment from God. He calmly responded with a simple statement, "Read Luke 13:1-5."

"What? Why?" they demanded.

"Read Luke 13:1-5," he repeated distinctly and carefully. And with that, he left, got in his old white minivan and drove back to the warehouse.

The mayor raced out front and in an action reminiscent of Mayor Dailey during the 1968 Democratic Nation Convention in Chicago, ran his finger across his throat signaling "cut" to immediately end the press conference – and so it ended.

CHAPTER 10

DIFFERING RESPONSES

Saturday, February 2 – MD minus 113 days

IN THE BEDLAM that accompanied the end of the press conference, hundreds of frustrated media employees around the world were scrambling to find Bibles. "What is Luke 13:1-5? What does it say? What does it mean? Who was that old man?"

As they scrambled to find something to say about what had just been televised to the world, millions of people were asking the same questions and were reaching for Bibles. Among the searchers were Paul and Samantha, who had interrupted their reading to watch along with most everyone else in Williams. Paul had been shocked when the Bookseller appeared at the floor microphone, but he had listened intently because he believed what was said would be important. It was so unlike the Bookseller to seek the spotlight. What could have motivated him to go and speak?

The answer to that question, along with why was he invited, why he went and how he knew what to say, was that direction had come from the light inside him to advance the Father's kingdom. The Father still sought to make all people searchers. This was an opportunity to create questions and cause people to want to search for answers.

The forces of darkness responded in a rage using every Keeper available who had influence over those in the media and in the audience to ridicule the Bookseller and to create anger at what he said. The sword of the Spirit had cut deeply [78] but now was the opportunity to deceive and pervert so that the verses could be twisted and used to attack Jesus and thus advance the Dark Master's agenda. Still, Argon thought, it is amazing how the Enemy takes what should be our victory and uses it against us.

Paul and Samantha Respond

"Luke is one of those red letter books," Paul explained to Samantha excitedly. "I remember seeing it when we were looking through for where to start reading. Here it is –

and here is Luke 13. Look, all but the first verse is red letters. That means Jesus said it," and he began to read.

> Now there were some present at that time who told Jesus about the Galileans whose blood Pilate had mixed with their sacrifices. Jesus answered, "Do you think that these Galileans were worse sinners than all the other Galileans because they suffered this way? I tell you, no! But unless you repent, you too will all perish. Or those eighteen who died when the tower in Siloam fell on them – do you think they were more guilty than all the others living in Jerusalem? I tell you, no! But unless you repent, you too will all perish."

"Samantha, get the dictionary. Look up 'perish' and 'repent.' I have no idea what, 'unless you repent, you too will all perish' means, but I know what 'all' means. If this is true and applies to today, we are included in 'all.' I know the Bookseller believes it applies today and is important, or he wouldn't have said it."

As Samantha found the dictionary and began to look up the words, the Bookseller arrived back at the warehouse, locked the front door and wrote a sign which he placed in the front window that repeated what he had already said publicly – "READ LUKE 13:1-5." And with that, he turned off the phone and found a quiet place in the back to pray. He had no intention of talking further with the media unless he received guidance to do so. He knew this was not about him, but rather about what Jesus had said that the world needed to hear once again.

"Perish," Samantha began. "Perish is defined as, 'to become destroyed or ruined.' "

"Did you notice, Sam, that Jesus did not use the word 'die' or 'death?' To perish must mean something different from death."

"Your right, the dictionary defines 'die' as 'to pass from physical life.' Perish is something else – must be something much worse. Do you think 'perish' is a reference to the 'second death' the Bookseller told you about, something after physical death? Could Jesus have been referring to the eternal destiny of those killed by Pilate or those killed when the tower fell, like the two towers that fell on 9/11?"

"It has to be more than that, Sam. Jesus is talking to the living about their eternal destiny, using the example of those who were killed in a horrific act to emphasize His point that there is something more important than physical death. He also is giving a key to avoiding this second death. 'Unless you repent, you too will all perish.' What about 'repent,' what does it mean?"

"Repent," Samantha read from the dictionary, "means 'to turn from sin and dedicate oneself to the amendment of one's life.' Hold on a minute, let me find out what the dictionary says 'sin' means," and she rushed to find the final puzzle piece.

"Sin is defined as 'an offense against religious or moral law.' What is religious or moral law? Who makes that law?"

"Stop just a minute, Sam. I think I understand what the Bookseller was trying to say. He was using what Jesus said to warn that something worse than 9/11 might happen if we don't find out what offense we have committed against what God considers religious or moral laws, and turn from it, dedicating ourselves to change our lives. But it is worse that that. He is using Jesus' words to also warn us that if we are a victim of the next attack unless we have repented, we will not merely die physically, we will eternally perish. I'm not sure I can handle this. No wonder Chaplain Forrest was afraid of him."

"It frightens me too, but I think you missed something," Samantha responded. "You said that the Bookseller always carefully selected his words, kind of like an artist painting a picture selects colors and tones. He did not say that 9/11 was a judgment for the sin of the America people or that God was mad because of some particular sin, like those who attack homosexuals would say. He said that these were judgments 'on His people.' That means the Christians, doesn't it? We're not Christians. You said you didn't even know if you believe in the existence of a God. What does this have to do with us?"

"It has everything to do with us, Sam. Regardless of whether you accept that it is the Christians who are at fault, what the verses say is "all" – that is us – if we die in one of these judgments on the nation because of the Christians, we will perish too. That is frightening. We have to find out what is true about God. We can't risk dying in ignorance."

"Slow down a minute, Paul. The Bookseller didn't just say read the verses. He called on believers everywhere to pray for God's deliverance and for wisdom to understand why God has allowed this to happen. We may not be believers right now, whatever that means, but he told us to pray. Remember, he said pray that you be shown the rest of the dream. Let's pray for that, but let's also pray what he asked the believers to pray and let's pray now. If this God is real and these words are true, He will hear and answer our prayer. If not, we will know that none if it is real and we can disregard it all."

The forces of evil had endured all they could take of this rational discussion seeking to understand what Jesus meant and their threat of more prayer. Molech issued a one word command to the three who were formerly worshiped as gods, "Now." And with that, the attack began in earnest to destroy these two and take them outside of the Enemy's protection. The attack was launched when they would not expect it – as they tried to pray.

Suddenly and unexpectedly, Paul's mind exploded with sexual fantasies about Samantha. As the Tempter named Lust descended on him, Paul found it difficult to focus on anything other than physical desire for Samantha. He was uncomfortably excited by her presence, her appearance, her smell. Even as he listened to her pray, the battle was in full force.

He was shocked at the thoughts racing through his mind. She had always been beautiful and physically desirable to him, but the thoughts he was having were crude and selfish, completely apart from the love he felt for her. It was as if he had gone from thoughts of marriage to reducing her to a piece of meat to be consumed to meet his immediate hunger. He had had those kinds of "relationships" before and wanted this to be different.

Revolted by himself, he cried out in silent prayer for deliverance from these thoughts rejecting them as the selfish evil he knew they were, and in the invisible, a blow was struck which freed his mind. The blow not only drove the Tempter away; it temporarily disabled Paul's self as a motivating force, enabling him to give love and not just take what he wanted. His prayer had been answered and he was able to continue in prayer with Samantha.

Unknown to Paul, Samantha had fought and won a similar battle with another Tempter also named Lust. These two were committed to the search and God had declared they would have this opportunity to choose. As they prayed for the rest of the dream to be revealed, in the darkness a defeated but determined cry was heard. "Wait till tonight. We will still prevail."

ITN Decides

It was decision time for media producers and executives. What to do with what the world just saw? How can we build a bigger audience using the events in Williams? How do we picture the Citizens Militia and the old man? The answers were as varied as the agenda which drove the questioners. Some chose to ignore the old man altogether and focus on the danger of encouraging citizens to be armed. Others chose to attack the incompetence of the police at not being able to find the killer. Perhaps they could force a resignation or a political fight that would interest the audience. They would keep the pressure on the authorities through attack interviews and daily coverage.

Some saw the old man as an opportunity to continue their attack on all religion in general and decided that the story theme was the danger of those religious fanatics who sought to blame what had occurred on 9/11 as a judgment of God on social issues – abortion, homosexuality and so forth. These people were as dangerous as the terrorists, so the storyline would go. The old man was a bit of a problem since he didn't look dangerous and wouldn't cooperate, but there were always those who could be put on camera who would be more concerning – and then there were the paid "experts" who could draw on their version of history to say that all religions had been violent and cruel throughout the centuries against any who did not share their beliefs. The debate would be fun and fully one-sided.

The political cartoon industry immediately saw an opportunity to portray the old man as a nut carrying a "the end is coming" sign and red-jacketed baboons shooting children and mothers. None in these crowds were interested in what was actually said or in whether it could be true. It was theater to promote their agenda and sell papers. It was all about the opportunity.

One network had a different take. In their New York City headquarters, Jim Hunt, the head network news producer and Carl Stern, the executive vice president of News of ITN considered the events in Williams and how to respond. "Carl, I am struck by the idea of this Citizens Militia. This is an important first. A way for ordinary people to strike back when they feel at risk and it is being done in full cooperation with authorities. This is not the picture most have of the average gun toting NRA member."

"Agreed," Stern responded. "If this works in practice, it could actually deter violence and if it expanded, could be an important option in the future when the terrorists strike again. Everyone knows they will. The question is not if, but when, and how, and how many are dead."

"That's a depressing thought," Hunt answered. "But what of the old man, do we cover him and what he said?"

"I am struck by the whole scene," Stern said. "How did he even get into the press conference? Did you notice, he did not speak in anger and was not seeking to promote violence or hate against any group. The only action he called for was prayer and he wasn't blaming everyone for what he said was God's judgment. He was blaming the church people, the people who called themselves Christians. I am afraid if we don't do this right, what he said will be lost in the anti-religion spin so prominent in the other mainline media. I believe that what he said deserves a hearing and constructive debate."

"Agreed," the producer answered. "But we have already found out that he isn't going to cooperate. Our runner found a locked door with a sign saying read that Bible reference on the door. He is not answering his phone. How can we do this without him?"

"Jim, you missed the point. It is not about him. It is about whether or not what he said was true. He doesn't want to become the issue. He wants the issue to be the Bible reference and what he said. To me, that increases his credibility and it should be played that way."

After a pause to think and pencil out an idea, Stern, as the network's news executive, made the decision. "Here is what we are going to do. We are going to cover this press conference – all of it – and the events in Williams as a hard news story. No commentary. I want follow up as often as the story merits. For example, cover the initial patrols Monday. After you show what the old man said including the answer to questions, put the Bible verses up and have the anchor read it without further comment. Close introducing a special on Williams, which I would like to do Wednesday night. Call it something like, 'Williams Fights Back – A City Under Siege.'

"Jim, put our best people on this. There is real news here which the whole nation will want to follow. I sense that this could be really important in the future. We want to get to know the players and let the audience come to identify with them and with the victims and their families. The special can conclude with questions about citizens and the police cooperating like this in other cities. "The response of the churches to the old man's call for prayer and his warning should be a part of this. Let's limit the opening special to the local churches in Williams and keep it constructive. We'll let the other networks ridicule the man. For some reason, I don't think this is a matter to be dealt with that way. We need to understand what he is saying and anyway, after 39 deaths or injuries without a clue, it is about time somebody suggested we pray. I want to see the script and the interviews before the broadcast."

"Done," was Jim's response and off he went to gather his team to begin. This project has potential, he thought.

An Unexpected Discovery

After the press conference had ended, the local press and TV media in Williams were both shocked and excited. Many rushed forward on the spot to sign up for the Citizens Militia. The two phone numbers had been swamped since they were first revealed. Calls came in from all over the country on the 1-800-helpnow line as people wanted to take their vacation in Williams to stand with the Citizens Militia. The local response was the same. The calls could not be immediately handled because of the volume which did not let up until late in the night. The logistics of processing applications and police clearance would be massive. The effort had hit a nerve nationally. People were fed up and were looking for a way to strike back.

The calls on the 1-800-safenow number were also many more than anticipated, as seemingly every place where the public gathered to shop, eat or meet wanted a patrol. Even a local daycare called, but strangely no churches except for Temple Shalom. The public transportation agency wanted patrols at the park and rides after the latest shooting. There was no way all the requests could be accommodated in the near term.

There were other reactions in Williams, in Washington DC and in Tehran where the press conference had been watched with more than passing interest. Abdul Farsi, the leader of the Jihadists in Williams, took note of a possible new enemy and decided that his best response would be to join and find out what they did. He made the call to join and, as a local junior high history teacher, he was welcomed. He expected no problem with the police clearance. His instruction to his team leaders Kalab Sawori and Alharad Doeg was simple, "If while on a mission you see anyone in the red jacket, shoot them first."

In Washington DC, members of the Survival Commission were excited at the possibilities of taking this idea nationally in the event of another 9/11 crisis. One member was dispatched to Williams to get the details and follow up. The president too was encouraged. Americans don't give up, we fight, but how do you fight the seemingly invisible enemy, he had to wonder. He liked the old man's call for prayer. "That needs to be a part of whatever we do," he said out loud in the empty office. "This fight is way beyond our ability to contain. We need divine guidance and revelation. I would like to talk to that old man some day. I wish the nation would wake up to the risk." he declared in frustration.

The leadership of Together Tomorrow wasn't pleased. Anything that might increase a focus on security could be problematic with their open borders agenda. They would be placing calls to senators and representatives to whom they had made sizeable contributions see if there was some way to stop this Citizens Militia idea. "Let's get former President Cox to make public statements about the danger they pose to the citizens," was one suggestion. "He ought to do something for the $2 million we pay him."

Others in Washington with specific social agendas were seeking to find a way to have the old man arrested and charged with a hate crime or at least removed from the airways. "We can't have him harping on possible judgment for sin and calling on people to pray. Next, he will be defining sin, and we know that the Bible describes us specifically as sinners," complained one homosexual activist.

"He said this on TV," chimed in another, "maybe we can encourage congressional hearings into the fairness doctrine and get our chance to call him what he is or expand the hate crimes laws to cover his conduct and shut his kind up once and for all." And so it went with those opposed to what was said in Williams.

Across the ocean, it was already Sunday, and in Tehran a convoy was getting ready to leave for Kerman Province in Northern Iran. The training camp located there was thought to be the safest place to hold the meeting and finalize the plan. The agenda was out and Monday would be the day to finalize plans and set the date. Before leaving the hotel, Ahem El-Ahab had watched the cable news coverage of the Williams press conference by satellite. Initially, he thought that the Citizens Militia was a troubling development but then decided that the attacks planned in Williams could not be stopped by this group. "After the attacks occur in the face of this group, they will see that nothing they can do will protect them from our wrath. Anyway," he concluded, "they looked silly in the red coats and that ranting old man and the mayor's reaction made the whole thing comical."

As they boarded the vehicles to leave, Hushai, a seemingly nondescript hotel doorman watched carefully, seeking to memorize faces and names that he heard. Going through the trash, he had found a copy of the agenda with some draft notes which made no sense to him. What could "G", "AW", "FS", "O" or "MD" possibly mean? What about "J-2" or simply "in 1?" He had to know all he could about this group and what they intended so he could report accurately to those he really worked for.

CHAPTER 11

MASQUERADING AS AN ANGEL OF LIGHT

"And no wonder, for even Satan disguises himself as an angel of light."

—2 Corinthians 11:14

Saturday, February 2 – MD minus 113 days

NIGHT FINALLY CAME and for some, it was an end of the day's proceedings, while for others, it was just the beginning. Molech was always more comfortable in physical darkness. He had learned over the centuries that the human creatures were more vulnerable when they thought no one else could see. Night was the time to prepare them for what the Dark Master wanted to do with them during the day. "The agenda is full tonight," he thought as he observed the city before leaving for the cabin on a lake north and west of it. He had work to do in the city this night, but first, attention must be paid to retrieve the shooter. There was still work for her to do.

In the invisible, a fierce battle had been raging since the moment Paul had agreed in his heart and mind to join with the Bookseller and commit to pray that his eyes might be opened to see the forces of light at the funeral. Like Daniel of old, the answer had been sent, but the forces of darkness sought to delay or prevent delivery so that Paul would be discouraged and perhaps give up on his prayer, assuming either that there was no God to answer or that the answer was "no."[79] Because of the importance to the dark forces of keeping the Curtain closed, an alternative answer had been sent and was scheduled to arrive tonight.

Paul and Samantha remained faithful to pray as did Chaplain Forrest and the Bookseller. The events of the day had only increased their determination to continue to pray until God answered. Deception or death was now the Dark Master's only hope, for Michael the Archangel had been sent to clear the way for God's answer to be delivered as he had in the days of Daniel.[80] The darkness had withheld against Daniel for 21 days, but the answer was ultimately delivered once Michael had been sent. Time would be short.

Paul struggled alone in his bed wanting to know what was true and what was false. His prayer was motivated by real passion and desire. He and Samantha had now completed all the red letter books and there was so much to ponder and to seek to understand. This Jesus had said and done amazing things. Paul was frustrated waiting for Monday to come and another chance to talk with the Bookseller. He was filled with questions.

Elsewhere in the city, others also wondered at what they had seen and heard this day. The battle for hearts and minds was fully engaged everywhere. It would be a long night for the forces of darkness and light.

The Forces of Light Gather

As Molech traveled to the cabin, Argon searched for an instrument to use to fulfill the Dark Master's command to kill the Bookseller. He left the effort to move him outside the Enemy's protection to those who had shown themselves capable of deceiving these humans even to the extent of being worshiped as gods themselves. They were clearly the experts. He was more of a physical force. Violence and terror were his preferred areas of operation. He had a lot to work with in the city at this time. He was thankful and proud that Williams had been selected to launch the assault on "Christian" America. How was it possible – the shooter and terrorists both here at the same time in his dark domain? He rejoiced at his good fortune and the opportunity to strike at those made in the Enemy's image. He would not fail the Dark Master.

The forces of light had a much different agenda this night. Barnabas was aware of Argon's plans and of Molech's activities. They would be dealt with in due time, but their activities this night would not determine the outcome. The real battle was much larger and was at this moment being fought in the hearts of those who carried the light inside, and in the Father's effort to free millions, even billions, bound and blinded by the Dark Master's massive army of Keepers. The forces of light's agenda was not about death and deception; it was about choice. They were charged with doing as the Father commanded so that those made in the Father's image would be enabled to understand their choices and be provided the opportunity individually to make their choice. They could choose light or darkness, but not both, and they would live in their physical life and for all of eternity with the consequences of their decision.[81]

As Barnabas came together with Lucius, Niger and Manaen high above the city, he was troubled. "My heart is full tonight. There is so much at risk and most with the light inside are asleep – physically and spiritually. They seem to be like the religious crowd in Jerusalem when Jesus was on the earth. In that time, they were in the very presence of the Son of God and yet they were blind to the truth. Remember, He cried over Jerusalem knowing what would come. Jerusalem would be totally destroyed by the Romans because they made the wrong choice and rejected the Son.[82] Is this another time like that or is it already too late for these Americans?"

"Only the Father knows that and only He knows the timing of the consequences of wrong decisions," replied Lucius. "I don't think it is too late because of what He did to cause truth to be proclaimed today. Why would He have motivated the Bookseller to go to the press conference and speak as he did if there was not still some time? Why would He open Paul's eyes to see behind the Curtain if the future was sealed? Jesus spoke truth and people made a choice – unfortunately, the wrong choice. Now peoples' eyes are being opened to see they have a choice. I believe that the Father's love will compel that they get to make that choice."

"How I wish these humans understood the gift of a second choice," Niger added. "Most are unaware that all the forces of darkness were once angels ministering in the Father's presence until they made that single wrong choice. Their choice was to attempt to overthrow God and support Satan becoming his own version of a god – exactly what these humans have done. They fought fiercely but were defeated. Their single wrong choice sealed their fate for all of eternity.[83] The consequences of their rebellion are that when time ends, they will all perish.[84] One wrong choice with no second chance is all they had. Not so for these humans. Because of what the Son did, their rebellion can be forgiven.[85] They have a second choice. I wished they understood the love that the Father has for them over even us. If they did, no one could make the wrong choice twice."

"Yes," added Manaen, "but even more, why are those with the light inside blind to this reality? They are not under the influence of Keepers. Time is short, whatever it may be. The Dark Master's plan is for their complete destruction and that all those without the light perish – and yet they do nothing but meet and sing. Why don't they trumpet the choice everywhere before it is too late? I sometimes wonder why the Father has any patience with them. He could in righteousness destroy all of them now, even as in Noah's time, had he not made that promise of the rainbow[86] – or He could lift his hand of protection and allow the terrorists to have their way. They could not in truth complain of either."

"Correct," said Lucius ending the discussion. "But don't forget that God is love [87] and that part of His character compels Him to seek to give them a second choice. That must be our desire as well." And with that, he raised his arm and rang out with the cry, "For the Light!" which was immediately echoed by the others as they dispersed to this night's assigned places of service.

Molech's Deception

For Susan Stafford, the day had been miserable, alternating between throwing up and paralyzing terror from witnessing her victim's eternal sentence. She was a helpless wreck. Wishing for death to end life, she still feared the second death and so desperately clung to life. She had played the game and lost. There was no future for her, alive or otherwise.

Suddenly the room where she sat exploded in unnatural light. She was almost blinded by the brilliance of the glow that surrounded her and she fell on her face to escape whatever had taken the room. Out of the cloud of brightness came a voice she would never forget. "My child, do not be afraid. I have come to open your eyes so that you may understand. You have been commissioned to execute god's judgment on those whose lives have made them worthy of the second death. Although you were unaware, your previous actions have all been in his direction. I have been sent now because you have been chosen for a mission on which the eternal destiny of tens of thousands rests."

"Who are you?" The question rang out in fear.

"I am an angel of light sent by god as his messenger to guide you on your way. In the town of Williams, there is a dangerous young man who will soon assume a false mantle of religious authority. If he is not stopped, he will lead thousands, perhaps tens of thousands, even millions to the second death. His name is Paul Phillips. You will be told when and how to execute god's judgment."

"How do I know you are what you say you are?" was her only response.

"I will prove who I am this once, but never question god again, or you will be the immediate object of his judgment. Watch, be healed," and with those words, she felt immediately well and rested and the fear that had terrorized her departed.

"I believe and will obey," was Susan's shocked but relieved response. "Thank you for choosing me. I will not fail you." She would now live with a different kind of fear – fear of failure.

The room went dark and Molech left for the city. There was still much to be done before morning came.

Darkness Fails

As sleep came to Paul, he began to dream, and in his dream, he was back in the cemetery at the funeral. All he had seen in his dream was present as before, but he now saw a small band of what appeared to be the forces of light at the edge of the scene, cowering together as an enormous dark being descended on them, placing his foot on their necks. He cried out in a voice that seemed to be heard across the whole earth, "Be gone. Williams is ours and its people. Never return." And they departed quickly in obvious fear before they were destroyed by this all-powerful dark being.

Looking to the crowd, Paul saw the few with the light inside, but that light was diminishing and was soon extinguished in all of them. It was becoming dark everywhere and he heard the sound of unholy laughter in a victory celebration. The giant dark being declared to those who were obviously his servants, "It is finished. Our victory here is complete. Nothing can defeat us now." Then Paul saw again clearly the great yellow hands of a wisp of darkness descending on him, reaching its fingers deep within his skull. Just before his eyes crusted over, he could see Samantha, totally captured in the hands of another of the dark beings, and then nothing but black darkness.

He awoke as before, screaming in terror, wanting to find Samantha immediately and run for their eternal lives. This city was cursed. God had abandoned it to the forces of darkness. It seemed as if everything he had been told was a lie. God was not able to protect His servants from the black wisps. Having been drawn toward God and wanting to believe the Bookseller, there was a feeling of helplessness. Thoughts flooded his mind that he had never considered before. If indeed this is true, then what is the reason to live? But like the shooter, he feared the second death. Tempters named Despair and Depression attacked him; he began to shrink from life, but then other thoughts began to fill his mind and he paused.

"Wait a minute," he cried out to the no one visible in the room. He continued speaking audibly because he felt a need to say what was now in his heart and mind out loud to whatever was there with him at that moment. "I read the red letters in the Bible, and if they are true, this dream is a lie. Jesus cast out the forces of darkness from men and women at will. His servants were not left helpless. He empowered them to cast out evil spirits.[88] It was the demons who cried out for mercy from Him and who went where He sent them.[89] It was Jesus who said that He had all authority in Heaven and on earth.[90] He taught his disciples to pray for protection from the evil one because He could protect them,"[91] and with that, Paul prayed to Jesus for that protection.

In the invisible, there was again a scream of pain as the sword of the Spirit cut deeply, which combined with prayer, made staying in the presence of this one, a human made in the image of God, impossible. Rushing from the room were Tempters, a Keeper and others of the black wisps along with Molech, Baal, Asherah, and Ashtoreth. The room was now a place of peace and light.

Paul did not understand what had happened but felt the peace. Had he read more than the red letters, he would have come to a passage in the Book of James that explains the events he had just experienced. James wrote, "Submit yourselves, then to God. Resist the devil and he will flee from you."[92]

Paul rejoiced in being able to remember the red letters, very thankful that they were in his mind before he had this false dream. God had rescued him from what he now clearly perceived to have been an attack of the darkness. This God must be real, he thought, as he prayed for Samantha's protection from the evil one and then fell back into a restful sleep.

In the darkness, now far away, they knew Susan was their only option to deal with Paul Phillips, so they planned and prepared accordingly.

Hushai & Ittai

The hotel doorman smiled as he helped a couple with their bags. He scanned the room for familiar faces – as well as unfamiliar faces as he always did. His trained eyes and sharp memory would preserve what was playing out before him for Hushai was not really a hotel doorman; he was a double agent working for the Iranian government and for the CIA. In the underground world of Middle East intelligence, he served an important function and both of his employers were well aware that he worked for the other. He was careful to be sure that each got the same information. That protected him, but also made him an invaluable source of communication between two nations that had no diplomatic relationship. It was like the cold war days as two enemies sought to be sure that the other understood the facts and did not over react to the rhetoric. As a result, Hushai had become the pipeline for disclosure of information one side wanted the other to know, but also the source of information on what the other side knew.

His CIA contact was a cab driver who went by the name Ittai. They had arranged a simple way of communicating a need to meet, which the Iranian government knew about but did not care as long as they remained confident they were getting the same information. The signal was a small

Iranian flag on a particular table at an outside restaurant located in the hotel. When the flag was up, the one who hadn't placed it knew a meeting was needed. They checked daily and met at prearranged locations and times where Ittai would pick up Hushai in the cab. The cab was their moving office, a place of confidence. The local CIA operatives swept the cab for listening devices regularly. None had been placed for neither side felt the need. They both trusted Hushai.

Ittai picked up Hushai at the hotel this day because they had known speed would be essential. "Here is what I have learned," Hushai began as they pulled away from the hotel's circular drive. "There is a large group traveling today to the Kerman Providence in Northern Iran. There is a training facility of some sort located there. I could identify Ahmed El-Ahab, a close associate of the Sheik. Most of the others I did not know, but it was a strange crowd. It appeared to be more of a meeting of white-collar professions –lawyers, accountants or business people than Jihadists. These are planners, not field operatives. They don't plan on dying or killing. They are planning for others to die and kill."

"Iranian officials know about the camp and that Jihadists training is going on there. They don't know about the plan or how the training fits into the plan. They say the preparation is like nothing seen before, but at this point, I have no information beyond that on the training. I did find this," and he pulled out a wadded up copy of the agenda with some handwritten notes in English. It read:

Purpose – *FS*
Weapons – *AW*
Targets – *in 1 - __*
Personnel – *J - 2*
Coordination & Communication - *O*
Timing – *MD*

"Hushai, do you have any idea what these letters mean? Why are they in English?"

"The English part would seem to indicate that they have recruited either Americans or those educated in America to join in their plan. The letters have to be a code which would reveal the plan, the timing, the weapons, targets, how they intend to communicate – everything needed to stop it. I don't know. I have never seen anything like this from them. To me, it shows a change in approach that concerns me. There is something really dangerous about this plan whatever it may be."

"I assume you have made a copy of this for the Iranians," Ittai asked.

"Yes, of course," was the response.

With solemnity, Ittai added, "Be sure they know we know and remind them that it is the policy of the American government to hold responsible those who sponsor terrorists, even if they are not part of the plan. Perhaps that will motivate them to stop this themselves."

"They know, but remember who leads in Iran and what their response will be," Hushai added. "If you attack them, they will seek to block the Strait of Hormuz, cutting off the flow of oil to the west while attacking the oil fields of governments friendly to America. They would also seek to unleash total hell on Israel to create chaos throughout the region and would strike at your forces in Iraq. If they had nuclear weapons, they would use them or supply them to the terrorists or both. There would be no clear winner of that conflict. There has to be a better way."

"True," Ittai answered, "and it is not a fight we would desire, but America is not going to take an attack and not respond. If these killers are known to have been trained in Iran and that the planning for the attack was done in Iran, you can be sure that Iran will feel the full weight of an angry response which the American people will demand. Remind them of what happened after 9/11."

"What a nightmare," was Hushai's response. "I will see what I can learn from the Iranians and others about this plan. The fact that they are going to the camp to have their meeting makes me believe the Iranians are telling the truth; they don't know much and the Jihadists are seeking to keep them from learning more."

"The scary thing about this is that the agenda itself implies the operatives are already deployed in America and elsewhere. Even if you took out the camp and all those present for the meeting, you would only delay the attack, not prevent it. We have to find a way to stop the attack. Watch for the flag."

The cab turned around and returned to the hotel with both occupants silent in their thoughts.

A New Assignment

When the agenda with the handwritten notes arrived in Washington, the response was immediate. The Pentagon was ordered to locate and prepare attack scenarios on the Iranian camp. Every agency with a code-breaking unit was employed to try and find out what the handwritten notes meant. At the president's instruction, David Barnes was detached from the CIA and assigned to the Survival Commission. They found an office for him in the White House basement and he was told that he was full-time on deciphering the Jihadists plan. Intimidated and feeling very insufficient he searched the internet for possible clues and set to work storyboarding what the initials could mean.

CHAPTER 12

PAUL DREAMS AGAIN

Sunday, February 3 – MD minus 112 days

IT WAS CLOSE to dawn when the solidly sleeping Paul Phillips again began to dream. He returned to the cemetery during the funeral where what he saw was as he remembered. Suddenly it was as if the second layer of a curtain opened and he could see among those in attendance the few with the light inside. The glow was not uniform. Each differed somewhat in the degree of brightness within. There seemed to be a universe of sadness among them, even in the presence of Pastor Holt's comment that Taylor Jones was "now at rest in a far better place." Over each was a great and powerful being of light who shielded them from the reach of the great hands and long fingers of the dark beings reaching out for them.

Strangely, most of those with the light inside also had smaller dark wisps attached. The larger and obviously more powerful beings of light did not block these, although they easily could have. For those with many of the small dark wisps attached, the light inside burned dimly. It seemed to be an inverse ratio, more meant less.

Moving his glance from the crowd to Pastor Holt, he saw no light within. The great hands and long fingers of a large dark wisp covered his head, piercing his skull, holding his brain securely even as he quoted Jesus. Actually, it was the dark wisp who was quoting Jesus. Pastor Holt was merely repeating what he was told by the one who held him, covering his ears. Just like the others, his eyes were crusted over so he did not see anything beyond what his Keeper allowed.

Turning again to look for Samantha, he encountered a blur. He could not focus on her. When he looked where she stood beside him, all he could see was something like a fog. He knew she was in the fog. He was even holding her hand, but he could not see her face and was unable to tell whether she was protected by a powerful being of the light or held in the great hands of a dark wisp.

Also over the cemetery, but away from the gathering of darkness, was a gathering of those of the light. They seemed sober, even sad, but resolute with a fixed gaze looking up. The leader let out a great sigh, lifted his hand and said loudly, "For the Light!" which was immediately echoed by others in the gathering and by all the Guardians among the crowd. With that, they dispersed with apparent purpose.

Again removed from the scene and looking down on it, he was able to see himself. There was no light inside, but one of the guardians of light was pushing away the great hands and long fingers of a dark being. The crust fell from his eyes and he heard the being of light speak with power to the dark being with whom he struggled. "Away from this one in Jesus' name, he has been chosen to search." The dark being immediately backed away and the gathering of darkness turned toward him in anger. The dark leader wrote another note which a smaller wisp was given. He departed with speed.

Paul woke excited, wanting to understand everything he had just dreamed, particularly the part about Samantha. He grabbed the phone and called her. "Sam, I have to talk with you. Can I come over? I had two dreams last night, but our prayer was answered in the second. I have to tell you."

"Please come now," was her response and Paul rushed to get dressed to go.

Darkness Prepares for Church

"And he [Jesus] said to them, 'Well did Isaiah prophesy of you hypocrites, as it is written,

This people honors me with their lips,

but their heart is far from me;

in vain do they worship me,

teaching as doctrines the commandments of men.

You leave the commandment of God and hold to the tradition of men.' "

(Mark 7:6-8)

Early Sunday morning before church services were held anywhere in the continental United States, Molech gathered the rulers of darkness over all the cities in America as was his custom. Similar gatherings had been held throughout the world in preparation for the day which the forces of darkness considered their best and most important in every week. Molech used this time to refocus his forces to carefully be about the work before them. It was almost the same speech every week, but it needed to be made so that no opportunity to advance the agenda of darkness would be missed.

"Listen carefully. This Sunday is even more important than most. The Dark Master expects the comments of that crazed old man to bring many more to the meetings this day, and many of the pontificators will be trying to explain what he meant by what he said. We have a great opportunity before us to answer the questions that now exist in these human's minds. Don't miss it. We can put many on a guaranteed path to the second death if we use this opportunity. Your Keepers have been given the specific message the Dark Master wants to be shared. See that they obey and pour that message into the minds of those they influence both as speakers and hearers."

"We are prevailing in America, so continue to be aggressive. We easily have as many meetings and pontificators as the Enemy has. We have more church members than He does, and if we work hard today, that number will only increase. Don't lose focus. Here are the simple rules. The key is appearance and emotion. Lots of singing and noise – no quiet moments when the Enemy could speak – limit prayer and Bible reading. Cause your pontificator to sell lots of fire insurance. Cause these people to believe that they are saved from Hell by joining a church or by living a better life than others. Let them talk about Jesus, but not about what He taught except intellectually or historically, and never let them declare that Jesus is God or that He is their Lord. Limit their thoughts to Jesus as a great teacher and example. Let them tell stories – keep it simple and non-offensive – positive so the people will leave feeling good about themselves. Make their religion personal and private, separated from the 'real world' of work and relationships. We don't care if they study it as long as they don't live it."

"Have your pontificator focus on the Enemy's love and grace – nothing about righteousness, holiness or judgment. If they mention sin, make sure they are talking about someone else's sin and don't let them mention any particular sin. Have them emphasize that Jesus said not to judge others.[93] Be sure they tell the gathered crowd that tolerance of others is the measure of real love. Have them teach that a loving god gives them what they want because he wants them to be happy. If they teach about prayer, have it be that prayer is how you move god to give you what you want."

"In the buildings where the pontificator has the light within and still continues to speak boldly, destroy them and their church. It's not hard – division – division – division – attack – attack – attack – discourage – discourage – discourage. We have run thousands out of the ministry this year, divided churches by causing splits and frightened others into playing the game by our rules so they will survive. Kind of like that Chaplain Forrest in Williams until these last few days. He will merit some future attention. Anyway, no excuses! Only results. Turn your Tempters loose on the leadership and every single member with the light inside – absolutely no exceptions. Ruin them using their fleshly desires and make it public if possible."

"If you follow those rules, making their religion about what they want – what they do – what they decide – what they feel. We will not only escape this day without the Enemy gaining very many more with the light inside, but we should be able to attach Tempters to those who already have the light inside while dimming what light there is. We cannot put it out if it is really there,[94] but we can dim it such that it has no impact on reducing the spread of darkness. Remember, darkness is the absence of light. We have to reduce what light there is and not allow it to increase. We are to continue to advance the darkness. Now get out of here and go to work. Send them all to Hell."

Plans for College Church Attack Advance

The crowd in the old rent house off Bell and 17th were active. Abdul Farsi had come over to meet briefly and separately with each of the teams. It had been several days since he had instructed the three Palestinian students to begin purchasing the white king size cotton sheets and pillow cases and they had two sets. Work was ongoing in the upstairs room by Kalb's team preparing the disguises for next Sunday's church attack. They looked promising.

Farsi was glad that making and using disguises had been added to the subjects being taught at the training camps. If they were to survive their attacks and be able to hide in preparation for the next, a disguise was essential. "Good," he observed after trying on a set. "These will work. They hide you but give you a good line of sight and freedom of movement. Well done. Just get the rest finished by Saturday. I want people to be comfortable in them before the first attack."

"Now listen, all of you," he continued. "The first service at College Church is at 9:30 AM. Kalb and Salamis are going to that service to make final plans for next week. They will determine the final schedule, make the targeting decisions, outline how the attack will proceed and prepare the plan of escape. Remember, this is not about a fight to the death. This is to kill a few of the infidels and escape as we have a date soon thereafter at Temple Shalom to begin a campaign to do some real damage to the occupiers of the Palestinian homeland."

Pulling Kalb and Salamis aside he warned, "Be extremely careful. Do nothing to attract attention. Dress like a college kid. Remember – take no notes – no drawings. Do whatever the infidels do in their meeting and be friendly if approached by anyone. You are glad you are there. Show it. You are curious to learn about this Jesus; after all, He is one of our prophets too. Be careful to observe if any of those red jacket people are around. We will talk tomorrow night and finalize plans."

Doeg's Rebellion

Going downstairs, he met with Doeg's group now gathered. "You are going to have to be patient for a little longer. We are probably two weeks from your first attack. I want to monitor the red jacket people and see how they respond to Kalb's attack to be sure we are successful. If these red jacket people become a problem, we may have to target them in mass. I will know their plans for I have applied to join them. I expect to be accepted and assigned a patrol by midweek."

Doeg thought, "Killing a mass of the red jackets – what a good idea. Why wait?" He would make his own plan to proceed against this red-jacketed bunch. They needed to be discouraged and he knew from experience that terror and fear were great instruments of discouragement. He wanted to end this Citizens Militia thing here and now and not let it spread. There were even women in that red jacket bunch. They have no shame. They would be the first to die. Anyway, he didn't like taking orders from this school teacher. Where was he when they were killing Americans in Iraq and Afghanistan? Perhaps Saturday at their so-called Security Fair would be good timing. There should be many targets.

Both the forces of light and the forces of darkness were present when Doeg began to plan his rebellion. Those of the darkness were there in mass because all present were under their influence, and the activities under discussion were taken from the Dark Master's agenda. Those of the light were present because the Father seeks to enable even His greatest enemies to have the second choice, the opportunity to be changed.[95] In a human sense, the response would be to destroy them all, but God is not human. He had once taken the greatest enemy of those who followed Him, a man named Saul of Tarsus, and transformed him into Paul the Apostle.[96] And God desired to once again take the passion of hate and turn it into a passion for the light.

There was another clear distinction between these competing forces fighting over the very nature of the evil present in the Jihadists. Although the forces of darkness could use Keepers to influence thought and behavior, they could control neither unless they possessed the human instrument. They possessed no one here. The real problem for the forces of darkness was that although they were in the presence of Doeg's rebellion, they were unaware. The forces of light know what is in a heart and mind because God knows.[97] The forces of darkness can only try to influence what is before them. As a result, Barnabas was aware of the beginnings of Doeg's internal rebellion while Argon only saw what appeared to be disgruntled obedience.

Internal Struggles

Others this morning were still struggling with the Bookseller's message. Having read Luke 13:1-5 as he had said, many were troubled and did not understand what Jesus meant by, "Unless you repent, you too will all perish." Most had never seen the tie between a tower falling in Siloam killing eighteen and the twin towers falling in New York killing over 3,000. There was something eerie and troubling about the comparison, but it could not be ignored. Had 9/11 been a judgment? Was something worse possible? It set people to thinking which is why the Bookseller had been influenced to speak.

Those with the light inside wondered at the call to pray for protection and for wisdom to understand why God was angry at His people – at them. The protection part they understood, but why would God be angry at church people, at those who claimed to be Christians. What about the real "sinners," those whose chosen lifestyles were obviously evil – totally against what was taught in the Bible? The idea that terrorism was a judgment, and not simply evil people killing innocent people, was foreign. The claim that it was somehow their fault was shocking. Most dismissed it as the musings of an old man, but some struggled with a sense that it was true and they returned to the Bible seeking to read the prophets to gain an understanding of what made God angry. The prophets had warned their generations who ignored the warnings and were subsequently destroyed or taken into captivity. Was the Bookseller's warning really God's warning to this generation of Americans?

Chaplain Forrest struggled too. Like everyone else who heard, he was troubled by what the Bookseller had said, but he was more troubled by himself. The light inside had grown dim over these past years and he saw clearly that he was the cause. It was as if he was sitting in a theater watching a replay of the last years of his life, and it was a horror story. How could I have been so blind? Like the Apostle Peter when confronted about his denials of Jesus, Chaplain Forrest "went outside and wept bitterly."[98]

Paul & Samantha Try "Church"

Paul rushed to see Samantha to tell her of the dreams and they came pouring out of him. "Sam, that first dream last night was obviously not from the same source as the earlier one. It conflicted with everything we had been reading in the red letters in the Bible. It presented the darkness as all-powerful and completely in control in Williams. The statement of the giant dark being, 'It is finished. Our victory here is complete. Nothing can defeat us,' was chilling, but I believe it was a lie. We read nothing about a victory of darkness, although we read a lot about a fight with darkness. Let me see the Bible a minute, please."

Paul went through the last of the red letter books looking for the comments of Jesus about light and darkness. They were stuck in his mind. "Here it is, remember? Jesus said, 'I am the light of the world. Whoever follows Me will never walk in darkness, but have the light of life.'[99] Earlier he said something else, just a minute; I will find it."

"Here, 'This is the verdict: Light has come into the world,' – that would be Jesus the light of the world," he said with emphasis to Samantha, "'but men loved darkness instead of light because their deeds were evil. Everyone who does evil hates the light for fear that his deeds will be exposed.'[100] The Bookseller had read me a verse about being called out of darkness into the light. I don't remember where it was, but it's in there somewhere."

"What about the real dream?" Samantha asked. "What about me? What does it mean that I'm a blur, like in a fog?"

"I don't know," was Paul's honest reply. "All I know was that I didn't see any great hands on you or reaching for you, but then I couldn't see your face. There has to be a reason. I have many questions for the

Bookseller about the dreams and about what he said on TV. Tomorrow cannot come fast enough."

"Look, today is Sunday and it is still relatively early. Let's go to church. Maybe we can learn something there," was Samantha's reply.

"Great idea, but which church should we go to? I haven't been to church since I was a kid and then only on the special occasions. You know, Christmas, Easter and sometimes New Year's Day if they had a service that didn't interrupt the football games."

"I have actually been thinking about this since we started looking at the red letter books. I really do want to know more, so I asked some of my classmates and they suggested Faith Church of Joy. That's the place where Professor Thompson teaches and Roy Elkhorn is the Senior Pastor. Everything I hear about it is good. It's positive – got great music – a short inspirational message – the people are friendly. That is just what I need this morning to get out of the fog," she said nervously trying to make fun of her fears.

CHAPTER 13

DARKNESS VS. LIGHT

Sunday, February 3 – MD minus 112 days

ITTAI MADE ANOTHER swing by the hotel looking for the flag on the end table at the outside restaurant. The flag was still there, but it wasn't up. He was frustrated. The Iranians had to know something, he thought. That camp did not simply appear in Kerman Province. He pulled over to the curb to pick up a fare waving wildly, obviously in a hurry and raced off to the designated destination.

In Kerman Province, preparations continued for tomorrow's meeting. El-Ahab was excited that he would hear from the planners and coordinators on the status of preparations. He tired of the operatives. All they talked about was killing and martyrdom – the eternal rewards they would receive. It was nice to be around people of intelligence who would send others to their death but had no intention of dying themselves. He had to admit that was how he felt. Death to the Americans now, but he wanted to share in the new Middle East after their humiliating surrender. No Americans – no Jews – no infidels – only true believers. He would have a place of honor in the new Middle East with the Sheik. For now, he was content to be the messenger and let others lead and die.

He wondered about this new one, apparently invited at the last minute. Why suddenly an Iranian? Where did he fit in the plan?

Washington

In Washington, David Barnes was adjusting to his new schedule and new focus. Nights were over, now he would begin working days into the nights and would participate daily in working groups of the Survival Commission. Tomorrow they would tackle the agenda as a group for the first time. That was interesting timing, he thought, since the agenda would be in use in Iran for another discussion. Closing down his computer and preparing to leave for church, he wondered if he had found something. It didn't exactly fit the handwritten codes, but it was close. Too obvious, he thought, and what could all that gibberish mean? It was interesting that none of this had made the usual sites. There were no threatening videos, no warnings, nothing. The silence troubled him. Something was imminent.

Williams

Back in Williams, ITN Network Producer Jim Hunt was hard at work. He had come himself because he just sensed this was important and Williams was the place to be right now. The immediate task before him was the Wednesday special, and there was much background work to do. He had an unprecedented five camera crews here to film interviews and a staff of researchers to gather information on what was being called the "Siege of Williams." They had brought in such large resources because they had only days to do what normally would take weeks. Today they were scheduled to do victim family interviews, to film sites of the shootings and interview survivors. That was the afternoon schedule. This morning there would be five crews in five churches by permission, filming services looking for what was being said about the siege and about the old man's comments. Only one church had turned them down and all five where they were filming had consented to on-camera interviews after the services. He wondered what would be said and hoped it would be balanced.

Samuel Evans White, the Bookseller, was to have preached this morning at a church in Greenville that was without a pastor. It didn't happen. After his comments at the press conference, one of the messages he found on his phone recorder was from the deacon chairman of that church uninviting him. He was disappointed, but not surprised. But then, he didn't serve the church; he served the Lord. The fact that the leadership of this church rejected him was not a concern. He had complete peace that he had said exactly what was given him to say. That is why he hadn't said anything else.

"Margaret," he said to his bride of many years, "let's do something different. Let's go to College Church this morning. I want to see if God has touched Pastor Scribes. I have felt for many years that he could be a leader among the pastors if he was willing to stand and fight the good fight. Scribes have always waited for a consensus which never came. Perhaps now, with all that is going on, he is ready to lead by following Jesus."

"Are you sure it is wise to go anywhere this morning?" she responded. "Look outside. You would think you are a homicidal maniac by all the news trucks and reporters waiting to spring on you. Do you really want to face all that and then hear someone probably preach against what you said? Fredrick Scribes has never had the courage to stand against opposition."

"You weren't listening carefully, Margaret. I don't expect him to change. I want to know if he has been changed. That is what I am looking for – the activity of God in him. If that happens, there is hope for Williams, but I truthfully don't think he is ready yet. I hate to think what God will allow here and in America as a whole if His people don't wake up – and soon.

"As for your concern about the reporters and cameras, this is not about me. They are just doing their job. They expect me to act like some politician or religious 'star' seeking the microphone. I have no problem walking silently by them. I haven't been given anything else to say to them, so I have to be silent for now. I don't want to be unkind, but I don't want to be disobedient. I don't expect they will be here tomorrow. I'm old news and I am not looking for a microphone."

In the Invisible

Argon took great pride in his work among the churches in Williams. With few exceptions, they were under his control. Each had been assigned to a specific demon whose responsibility it was to advance the Dark Master's agenda in those who attended while seeking to limit the number of those who would receive the light inside. To accomplish this, they had created both a false church and a false gospel. The results were obvious. They had been able to produce pastors like James Holt and Roy Elkhorn, and religious hypocrites and false teachers like Taylor Jones and Professor Daniel Thompson – one having already perished and the others well on their way. The wonderful thing about these fools, thought Argon, was that they were not even aware they were leading people to their eternal destruction, which is exactly where they were going. They just liked being followed, so they led where the people wanted to go.

The forces of light held no meetings to decide what to do on Sundays, and they had no individual assignment to particular churches. There was no need. The Holy Spirit received direction from the Father, which He passed on to all with the light inside. It was also the Holy Spirit who convicted people of sin, righteousness and judgment, so emotion was not necessary, although it was often the response to the real conviction of sin.[101] The Holy Spirit also enabled people to hear and understand teachings from the Bible.[102]

Since God both called people to search and enabled them to search, [103] the forces of light had a different function. Their principal responsibility was to protect those with the light inside and those called to search who had been freed from the grasp of the forces of darkness. That was the Guardians' job. Beyond that, they waited for instructions on what they were to do to advance the kingdom of light and obeyed immediately whatever instructions were received. God the Father was sovereign.[104] They didn't need to know God's overall plan, only what they were to do at the moment. With that they were content.

Faith Church of Joy

Faith Church of Joy was huge. It housed thousands for numerous services every week and was one giant media event. There were big screens to televise live what was happening on the stage and to put up the words to the songs. They had a band and "praise team" as well as a choir, dancers, and a drama team. People clapped, jumped, raise their hands, and shouted during the "praise" times. They had healing services, a gym, church athletic leagues for most sports, and help groups for everything from drug issues to working through a divorce. People came in mass if only to watch the other people. It was an event planned to send the folks home happy, having had a fun time and been made to feel good about themselves so they would come back for more.

Pastor Elkhorn was young, handsome, and charismatic with long flowing black hair. He had the beautiful thin blond wife and the rich baritone voice. He was the author of numerous feel-good books on a variety of subjects and their services were available live on the internet, on radio, and were replayed later in the week on one of the Christian TV networks. Today, however, he came on stage slowly with a somber face. This message would be different from the norm, partially because of events, but also because of the camera crew filming the service for possible use in a Wednesday night special. He was excited at the possible national exposure on secular TV. That would sell a lot of books.

About midway in the back sat Paul and Samantha, looking for the answers to many questions. Paul had a strange sense of danger which he didn't understand. Unknowingly, he was receiving his Guardian Simeon's warnings. There was danger here for someone who was truly searching for God. Deception was everywhere.

The whole of the praise time had seemed like a rock concert with the people reacting a lot like those at concerts he had attended, Paul thought. The words were different, but the music was the same. The musicians were performing just like those at a secular music event. It was exciting and fun; people were shouting and clapping, dancing and jumping. He found his emotions were fully engaged, even when they sang quiet songs. This sure was different from how he had felt when reading the red letters or listening to the Bookseller. He wondered what he would hear from the pastor as he walked slowly onto the stage. There was no podium, so he walked around looking at the massive audience who waited for his words as his unseen Keeper dug his fingers deep into his skull to be sure he got it right.

Beginning without a prayer, Pastor Elkhorn said, "Jesus declared, 'Blessed are the peacemakers, for they will be called sons of God.'[105] This week in Williams we have all heard from one who is anything but a peacemaker, he might more correctly be labeled a troublemaker. Everyone within the sound of my voice knows who I am referring to. Many of you have come this morning because of your confusion over what that old man said at the end of yesterday's press conference. I put away the message I had prepared for this morning in order to deal with this attack on your peace and joy. Please listen carefully.

"Jesus warned that we are not to judge,[106] and yet this man judges us all. He says God is angry with us and that we are responsible for 9/11 – you and me. But this book," he declared raising a Bible over his head, "says that God is love.[107] The old man uses Old Testament analogies as if God were not in Jesus. He would have you believe that the God of today is the same as He was when He directed Israel to destroy its neighbors and then was itself destroyed by His hand. Jesus did not die on the cross to imprison us with a new set of rules and regulations, threatening us with death and destruction in some future judgment if we disobey. Not us, the Christians. Jesus died to set us free to have a life now full of joy and peace, covered by the promise of abundance here and eternal life.

"I don't know what God this old man serves, but it is not the God of the New Testament as pictured in Jesus. The God of the New Testament understands us and our strengths and weaknesses. He too was human once. He is tolerant of our failures. He understands change and will meet you where you are. He does not expect the impossible from you. His way is easy. His burden is light.

"Consider the Bible verses the old man said go and read.[108] He should have done that himself. What did Jesus say? Nothing new, it is the same thing Jesus said throughout His ministry. All He requires is for us to 'repent.' That is not difficult and is probably something everyone in this room has done. All it means is to admit you made a mistake and are sorry. Anyone here who has not made a mistake and later been sorry? If you say you haven't ever made a mistake, you have a problem with your facts. Everyone blows it and the conscience inside each of us tells us when we are wrong. It is in those moments you understand your mistake and feel sorry that you are wrong. When that happens, you have repented. That's all Jesus meant.

"I don't understand the massive fear and discouragement that has fallen on this city and elsewhere around the nation over what the old man said. We are to be a people of joy. Rejoice in the freedom Jesus has given us and ignore this misguided old man. Forgive him and forget him, but don't let him steal your joy. Remember, a life without joy is living death.

"Now bow your heads and close your eyes. Some of you are not members of this church or any church. You need to step up to the reality that there is a Heaven and a Hell and Jesus has given us the way to choose Heaven. It is not difficult. All you have to do is to be honest with yourself and say a little prayer. Here it is – just pray with me right now. Admit you have made mistakes – perhaps you hurt people wrongly, lied or whatever your particular error may have been. Admit you were wrong and ask to be forgiven. Acknowledge Jesus' death on the cross and then invite Him into your heart. There is plenty of room in there for Jesus. Let Him come in and bring you peace and joy and then watch as your life gets easy and your burdens are lifted. All God requires is that you do the best you can to live a good life. He doesn't expect perfection, and best of all when this life ends and you are called home, you are assured of a home with Jesus in Heaven," he said pausing for the greatest possible effect.

"If you prayed that prayer, this book in my hand guarantees that you are now eternally saved, a member of God's church, this church, and you have been freed to live your life to the full; rejoicing as a Christian knowing that you have a place in Heaven when your life ends here on the earth.

"If you prayed that prayer, I want you to step out now and walk to the front where counselors will meet with you to enroll you in the church and rejoice with you in your decision to become a Christian."

The aisles were flooded with counselors and new members who rushed to the front. The band and praise team struck up loud and joyful music. The people began to shout and sing. In the crowd going forward were both Samantha and Paul, who wanted to be Christians. They were met by Professor Thompson, who came forward with them to be their counselor. Paul was confused by what had been said and troubled by the attack on the Bookseller, but he wanted to be a Christian and what Pastor Elkhorn said is required he had done. He didn't know. Maybe the Bookseller was wrong. He was relieved, but didn't feel much different, and there was a nagging doubt in his heart that he did not understand.

College Church

The one church which refused to allow a film crew was College Church. Margaret had been right; Pastor Scribes wanted nothing to do with making a decision on how to address the Bookseller's comments. He didn't want to offend and he was afraid to stand for what he knew was right. He had known for years that the churches in Williams, his included, had become more about their own programs and growth at the expense of others than about representing Jesus truthfully to the community. Internally he was in a state of turmoil. He knew that the Bookseller had spoken truth, but he could not publicly agree in the face of the firestorm of opposition that had arisen. He took the same approach he had taken following 9/11; he ignored the press conference and the Bookseller's comments and went on with the current series he had been preaching as if nothing had happened.

Looking out over the audience, he saw that the Bookseller was there. Conviction immediately fell on him as the light inside sought to provide guidance. He saw that Chaplain Forrest was also there sitting with the Bookseller and his wife, silently aligning himself with what had been shared yesterday at the press conference. He looked different somehow. The Bookseller appeared to be totally at peace as if he had spent yesterday with a good book. How can he be so calm in the midst of the storm he started?

Unnoticed, sitting in the back on separate sides of the auditorium, were Kalb and Salamis taking it all in, carefully observing the timing of the schedule, looking for targets. Their entry would be complicated because of the large open area before entering the auditorium. They would have to divide the force with one to control the door, two to clear the open area and two to enter the auditorium from different doors. They would have to recruit one from Doeg's group to drive. They would need all five as shooters.

The targets would be random at the door and open area. It would be whoever was there. The ushers were obvious targets to clear the way into the auditorium. Once inside there was only one worthy target: the music director, who was black and they were told to kill someone who was black. The speaker had said nothing worthy of wasting a bullet, but in the crowd was that old man Farsi had shown them on the video of the press conference. He and those around him would be good targets. There were none of those red-jacketed people, but they or any security force would obviously be the first priority should they be there next week. One automatic weapon and hand grenade should be adequate to clear the way for their escape.

Present in the crowd and armed was Tom Campy. He had a concealed weapons permit, so it was legal and he had a sense that the church needed protection. It was strange that he had this concern since the shooter had never targeted a church, but the concern was real. College Church was his church and he knew Pastor Scribes well. He would ask if next week several members of the Citizens Militia could be present in uniform.

Also present was a researcher for the ITN, who had been assigned to listen and take notes. One way Producer Hunt decided to get an overview of all that was being said was to send researchers to churches where they did not have a film crew. He wanted the largest possible coverage to gather the greatest amount of information so that the reporting would be as accurate as possible. She was surprised that the pastor had said nothing, even in the presence of the old man and an obviously questioning congregation. Where was he yesterday, she thought.

The Anglican Mission

Across town, meeting in a rented high school auditorium, one of the pastors of a small church associated with the Anglican Mission in the Americas was coming to the end of his message. The camera was rolling, filming the service by permission for possible use in the Williams Special. The pastor had agreed for the services to being filmed because they sensed the importance of this time and the opportunity to the movement to plant and strengthen churches in America. Their movement had been initiated under the authority of archbishops from Rwanda and South East Asia to address what they observed to be "the largest English-speaking collection of unchurched and spiritually disconnected people in the world." It was history reversed, other nations sending missionaries to America.

Pausing for effect and to get the full attention of those present, Pastor Wilson then began his closing. "Yesterday our brother, the Bookseller, said some extremely significant things which we cannot let this day pass without addressing. I listened earlier this morning to the first service of one of the big churches and their whole message was an attack on what was shared at the press conference. You need to be equipped to be a positive witness when this comes up in discussions this week, as it undoubtedly will.

"What did the Bookseller ask us, his Christian brothers, to do? He asked us to join together and pray. Nothing is more biblical than believers praying together. What did he ask us to pray for? There were two things. First, we were to pray together for God's deliverance. Can anyone take issue with a prayer for deliverance when in the Lord's Prayer Jesus specifically instructed us to pray that the Father 'deliver us from the evil one'?[109]

"The second prayer request was that we join together to pray for wisdom, specifically wisdom to understand why God allowed 9/11 and why He has allowed Williams to be terrorized by the shooter. Is that biblical? A prayer for wisdom is what James told us to pray for. He wrote, 'If any of you lacks wisdom, he should ask God, who gives generously to all without finding fault, and it will be given to him.'[110] A more significant inquiry might be why we didn't ask for wisdom sooner. Clearly no one in Williams has the answers.

"I guess the place where people are having trouble is with the idea that God was in any way involved in 9/11 or in the shootings here or the whole Jihadists effort to destroy us. The Bookseller did not say that God initiated these activities; what he said was that God allowed them. Is that a wrong view of scripture? Absolutely not. The whole of the prayer raised by the Apostles when they first encountered opposition was based on two words – 'Sovereign Lord.'[111] They understood that God was totally in charge and that nothing could happen unless He either did it or allowed it. It is absolutely proper to gather together and ask God 'Why?' provided that you are willing to accept his answer and change.

"What about the statement that 9/11 was a judgment of God on all people, could that be true? I tricked you there. He never said that. What he said was 'allowing 9/11' was God's judgment on His people. Big difference and the difference is whether God's wall of protection around America is coming down and He allowed those events to happen. The Old Testament is filled with examples of Israel rebelling against God and their protection against enemies being taken away.[112] Is that happening to us? It is a question worthy of asking and much prayer.

"Is God angry with His people? That is an easy one. If He isn't angry, then He isn't God. Those who are called Christians have chosen to ignore

His Word and to live as they wish for themselves. That is called rebellion. That is why Satan no longer is an Archangel. He rebelled and was thrown out of Heaven away from God's presence.[113] Can we expect to be treated any differently, particularly after Jesus' sacrifice on the cross?

"I watched the first service early this morning of Faith Church of Joy to see how another church in the city responded to the Bookseller's comments. Pastor Elkhorn surprised me. Actually, he shocked me. He said that the Bookseller was judgmental. Forgive me, but hogwash – all the Bookseller was asking was that we all (he included) submit ourselves to God's judgment. He said that the Bookseller wasn't a peacemaker – true on this issue, but then how do you as a Christian make peace with people who are at war with God? Peace is not surrender to or tolerance of evil. We are called to stand with God against evil and that is all the Bookseller suggests.[114]

"Pastor Elkhorn also said that all we needed to do was repent and that repentance means you feel sorry you were wrong. He was half right – repentance is what is needed, but repentance means a change of heart which results in a change in conduct. You go from enjoying a sin to hating the sin. If he had been right about repentance being merely a feeling, then Judas Iscariot, who was sorry for the consequences of his sin, would have been forgiven and restored to the eleven.[115] That didn't happen and he killed himself.

"I apologize if I have offended anyone by criticizing another pastor in the community, but there was nothing judgmental or biblically inaccurate in anything the Bookseller said, and someone needs to affirm that fact. He spoke in love, seeking to call God's people to stand before God together to hear and to change. Nothing could be more important this day or any day. I intend to contact the Bookseller this week and ask to join with him in those prayers, and I am asking, as your pastor, that you meet with me here Wednesday night to pray together as a church family. I believe that God has given us an opportunity to seek Him together, and we had better not miss it." And with that, he prayed.

CHAPTER 14

PREPARATIONS CONTINUE

Sunday, February 3 – MD Minus 112

UNKNOWN TO ABDUL Farsi and the other Jihadists working out of the old rent house off of Bell and 17th, there were cell groups throughout the surrounding communities and in Chicago, which had been established as part of the economic destruction effort. Operatives had been brought across the Mexican border two at a time and moved up to Carmen, Arizona where they had been placed aboard Brothers Trucking vehicles and taken to their assigned locale to await the attack. They had been trained in Iran and equipped in Mexico before the border crossing. Although the effort continued, most were now in place across the country waiting for the command to act.

It was in one such cell in Greenville that Argon found the one he believed was the chosen instrument to kill The Bookseller. He had a good Bible name, Demetrius, and like his namesake, he would be useful in trying to kill a boy named Paul along with the old one.[116] This instrument was filled with hate, a perfect candidate. He was enraged at having to wait for months hiding in a house, unable to go out except at night. He had been trained and prepared to die. He was ready. The rage he expressed at the Bookseller's press conference remarks boiled hot inside him – Argon could feel his wrath waiting to be unleashed. He was the one. "This one has publicly insulted all the martyrs," he had screamed at the television set, "he must die." Demetrius' Keeper had reported immediately what had taken place.

Argon knew that it would take powers and abilities that had not yet been given to him to direct this instrument of death into their service and so he fearfully sought an audience with Molech. Fear was the right word after his last failure at trying to solve the Bookseller problem.

"Exalted one," he began, seeking to calm the waters by feeding Molech's pride. "We have found an instrument of hate wanting to die by killing the Bookseller. I was careful to seek out someone without a current assignment. This one is intended for the later attacks and can be easily replaced in time. He is restless and angry and probably will not wait for the planned attack. He has seen the outrage, and from his own mouth came the desire to kill, which his Keeper assures me is from his heart. He is evil and can be trusted. He is called Demetrius, like the one who almost rid the earth of the man Paul who wrote so much of the Enemy's Book. That one was a hard kill, but back then our instruments did not have bombs they could strap to their bodies."

"I know this one," Molech responded. "He is worthy of the honor of killing such an enemy of the Dark Master. I will call him to his chosen task. Well done, little one. For now, you can stay," and with that, he was gone to Greenville.

It was afternoon and the sun shone brightly on the snow which reflected the light, giving the whole outdoors a sense of radiance. Molech hated the sun's light almost as much as he did the forces of light. And the feeling of cleanliness and purity which a fresh blanket of snow brought was repulsive to him.

Molech found Demetrius alone in a bright room with many windows sitting on the floor deep in meditation. Entering the room and rising above Demetrius, Molech caused the room to suddenly become dark with a darkness so unnatural and deep that it could be felt. It was as if Demetrius had been transported to a cave far beneath the earth where no light could enter. He could see absolutely nothing and was terrified.

Out of the darkness, a voice unlike that of any human was heard. "Demetrius, your desire to honor god with your life has been heard and your willingness to sacrifice has been accepted. Your reward awaits you. Listen as I tell you how you are to serve in death."

"Who are you?" Demetrius cried out to the darkness in fear.

"I am the one to whom you pray," was the answer. "No more questions, just listen and obey. Because of your faithfulness, you have been given the desire of your heart. You will kill the old man, the one they call the Bookseller, who blasphemed me and all of my servants. Your death will translate you to your reward and him to his eternal judgment. Tell no one, but prepare yourself for action. I will return soon with final instructions," and with that, the room was again bright as the light shined in from the windows. The others present in the house when Molech had acted saw nothing and heard nothing. Yet, Demetrius was convinced and awaited further instructions in silence. His time had come and he had been chosen. He would be ready.

The Shooter Returns

North and west of the city it had been a relatively quiet and almost peaceful day for Susan Stafford. Having been visited by what she believed to be an angel of light, the conflict and fears within had been replaced by a resolute determination to serve as god's instrument of judgment. Sitting in her boat on the lake in the early morning, she had been replaying the 39 shootings, seeking to understand how she had carried out god's judgment on each target. She had been helped in this search by her Keeper, who provided justification for every death and injury. By the end of the morning, she was convinced that everyone she had targeted was a person whose life either was or would be such that god had chosen to use her to intervene as the instrument of his judgment to end their lives for the protection of others.

It helped that the voice telling her about this Paul Phillips she was to kill next had explained that if he were allowed to live, he would lead tens of thousands into the second eternal death. This voice must be from god because it knew the future. That explained her killing a child. That child must have been one who, if allowed to live, would also have caused many to suffer eternal punishment. For now, she felt fully justified in what she had done and looked forward to future assignments. She remembered her plan for an attack on the daycare back in Williams and wondered how that fit into the judgment of god. She concluded that it would be made clear to her after she successfully completed this new assignment.

Driving back that afternoon to prepare for her classes tomorrow and to await further instruction, her peace was again disturbed by the memory of what she had seen in the park and ride as her last victim was transposed to a place of judgment, condemned to the fire. That reality was contrasted in her mind with the reality of the visitation she had experienced last night, the healing of her body and the assignment given to her. She was troubled but did not know what to do other than obeying what she had been told. This was now all beyond her and she knew of no other option. She could not risk angering the angel of light or she would suffer the same fate as the ones she had killed.

Demetrius is Called

The forces of light were aware of Molech's deception. They had been present as he masqueraded as an angel of light and when he brought the darkness on Demetrius. Visions and miracles, messages, healings and altering circumstances were staples of the arsenal of deception the forces of darkness had used over the centuries. Nothing new had occurred.

Although there would be earthly consequences for what had been done, the forces of light refused to yet surrender the shooter or the terrorist to the second death. As with all of the humanity, the battle raged. Barnabas had assigned Guardians to seek to open the way for each to search. The Holy Spirit sought to open their eyes to the evil of their sin and draw them to Jesus.

Barnabas turned to Susan's Guardian and observed calmly, "Don't ask me why, but I firmly believe that she will yet be useful to us. Continue to confront the deception. Don't let any of the lies go unchallenged."

Tom & Sally Prepare

Work continued in Williams on many fronts in preparation for the activities of the coming week. Tom Campy and Sally Johnson had reviewed a city map to determine the initial assignments for the Citizens Militia.

Tom's employer had given him the week off with pay to help organize the effort. There was much to do with the mass of phone calls received at both toll-free numbers and with the Security Fair planned for the weekend. Earlier they had met briefly with the representative of some presidential commission and with a network producer who was filming for a special to be broadcast Wednesday night. They did the best they could to shift the interviews to higher-ups, preferring to get done what was necessary to make this a success in the field.

"Tom, we really haven't had a chance to talk privately since the press conference ended yesterday. What happened? Who was that old man? How did he get into the press conference?"

"I am the guilty party if there is one," Tom responded. "I invited him because I believed that was what I was supposed to do. What he said is part of all of this in some way. I don't know how, but there is more at work here than the shooter."

"I agree with you," was Sally's candid response. "I sense that we better get ready quickly, although I don't know what we are getting ready for. At least we start tomorrow with all the schools covered. By the end of the week, we should have the manpower to really be a presence throughout the city. I don't know how long we can sustain this level of interest. Everything will depend on the shooter's reaction."

"Tom, I hope you appreciate the danger of walking around in a red jacket. All of you are first-line targets. That Bookseller too, there have already been numerous death threats made. He stepped on lots of toes, even though he spoke quietly and did not point the finger at anyone beyond the church people. What he said is being misquoted and restated to advance some pretty strange agendas. He is definitely at risk but refuses protection."

"It is true that he is at risk and so are all of us wearing the red jackets," Tom replied, "but we cannot allow fear to dictate our lives. I think I can speak for the Bookseller as well as for myself on this one. As Christians, we don't fear death because the Bible teaches that Jesus not only defeated death at the cross and has given us eternal life, but that He literally holds the keys to death.[117] We cannot die until he allows our death. If I am where I am called to be, doing what I am called to do, I'm bullet proof until I finish what I have been called to do.

"I don't know whether you are a student of history, but there are some really interesting stories about believers. One of my favorites is about George Washington's command during the French and Indian War. The unit he was with was wiped out and several horses were shot out from under him. His jacket had a number of holes in it, but he was never hit. The opposing Indian chief later said they quit shooting at him because the Great Spirit would not allow him to be killed. It is like that for all of us – if we are where we are supposed to be doing what we are supposed to be doing. We are safe until God accomplishes through us what He has determined to do. Don't mean to be preaching at you, but I believe that, so am not afraid."

Sally smiled and said, "I knew there was something different about you. I also am a believer, which is I guess why we seem to have the same heart and mind about what is happening in this city. Are there other believers in your group?"

"Some," Tom answered. "What about the police?

"Some also," was the response. "What would you think of setting up a time to pray even as the old man suggested? We desperately need God's wisdom and protection. There is so much that could go wrong with armed civilians on the streets looking for a cold-blooded, indiscriminate killer. And there is that other part, the 'why' part. We need to know that too. It may sound strange to you, but I fear the 'why' part more than the shooter. This has the potential to be catastrophic if we have really lost God's protection."

"You are so right," was Tom's sober response. "I have an unnatural fear for the churches of our city, mine in particular. I asked my pastor for permission to deploy a uniformed team there and he refused. He wants nothing to do with anything controversial. I hope my sense of danger is wrong."

"Let me change the subject for a moment; I have another idea. What about organizing a formal neighborhood watch program where there are block captains who would report on unusual activity in their neighborhoods or near where they work? This would be another way to involve the public in looking for any suspicious signs that might lead you to the shooter while also opening the door to widespread intelligence to alert you if there is more going on. We could work together on this using some in the Citizens Militia and announce it at the Security Fair on Saturday."

"I like that," was Sally's response. I will pass it on to the higher-ups. They shouldn't have any objection if it is presented positively. Now, what about praying together? You never answered my question."

"You are of course right, prayer is essential," Tom admitted. "I have to confess that it is easy for me to pray alone, but hard in a group. I don't know why that is, but it is. I think it is a silly man thing."

"Well, grow up and stop with the man thing," was her candid reaction. "We need to pray. Your Monday assignment is at Patterson Elementary. I will be there in a police vehicle at 6:30 AM to pray."

"Yes Ma'am," he answered. "I will be there tomorrow morning at 6:30, red jacket and all. Thank you for keeping the focus on what is really important. Can we pray for a minute now?"

Eyes Opened

Officer Sally Johnson was not the only one in Williams trying to organize a prayer meeting. Chaplain Forrest had been on the phone all afternoon trying to get pastors of churches to meet with the Bookseller for a time of prayer and to answer questions on Wednesday morning. He was shocked at the response. Only one pastor, Pastor Wilson from a little church associated with a Rwandan archbishop, was interested. Pastor Wilson was excited at the opportunity. Everyone else either didn't see the urgency or wanted to duck the controversy.

Chaplain Forrest thought if the Bookseller was right, it was apparent why God's protection was being withdrawn. The three of them would meet anyway. Jesus said, "Where two or three come together in My name, there am I with them."[118] That will be us. It is enough.

Frustration in Iran

"Hallelujah," Ittai screamed and his hand flashed in the air, "the flag is up." He raced to the designated rendezvous point to find Hushai.

As they drove through the city together, Hushai reported on his recent contacts with those in the Iranian government willing to talk.

"Your government must understand the extent of the division of the Iranian leadership. The Mullahs, who control, are radically anti-America and are glad to help anyone who seeks to destroy your country. They want Shariah law here and everywhere – a one world religious government not greatly different from that written about in the book of Revelation.[119] It is literally a 'believe like us or die' philosophy. Fortunately, it is not shared by the majority of the Iranian people who remain secular, or by all in the government.

"Unfortunately, the current elected leadership shares that view, particularly anger against America and Israel, and is actively seeking nuclear weapons to use against them. However, there remain those who seek to avoid conflict and facilitate a peaceful revolution to bring Iran out of this religious nightmare. They are our hope and the source of my information. We must be careful not to damage or expose them. Watch the rhetoric or your government will feed the hand that seeks to destroy it. I got the expected responses to the 'saber rattling' in our last meeting. They rattled back. Tone it down. Everyone knows what is at risk.

"Now, here is all I have learned new. The camp where the meeting is being held is not like any other terrorist camp, which is why you probably never found it in your review of satellite pictures. It is hidden in what appears to be an oil and gasoline terminal of some nature. It is massive for this part of the world. I don't know whether it is operational or merely a sophisticated disguise. It is unclear what kind of training has been going on there, but whatever it is it has been in place for at least two years and is different from what has been seen on the videos from the old Afghanistan camps or even those in Sadam Hussein's Iraq. This camp is also different in that the effort is totally secret – no videos, no internet postings. The training is for a definite operational plan of some nature.

"The Iranians don't know the details, but they know something about the plan and are aware of the meeting tomorrow. Part of the plan appears to be a coordinated attack of some nature on United States interests in the Middle East. I draw that conclusion because the terrorist leadership has asked for Ahmad Habid to attend tomorrow. Habid is the Iranian coordinator of the attacks against American forces in Iraq. He has supplied the technology and materials for the roadside bombs and suicide bombs. Imagine what would happen if that knowledge was used in the United

States proper. Habid hates America, but he is a loyal Iranian. He will tell the government what he is being asked to do. They will, at least, know that much.

"Don't get any ideas. Tell your people not to kill Habid now. He is the only available link to information on the terrorists' plan."

"What else about the meeting – the people in attendance – the agenda?" Ittai asked.

"Nothing much new; all we know for sure is location and the people I have previously identified. We know that the people are not operatives, with the exception of Habid, and that is significant. The other thing which becomes more obvious is that the communications are in English. The meeting tomorrow, with the exception of Habid's involvement, will all be in English. That has to mean two things: the participants don't want the Iranians or others to understand what they are saying and the leadership is either American or American educated. This is a different enemy than you have faced before. Is there anything new on your end from the Americans?"

"Nothing now," Ittai answered, "but you can be assured there is a major on-going effort to break the code and find out what the agenda means. Watch for the flag," and with that, they returned to the hotel.

Early Morning Assignment

El-Ahab didn't like early morning meetings. It must be really important to gather in the dark, he thought. "We have a problem and we have a solution," was the announcement. "I want these two messages posted. Address the first one to all and direct the second to Farsi in Williams." He was handed the text of the messages and left to post them to the site and get some more sleep. It took a while because he had to mix the real messages with misdirection. The intended recipients would know.

CHAPTER 15

THE PLAN

Monday, February 4 – MD minus 111 days

LEGION LOOKED DOWN on the gathering before him with a deep sense of pride. Speaking to the Keepers and Tempters, who were hard at work providing the Dark Master's guidance to those in attendance, he observed, "Humans don't appreciate real evil. They are such fools, always trying to find good in everyone and excuse evil people doing evil things. Look before us and you see real evil in all its beauty. These clean-cut frauds are calmly discussing sending others to their death and seeking to destroy America economically, taking it back 200 years in a single day. That is the beauty of real evil, no conscience about sending others to their death while planning for their own safety and prosperity. I love it. These are our kind of people."

The meeting had progressed for many hours when Demas Assad stepped to the front of the underground room to detail targeting decisions. The morning had been spent in a review of how the operatives would be directed, weapons and purpose. Ahmad Habid had long since left after he was advised of the request for coordinated attacks in Iraq and Afghanistan to tie down the American forces there while the attack proceeded in

America. He had embraced the idea but refused to work under anyone's direction. He wanted them to just tell him when and get out of the way. That was his approach. The "when" would come later; they didn't want Habid to have too much information. Trust no one.

Taking the floor, Assad asked, "How do you bring the greatest military power in the face of the earth to its knees? Certainly not by challenging its military and fighting on its terms. That is an absolute formula for a quick defeat. Killing them, even masses of their people, could bring a negotiated surrender, but not likely. We learned in 9/11 that the Americans only become angry and unite when attacked, unless it hurts them where they live and then their anger is channeled toward their government, demanding relief. Americans don't like pain. All of us have seen that during our years there. They are soft, looking for a quick, decisive solution. They gave up in Vietnam because they could not win quickly and suffered massive injuries and deaths that hit every American home either directly or through someone they knew. No one could escape the pain, so the people took to the streets and made it stop.

"The way to defeat America is to attack its way of life, not its government or its military. How they live – their ease, their pleasure, their toys. Even as Vietnam did, our attack must damage every American or take something from them. They must all be made again to feel pain or loss. Consider carefully what is essential to the American way of life? When you have that question answered, you know what the targets must be.

"America runs on vehicles – cars and trucks, trains and airplanes – electricity and communications. Destroy the means of transportation; attack their sources of fresh water, take away electricity and their ability to communicate and America falls under the weight of its citizens' protest. They won't even be able to grow, harvest, process or move food. It is really not that difficult.

"The targets are: all major oil refineries in the continental United States, all major dams, electric production power plants and distribution networks throughout the country, particularly in the large cities, exposed pipelines and finally, water purification and distribution networks. Think about an America where people cannot travel at will, and food, fuel, materials and equipment of all kinds cannot be moved. Think of an America without the ability to communicate, without heat or cooling, one where all the electric gadgets don't work, no entertainment and no assured source of food or fresh water. Think about an America without working indoor plumbing. After MD – that is the time when America will be screaming for peace at any price. That is an America to whom the Sheik will dictate terms they will accept gladly."

Then, with a precision that would have made Apple proud, Assad went through a power point presentation showing the major targets in each state. He showed how they would be attacked by the weapons of choice, the anticipated damage that would be inflicted on the target, and how that would impact the area of the country near the target and beyond.

Then the meeting turned candid. "Now we must consider some of the hard truths about this plan in the field. Our people have been being placed in their chosen target zones for the past year. We are probably two to three months from having them all located. All of us have invested two to three years in US schooling to obtain graduate degrees and teaching certificates. The plan's preparation has been successful thus far. We have teachers throughout the country who will be our coordinators. They are in place and waiting for further instructions to pass on to the operatives. Unfortunately, we have experienced an issue with the operatives which were the subject of an early morning leadership meeting. You should have received a copy of the instructions posted at the site. They must be obeyed. Note the leadership code and always obey when you see that code or one for an individual above you in the chain of command."

"The targets have all been numbered as have the locations. The complete list will not be distributed, but the coordinators will receive instructions on the targets in their areas. They will be given the numbers of those targets and the numbers of their locations. They will also be given information on the codes for the identity of the leadership so they will know when a message is posted with authority and must be obeyed. The communication process will initially have to be in person to protect the information. The teacher cadre will be used both to coordinate and then to communicate. We will handle the distribution of information to the teachers. The less you know, the better if something should go wrong. We are a little less than four months away from MD."

The meeting continued through the afternoon and ended before dark. Every attendee departed to their assigned tasks as the sun set. El-Ahab could not wait to return and report to the Sheik. Soon America would come begging. The thought of their proud and arrogant enemy being humbled excited him.

Another Perspective

Watching throughout the day were members of the forces of light, including Manaen, the leader in the Middle East, and Lucius, the leader in North America. They had no human representative meeting in this place of darkness, but nothing and no one was beyond the reach of God. As the last of the planning leadership departed, Manaen turn to Lucius and said, "This assignment is the most difficult God has ever given me across the centuries. Here these people live, fed by hate with no light and with no understanding of the love of God. There are such sadness and waste here, and it is all so unnecessary. God's heart breaks every time He looks here for He cares about every life, and here tragically it is almost universal. There is no peace. There is no real life, only darkness and death which they seek to export throughout the earth."

"True," Lucius responded. "But true also is the fact that their plan can only work if God allows it to work. They have put in place most of what it will take to succeed, all without discovery, for the Americans are blind. They cannot see beyond themselves and their pleasures. They foolishly fear nothing, believing their military can protect them from anything. I wonder whether God's people heard God's warning. The Bookseller was faithful to deliver it exactly as given."

"I haven't seen much to indicate that God's message was received," Niger, who was also there, answered. "With few exceptions, nothing has changed."

"Yes," Lucius replied, "but God ... Thankfully it is always, 'but God.' When God finally speaks, what went before Him matters not, nor does any seemingly physical reality, and few – even one person standing with God can be enough because He does not wish destruction unless His people will not hear and turn.[120] Remember the five loafs and two fishes?[121] That was enough when the Father blessed it. He took the little and multiplied it such that there was an excess of twelve baskets full after everyone ate all they wished. May that be repeated now, for there are the few who heard and sought to obey."

"That is America's only hope," was Manaen's sober conclusion. "They now know and they now have a choice. They are without excuse."

Petersen Elementary

As the sun set in Iran, it had only recently risen in Williams. There at Petersen Elementary, a police car had become for the moment a chapel as Sally Johnson and Tom Campy prayed. They followed the Bookseller's suggestions and prayed for God's deliverance and for the wisdom to understand why this was happening, to understand God's anger and to change. They prayed for protection and discernment, that the shooter is captured or killed, for safety in the community and in the country, and that God's people may be awakened to pray.

As they concluded, Tom met his partner for the day and the two red jackets divided to go to the drop off places to help reassure the kids and the parents that they would be safe. Tom watched carefully for any suspicious activity and saw none. The parents overwhelmed them with thanks and they got a lot of hugs from grateful kids who felt secure seeing them there. Tom raised a prayer of thanks for the privilege of standing for these kids. It was an exciting beginning.

Throughout the city, a collective sigh of relief could be heard at the visible presence of the Citizens Militia. The network cameras rolled not only for the Wednesday night special but for the daily news broadcast. A great story thought Carl Stern. A city fights back. If only it succeeds and the shooter is stopped.

The Survival Commission

In Washington, the Survival Commission was preparing to begin with its consideration of the agenda and the meeting in Iran. Before Chairman Knight could open the meeting, the president entered and everyone stood. "Please be seated."

"Before you start, I have something I want to read to you. It is a statement made by Ben Franklin to the Constitutional Convention as they met in Philadelphia on June 28, 1787. I believe that the wisdom of Franklin's request must govern your proceedings if they are to have a successful outcome. Franklin said:

> *In the beginning of the contest with G. Britain, when we were sensible of danger we had daily prayer in this room for the Divine Protection. — Our prayers, Sir, were heard, and they were graciously answered. All of us who were engaged in the struggle must have observed frequent instances of a superintending providence in our favor. To that kind providence, we owe this happy opportunity of consulting in peace on the means of establishing our future national felicity. And have we now forgotten that powerful friend? Or do we imagine that we no longer need His assistance? I have lived, Sir, a long time and the longer I live, the more convincing proofs I see of this truth — that God governs in the affairs of men. And if a sparrow cannot fall to the ground without his notice, is it probable that an empire can rise without his aid? We have been assured, Sir, in the sacred writings that, "Except the Lord build, they labor in vain that build it." I firmly believe this, and I also believe that without his concurring aid we shall succeed in this political building no better than the builders of Babel: we shall be divided by our little partial local interests, our projects will be confounded and we ourselves shall become a reproach and a byword down to future age. And what is worse, mankind may hereafter this unfortunate instance, despair of establishing governments by human wisdom, and leave it to chance, war, and conquest.*
>
> *I, therefore, beg, leave to move – that henceforth prayers imploring the assistance of Heaven, and its blessings on our deliberations, be held in this assembly every morning before we proceed to business, and that one or more of the clergy of this city be requested to officiate in that service.*

The president paused and then continued, "Respectfully, I would say that we are at that same place, and if a sparrow cannot fall to the ground without His notice, it is probable that our nation cannot be attacked or destroyed without His notice. I am not trying to force religion on anyone here. If you don't want to participate, then come into the meeting after the prayer. I am simply asking those of you who would to join together daily and seek God's protection for our nation and His wisdom to know how to respond to the threat we know is out there. I was struck by that old man's comments in Williams. I know he addressed them to church people and not all of us are church people, but the reality is that we need God's help and protection to address this threat."

There was no dissent for all nodded in agreement. Time was short and they were addressing a plan that had been moving forward for years. All they really knew was that the name of their commission described the threat they faced – survival. Even the doubters in the room knew that if there was a God they needed His help, and no one wanted to overtly disagree with the president. That first day, the president prayed and then left them to work alone.

Chairman Knight called on CIA Director Crenshaw for an update on intelligence. "Most of you are familiar with our Iranian efforts to obtain information on the meeting held in Kerman Province last night our time. Those in attendance included Ahmed El-Ahab, which solidifies the tie of the plan to the Sheik. The Iranians claim to know nothing, but we have learned that Ahmad Habid, the Iranian in charge of facilitating attacks on Western forces in Iraq and Afghanistan, was a last minute invitee. We are hopeful of getting some intelligence on the plan and the timing of the plan when he reports back to his Iranian contacts.

"Here is what we know. Those in the meeting, with the exception of Habid, were not operatives, they were planners and organizers. All had some tie to the United States. They were either resident aliens who were formerly foreign students in American universities or American citizens. Their communication was all in English. They met at a training facility that was either a working oil and gas terminal or a facility disguised as a terminal. All of their activities are secret. They are making no public threats or promises.

"David Barnes, one of our analysts, was able to discover what we believe to be the agenda for the meeting. After that, our Iranian intelligence contact found a copy of the agenda in a Tehran hotel occupied by participants who would travel to the camp for the meeting later that day.

That copy had handwritten codes in English. Barnes and others have been working on breaking the code. Barnes, have you found anything new?"

"Perhaps," Barnes began. "I have been working with the codes trying to find some tie to Muslim historical events or prior terrorist's activities of groups related to the Sheik. I can find no obvious tie, which again argues for American-educated leadership. These people are thinkers and planners from an American perspective, not a Middle East perspective. That should help us as we focus on both methods and objectives."

"The code appears to be the means of secured communication to many operatives and leaders at least throughout the United States and the Middle East. It argues for a widespread coordinated attack of some nature, different and much larger than 9/11."

"You are reading an awful lot into a list and the scribbles you are calling a code," one commissioner responded. "What concrete evidence do we have besides the list and the meeting?"

"Commissioner Thomas, we may have found the means of communication and the first posted instructions," Barnes answered.

"When did that happen?" Director Crenshaw asked. "This is new information to me."

"Late last night I was working on the codes trying to find something to relate them to when I discovered a website that seemed too easy and too logical, so I gave up and went to bed without reporting anything. The website was www.FS2.com. You will remember that the agenda with the handwritten notes had 'FS' beside 'Purpose.' It was close, but not exact, and when I looked over the site, it was filled with what appeared to be nothing more than gibberish."

"This morning when I woke up, I remembered how the Allies had sent coded radio transmissions to the Free French, which sounded like gibberish, and most was, but hidden in the gibberish was coded messages for particular cell groups throughout France to advise of the scheduled invasion. It was their instructions to do what they had prepared for. Remembering this, I went back to the site and found more gibberish, but two additions which appear to be messages. I say that because of their inclusion of some of the codes on the agenda and the incorporation of what, to me, seems to be a system of communications outlined in the codes.

"The messages I found first were: 'Some Gs crave delay and are cautious. Give them life recklessly and in public. J-14.' The other was, '0-1-later. J-10.' The 'G' reference is new, but must mean some type of operative. I believe that the 'J-14' and 'J-10' are references to particular leaders who sent the instructions. The '0-1' seems to be a reference is to a location where there is a target. Remember the agenda had this under 'Targets – in 1 –'? I am sure we've found something because this posting was made from Iran. Probably right before the meeting began."

"Great, but what does it mean?" asked Chairman Knight.

"I don't know yet," was Barnes' response. "It appears to be silly gibberish, but it is no sillier than what we used prior to the Normandy invasion. We will be monitoring police reports from across the country to see if we find anything happening that could be tied to the messages. That is all I know to do other than keep looking, and in light of the president's suggestion, keep praying. But there is one more thing which I hesitate to suggest."

"Speak up. Now is not the time to hold back on any theory, Barnes," Director Crenshaw instructed.

"Alright – I believe that the 'FS' which was on the agenda beside 'Purpose' may mean 'Final Solution' after the Nazi attempt to annihilate the Jews in World War 2. The 'FS2' symbol on the website simply acknowledges this is the second attempt. That Israel is also at risk here is no surprise. If I am right, the attacks they are planning are catastrophic. Effectively, the plan is the 'final solution' to the problem of America opposing their will in Israel and the Middle East. Think about that one for a moment."

Chairman Knight walked to the marker board on the South wall and said, "Enough. I don't want to think about it. What I want to know is what do we do next, and what do we tell the President?"

CHAPTER 16

DREAMS AND DECEPTION

"And it shall come to pass afterward, that I will pour out my Spirit on all flesh; your sons and your daughters shall prophesy, your old men shall dream dreams, and your young men shall see visions."

—Joel 2:28

Monday, February 4 – MD minus 111 days

PAUL PICKED UP Samantha to bring her with him to the meeting with the Bookseller. Now that they were both church members, he wanted her to meet the Bookseller and hear for herself what he said in response to the dreams. He couldn't wait to tell him the news and to learn more about the activities of the forces of light as revealed in the dreams.

When they arrived at the warehouse, they were greeted by Margaret, who brought them into the study where Chaplain Forrest and the Bookseller had gathered earlier that morning to pray. He introduced Samantha and before they even sat down, the Bookseller asked eagerly, "Was our prayer answered? Did you see the rest of the dream?"

"Yes. In fact, I had two dramatically opposite dreams," Paul began thoughtfully, choosing his words carefully. "One I rejected out of hand because it conflicted with what we had read in the red letter books of the Bible. The other stayed with me. I believe it was true, but it has raised a lot of questions about the nature of the conflict between the forces of light and the forces of darkness."

"In both dreams, I returned to the cemetery and saw what was there in my first dream except that now the forces of light were visible. In one dream the forces of light were pictured as defeated, held under the foot of an enormous dark being that ordered them to depart and never return. There were those in the crowd who had what appeared to be a light inside, but it diminished and was soon gone. The dark being declared in a loud and boastful voice that Williams and all of its people now belonged to them. The forces of light obeyed and departed in obvious panic, appearing to seek to escape with their lives. The forces of darkness held a great celebration, laughing and rejoicing, bragging about their victory. The giant dark one declared, 'It is finished,' as one of the dark beings descended on me to again establish control over me. I was shown Samantha before my vision was taken away. She was totally under their control.

"I awoke in terror and fear as before, but that only lasted for a moment because I suddenly remembered the words in the red letter books and knew this was all a lie. Nothing I had read supported demons having power over the forces of light, specifically over Jesus. It was He who ordered them around and cast them out of people at His will.[122] They begged Him not to punish them.[123] They were never able to force their will on Him. It was all a lie.

"I had a sudden, what I can only call a compulsion, to speak out loud, though no one was visibly present. I repeated what I remembered from the red letter books, and peace came as if a presence had departed.[124] I had a sense of joy and felt a new confidence that God was real. I easily returned to my sleep."

The Bookseller almost glowed with joy as he spoke, "Do you understand what you experienced in your response to that dream? Do you see how God has worked in your heart to open your eyes to truth?"

"What do you mean?" Paul asked.

"Before you began your search," the Bookseller replied, "you would never have known that what you saw in this dream was a lie. You would have blindly accepted it as true because you would have been under the influence of one of those dark beings as we talked about in our first meeting.[125] Now your eyes have been opened to truth[126] and you have been enabled to remember what the Bible teaches about demons. It was God by His Holy Spirit who reminded you of what you had read.[127] Think of the tragedy of those who never have read the Bible. They simply accept the lie as being true whether the forces of darkness use a dream or a false teacher to tell the lie. The forces of darkness control people by their lies, but you have been freed from their lies. Now tell me about the second dream and why you believe that it was true."

Paul began, "In the second dream I saw a few people in the crowd with what appeared to be a light in their chest. It seemed strange to me, for some lights were brighter than others. All had large and obviously powerful beings of light standing over them, fending off the great hands and long fingers of dark beings reaching for them, but most had smaller black wisps attached. The beings of light did not contest the smaller dark wisps, although they easily could have."

"Do you understand the light within?" the Bookseller asked. "That is the Spirit of God, which is put into everyone who is born again. It is the absolute evidence of the new birth."[128]

"Wow, that makes sense now," Paul responded. "But why are their different levels of light within and why did the more powerful beings of light allow the little dark wisps to attach themselves to those with the light inside?"

"Great question," the Bookseller replied. "The idea of choice and consequence is at the heart of the lives believers and unbelievers live in the flesh. Even after a person is born again, there remain choices on how to live. Jesus said that believers must deny themselves daily.[129] The forces of darkness tempt all believers to sin by inflicting us with demons that play to our passions and desires. The smaller groups of wisps can attach to any believer who gives in to the temptation, whether it is lust, greed, pride or one of many others. Love of money and pride, lust and sex are the big ones in our day. When a believer gives into temptation, the larger beings of light are not allowed to interfere with the demons because a choice has been made, and the one who made the choice will have to live with the consequences of that choice. One consequence is that the light of the Spirit does not burn brightly in that life until the believer repents and changes. When that occurs, the larger being of light will forcibly remove the temptation.

"I cannot tell you how exciting this is and what a privilege it is to hear what God has allowed you to see. I don't know why He has opened your eyes to the invisible world, but please, I want to know everything you saw."

"I tried to see Samantha and all I saw was a fog," Paul answered. "I could not tell whether she was in the hands of a dark wisp or protected by one of the forces of light. I could touch her, but not see her. What could that mean?"

"That is a hard one," the Bookseller answered. "I believe it must mean at that moment Samantha's future was in issue. Whatever work God was doing to prepare her to become a searcher was not yet completed, but clearly she had not been abandoned to the forces of darkness."

"What does that mean," Samantha asked almost in a panic. "Am I in the hands of those evil dark things?"

"I honestly don't know," was the candid reply, "but I do know that even if you are, you don't have to remain under their influence."

Samantha was silent, contemplating which she had heard as Paul went on seeking to know all he could about the dream. "One more thing, I got an answer to the first of the list of questions we put together. I asked whether everyone who is a member of a church and claims to be a Christian is a true Christian. I looked at Pastor Holt and there was no light inside. One of the large dark beings held his head and its long fingers pierced his skull. The dark being seemed to lean over to whisper what the pastor was to say even as he was speaking. His eyes were crusted over and his ears covered just like the vast majority of the others. It was frightening.

"I saw others of the forces of light gathered over the cemetery. They appeared sober, even sad, but resolute. The leader said, and I heard him clearly, 'For the Light!' which all the forces of light repeated and then they left purposefully."

"Really, you heard 'For the Light'?

"Clearly – Yes, I heard it clearly," Paul responded.

"That is incredible," the Bookseller answered. "For the Light! Jesus is the Light.[130] What a battle cry. I'll have to remember that. If it is their cry, it should be ours. For the Light!" he exclaimed excitedly and then turned sober. "Paul, I need to explain the significance of the sadness you were shown in the forces of light because I know what you saw was real. The Bible tells us that the Father wants all men to be saved,[131] that He wants none to perish[132] and when they chose wrong and do perish; there is sadness.[133] You were at a funeral of a man that perished. The forces of light were sad, but they left determined to fight for every other breathing human, even including the killer. God is like that."

Samantha began to cry quietly. "I didn't love him, but I would never have wanted him to perish."

Margaret moved to her side and began to hold her tightly.

"What about you, Paul?" the Bookseller continued with a single-minded focus. "Were you shown yourself in that moment in the cemetery?"

"I was," Paul began and he too had become sober. "I saw myself and there was no light inside, but one of the large beings of light was pushing away the great hands and long fingers that had obviously held me. He spoke and said, 'Away from this one in Jesus' name. He has been chosen to search.' The dark beings backed away and the leader of the forces of darkness gave a note to a small wisp that left quickly. I know I am in play, just like Samantha. The forces of darkness want to have us for their purposes."

"Paul, consider what you just said God showed you about yourself," the Bookseller responded excitedly. "Think about it. The creator of heaven and earth reached down and declared to all the powers of darkness that you were chosen to search. No greater honor could have been paid you. God obviously has a plan and a purpose for your life. Don't miss it."

Confusion Reigns

Satan "is a liar and the father of lies"

—John 8:44

Paul left shaken at the reality of what he had just heard until Samantha stopped him on the sidewalk outside and said, "Paul, wait a minute. Wake up. We are Christians now. We joined a church yesterday. The dream was not about us as we are today. It was about us at the funeral. We must have the light inside. The dark ones do not control our lives."

"Yes, you must be right," Paul agreed and turned back to knock on the door which was opened by a somewhat confused Bookseller, who let them in.

"The dream can't be right about us today. I forgot to tell you Sir – yesterday Samantha and I joined a church. We prayed a prayer and invited Jesus into our hearts. We are Christians just like you. We have the light inside. The dark ones do not control us."

"And who told you all you had to do to become a Christian was join a church, pray a prayer and invite Jesus into your heart?" was the Bookseller's unexpectedly stern response.

Defensive now, Paul replied, "Pastor Elkhorn at Faith Church of Joy."

"Is that all he said?"

"No," Paul answered now stammering, "he – he told us that from now on we had to do the best we can to live a good life which would please Jesus."

Slamming his fist down on the table and raising his voice, the Bookseller declared, "That son of Hell, he isn't saved and has no idea how to lead anyone else to salvation.[134] May he be eternally damned!"[135]

Samantha began to cry again and Margaret reached over gently to hold her close as she sobbed. Turning to the Bookseller, she said quietly, "Samuel slow down and explain. These kids mean well and are clearly being drawn to the Lord. Don't be angry with them."

"I am not angry with them, Margaret. I am angry with that fraud who claims to be a servant of God, but is nothing more than an actor – an entertainer building his little religious empire in that place of noise and confusion he calls a church. He deceives for a living even as he has deceived these two. He convinces people that they can manufacture their own salvation by praying a little prayer and opening a little part of their life to Jesus while continuing to live as they were – only now as church members. He gives them just enough false assurance in their eternal security to guaranty they will ignore truth and one day experience the second death. He is evil – evil – evil, every bit as bad as the worst terrorist on the face of the earth. I wish all those frauds who don't really believe the Bible would be removed from pulpits and thrown out of churches."

With that, he sighed and turned to Paul and Samantha, speaking almost tenderly, "I am sorry that my words hurt you, but they were not my words. The words I used to describe that monster were actually the words of Jesus and the words of the Apostle Paul, which they spoke in similar circumstances describing those who deceive lost people into believing they were saved. To the teachers of the law and the religious authorities of His day, Jesus said, 'Woe to you … you hypocrites! You travel over land and sea to win a single convert, and when he becomes one, you make him twice as much a son of Hell as you are.' [136]

"The Apostle Paul was equally candid in his expression of outrage at the deceivers. He said, 'But even if we or an angel from Heaven should preach a gospel other than what you accepted, let him be eternally condemned.' [137] Please understand, my anger is not at you, but rather at those who proclaim a false gospel leading people away from a real relationship with Jesus, substituting a relationship with a church."

Taking his Bible, the Bookseller said, "Let me show you what I mean. There is absolutely nothing in the Bible which supports the idea of praying a prayer and inviting Jesus into your heart as the means of salvation. You have read the red letter books. Jesus said nothing like that and if you went on into the book called Acts, you would never find the Apostles saying that. They didn't say it because it is not true."

"Do you remember when Jesus encountered Nicodemus, the religious authority that came to Him at night? This man was described by Jesus as 'Israel's teacher,' and yet Jesus did something to him which we might consider rude. He interrupted his questions with a declaration. Jesus said, 'I tell you the truth; no one can see the Kingdom of God unless he is born again.'[138] Nicodemus, a man who thought he was already in the Kingdom of God and was teaching others how to join him, there was dumbfounded and began to ask about this new birth. As Jesus explained, it was clear that this new birth was an action of the Holy Spirit, not something Nicodemus could do on his own."

"But I have heard at least one politician's pastor, a former president, in fact, say that he was saved, only he wasn't born again. How do you answer that?' Paul asked.

"Easy," the Bookseller replied. "You have to make a choice. Either the Bible is true, or it isn't. Either Jesus was the greatest liar that ever lived or

He spoke truth. Jesus said, 'No one can see the kingdom of God unless he is born again.'[139] No one is everyone, so unless Jesus is a liar, that politician's pastor is either a fool or a deceiver. Either way, he should be out of the pulpit because he calls Jesus a liar and says the Bible is not true."

"I joined the church and invited Jesus into my heart; doesn't that mean I have been born again? I have certainly changed the way I live some," Paul asked.

"Paul, did you hear what you said? You said you had joined a church and you had invited Jesus into your heart and you had changed the way you live some. What did God do? Sounds to me like you expect to be rewarded for what you have done."

"Wait a minute, Mr. White. We are trying hard to do the right thing. We are reading the Bible, praying, going to church. You mean to say, that after all that we are still not born again?" Samantha asked in disbelief.

"The Old Testament prophets answered that question. And they answered it before the new birth was even possible, for Jesus had not yet come and died and rose again. A prophet named Ezekiel wrote about what God would do to bring about the new birth in a person. God declared, 'I will give you a new heart and put a new spirit in you. I will remove your heart of stone and give you a heart of flesh. And I will put My Spirit in you and move you to follow My decrees and be careful to keep My laws.'[140]

"Do you see how silly it is to invite Jesus into your heart? He doesn't want to come into your heart. He wants to remove it and replace it with His heart and put His Spirit, the Holy Spirit, within you and give you a desire to follow Him in obedience.

"To understand the enormity of what that means, look at what the Apostle Paul wrote about how you will be after experiencing the new birth. Paul writes, 'If anyone is in Christ, he is a new creation; the old is gone, the new has come.'[141] The word for 'new' is very intentional. It means 'never been in existence before.' Do you get the picture now? When you are born again, God makes you new. He does not merely occupy the old, for the old is gone and the new has come and with it comes new desires. You will want to know what God says so you can obey Him."

"Now about that prayer, it was nothing more than absolute deception, an emotional response to the moment, sincere but mistaken. In the Bible, there is only one spoken prayer that is followed by an acknowledgment of that person's salvation. It is in a red letter book. Do you remember?"

"I don't remember any spoken prayer," was Paul's honest answer.

"What about the request made of Jesus by one of the thieves on one of the crosses?"

"That wasn't a prayer," Paul responded. "The thief didn't pray to God; he only asks something of Jesus."

"Yes, but Jesus was God in the flesh, and any request made to Him was the same as a prayer to God the Father, for they are one. What was it in the prayer that led to the thief's salvation?"

"I don't know," Paul answered. "The thief just asked to be remembered when Jesus came into His kingdom."[142]

"Right, but what had happened before that moment? Do you remember?"

"I don't. I'm confused, please help me understand," Paul pleaded.

"If you read all four of the red letter books, you will find that when they were all initially on their crosses, both of the thieves ridiculed Jesus. This one as well as the other, but he was changed as the day went on such that by the end of the day his eyes had been opened to the amazing truth. Consider what he said and think about how it was possible for him to learn that during a few hours on a cross while deteriorating and dying."

"He rebuked the other thief saying, 'Don't you fear God since you are under the same sentence? We are punished justly, for we are getting what our deeds deserve. But this man has done nothing wrong.' And then the prayer, 'Jesus, remember me when You come into Your kingdom.' Jesus' response, 'I tell you the truth, today you will be with me in paradise.'[143]

"Look closely and you will see the new heart and the new Spirit of the new birth evident in this man before he prayed. The Spirit within had shown him his own sin and that he deserved the cruel death he was suffering. This one had been shown that Jesus was the innocent sacrifice and that Jesus was the king who he would follow anywhere. He was bold and public in acknowledging his sin and in proclaiming his faith in who Jesus was while confronting another's need for Jesus. His desire was for an eternal relationship with Jesus, which in his mind was impossible, so he asked only that he be remembered. He went to paradise to be with Jesus not because he prayed, but because he had been born again."

"It will be the same for you. It is clear that God the Father is calling you and Samantha into that eternal relationship which one thief now enjoys. Let Him finish what He began in you. Just continue to search for Him and pray for your eyes to be open to truth. Get out of that false church and away from that pastor of deception. Continue to read God's word and you will know when the Spirit has completed His work and you are a new creation in Christ Jesus."

"How will we know?" Samantha asked.

"You will know because you, like the one thief on the one cross, will have never been like that before and everyone close to you will know, for you cannot hide what you have become. They will see the difference without you ever having to open your mouth. You will sense the difference by a change in desires and priorities as God's heart becomes your heart and you want what He wants, but most of all, you will want to be with Him and to obey Him.

"Let's get together again Wednesday morning at 8:00 AM? In the meantime, I want to give you a verse to guide you in your search. Through the Prophet Jeremiah, God made a promise which you should embrace. 'You will seek Me and find Me when You seek Me with all your heart.'[144] Jesus said, 'Seek and you will find.'[145] Make your search for God the object of your heart and you will find Him.

"Before you leave, let's pray together," and they held hands and took turns each praying from their heart.

"Until Wednesday," the Bookseller declared and then raised his hand and said, "For the Light!" and they all spontaneously responded, 'For the Light!' which was echoed in the invisible world.

Reflections in the Visible

After they had left, Chaplain Forrest turned to the Bookseller and said, "I believe that the light will soon burn within young Mr. Phillips. God is clearly drawing him. It was God who drew him to read the Gospels (the red letter books) and it was God that brought the works back to his mind and enabled him to overcome the deception. It appears that Samantha too is close."

"I believe you are right," the Bookseller responded, "but that is something they must discover for themselves. We must wait and be sure. When it happens, they will know. Remember, 'The Spirit Himself testifies with our spirit that we are God's children.'[146] When God's Spirit affirms, we will know too for we will see the fruit of the new birth in their lives."

"Samuel, after you meet with Paul and Samantha on Wednesday morning, would you come over to my office and join with me and, at least, one other pastor in a time of prayer even as you called for after the press conference?" Chaplain Forrest asked.

"I would be delighted to join with any who truly wish to seek God's face for wisdom and deliverance," was the Bookseller's response. "Thank you for your efforts to bring together the leadership of the real churches in Williams to pray. It will happen. Do not be discouraged by the lack of response or surprised at what God will allow to force His people to seek Him."

Chaplain Forrest left wondering what that last statement meant, but sensing that it was true, it frightened him.

Rage in the Darkness

Shaking with anger and pain, Molech turned to Argon and screamed, "Wednesday morning they will meet again, but not alone. Their meeting will include two uninvited guests. We will send both Susan Stafford and Demetrius here on their missions of death. We will end this threat then," and he departed to issue the necessary instructions to his waiting instruments.

Observing everything were Barnabas and Lucius, along with many others in the forces of light. They wondered at the arrogance of the Dark Master to again directly confront God. They wondered what the Father would allow as they awaited their instructions.

CHAPTER 17

EVENTS ACCELERATE

Monday, February 4 – MD minus 111 days

JIM HUNT HAD to admit that it was with some trepidation he placed the call to Carl Stern to get his views on the edited videos taken thus far for the Wednesday night special, and for use in tonight's news broadcast. He could not understand why he felt that out of the hundreds of productions he had done over the years, this one was so important. It made no sense, but the compulsion was there. Stern shared that view and had been anxiously awaiting the call.

"Carl," Jim began. "What did you think of the interviews? Did we get it right?"

"I am impressed with the depth of the coverage of the victims and their families, the fear in the community. You really bring that into the living room and personalize it. I believe it is important to show that clearly and put a face on it so people can think about what those who live under the daily threat of terrorism experience. America as a whole may face that someday and people need to be shaken out of their false sense of security. Perhaps we should add a terrorism expert to comment on the reality of what people who live under this threat experience, and to emphasize that terrorism is a real danger to America, something we cannot fully protect against?"

"I agree," Jim added, "but we also need to emphasize the Citizens Militia. This community is fighting back and people need to see that they are not powerless against a phantom enemy. The video on the first day covering schools and the interviews with parents should work well on tonight's news and for the special."

"That was particularly effective," Carl commented. "It will be a great kickoff for the series we will do to follow the story as it continues to develop until they get the shooter. It should attract viewers to the special. What have you learned about that Neighborhood Watch idea discussed in the interview with the woman police officer and the Citizens Militia spokesman?"

"These people are determined to find the shooter and are preparing for something worse," Hunt answered. "I don't want to put that out, but privately both Officer Sally Johnson and Tom Campy believe there is more to this and are preparing to face a larger threat. Their idea is to organize the city so that people have someone on their block to coordinate with when they see something unusual. The block captains would be the contact with the police who would communicate by email. Obviously, anything major would be reported by phone and they will have a special phone number for that purpose. They planned on announcing the idea at the Security Fair on Saturday but introduced it in the interviews. These two really don't want to be out front, but they are the driving force behind what is happening here. We have to use them."

"A question, Carl, how do we spin the police and political leaders? They can be attacked as incompetent or the shooter held up as someone who is really skilled despite their best efforts. We don't want to be unfair to the authorities while at the same time we don't want to build this killer up to the point that we create copycats throughout the country."

"Jim, let's make the story the people, not the killer. Let's emphasize their fight and praise the cooperation between the police and citizens groups. If there are any copycats, let it be other Citizens Militia groups or Neighborhood Watch programs. Maybe we can get someone from Homeland Security to praise the effort. I know they or some governmental group sent a representative to evaluate this after the press conference. Find that person if you can and get some tape for the special."

"Now, let's change subjects and address the religious aspect of the story. It can't be ignored. You got unbelievable contrasts from the pastors. I have to say after listening to their opinions on what the old man said, they don't appear to serve the same god and sure don't read the same Bible. No wonder there is such confusion out there with those kinds of conflicting messages."

"True," Hunt interrupted, "but the story is not the difference of opinion on religion. The story is about the people and how they respond to the threat of the shooter. The old man called for a response and even laid out a possible reason for the overall terrorist threat. The story has to center on what was said and how people respond. We want to share opinions, but not give an opinion or take sides on which opinion is correct. Let the facts speak for themselves."

"What we really need to close this out is an interview with the Bookseller so we can ask him all the questions the American people want to ask, get his views on the contrasting opinions of the pastors, and clarify what he is asking church people to do. We have tried but cannot get to him. His wife answers the door and only a few friends are allowed in. He will not speak to the press. His position is that he said exactly what he was told to say and has been given nothing further to say."

"Look, Jim, who are these friends? There has to be a way to get to him. If we could advertise that he will be interviewed as part of the special, I believe all America would watch."

"You may be right. The only friend I know for sure is Chaplain Forrest," Hunt responded. "He was seen earlier today going to the warehouse to meet with the Bookseller. I will try him. Perhaps we can, at least, get his interview about the Bookseller."

"Candid honesty time – this special doesn't work without the Bookseller. All America is wrestling with what he said in those few minutes at the end of the press conference. There are those in Congress who are threatening to open hearings on hate speech and subpoena him. No matter what people say about him, there is a fear he may be right and that something must be done to appease God. Find him and get an interview.

Agree to whatever conditions he sets within any reasonable limits. We need him to complete the story."

"I will try," was Hunt's only response and he left to seek out Chaplain Forrest.

The Presence of Darkness within the Survival Commission

Over the last several hours, Chairman Knight had guided the commission's discussions of what to do next. There was great frustration with the limitations of intelligence and the lack of a viable military option in Iran. CIA Director Crenshaw had been asked to issue immediate instructions to Ittai to push for additional information on specific targets, on the identity of the planners, or at least where they were flying to now that the meeting had ended. He left briefly to make sure that was done and the flag was soon up at the corner table in the outside restaurant in Tehran.

The commission had requested a maximum effort to study the camp using spy satellites to determine what kind of training was being done there. Director Crenshaw reported, "We have never encountered anything like this. As has already been described, this camp appears to be nothing but an oil and gas terminal. Lots of activity with trucks going in and out, but nothing that appears out of the ordinary. We know there are underground rooms, but that is about as sinister as it gets looking at it from the air. We still have no one on the ground and no one inside."

"I don't get it," Commissioner Matthews said, expressing the undercurrent of disagreement present in the room. "How can this have anything to do with a threat to the survival of America? Maybe we are overreacting and ought to back off. This code thing seems a bit much too. FS as 'Final Solution,' that is a bit much. Why would they use that when they deny that the holocaust even happened?"

"That really isn't much of a leap, commissioner," Barnes replied, "when you consider the public statements of the president of Iran. He has said as much about Israel on a number of occasions. He has also said that about the United States. He may deny the holocaust as a historical event, but he has made clear that he intends for it to be a real life future event."

"Yes, but Iran is not running this operation," Commissioner Matthews continued. "We need to back off until we have more information. If we let the president go public even with the name of the commission, it will create a panic. We may be at risk for Iraq kind of car bombs and terrorist attacks, but we have nothing concrete that says the nation's survival is at risk."

"Respectfully, Commissioner Matthews," Barnes replied, "the meeting happened on Iranian soil with the knowledge of the Iranian government and some active participation. Remember the report that one of their leading operatives in Iraq was invited at the last minute to incorporate attacks against Western interests in the Middle East. These people are not planning a party."

Matthews responded angrily, "We have known of the Iranian involvement in Iraq for years. That is evidence of nothing new. They would kill us all if they could, but they can't. We need to get concrete proof or shut up until we have proof. We don't need to alienate friendly Arab governments."

"When we have concrete proof, we will be digging out from what is left after the attack and burying our dead," Chairman Knight responded. "We did that once and we call it 9/11. Since then, the diligence of our security agencies in cooperation with our allies in this fight have stopped literally hundreds of planned attacks against the West, but nothing like this. Those were individual cells or small groups against specific targets. This is different. This may be an attempt to destroy the nation somehow and we cannot ignore it. They have been planning and implementing for years. We are behind. They have a plan and a date and many people already in place. All we have is an argument over whether we should wait and clean up the mess after the attack or try and prevent it. That choice is simple."

"Listen closely people; I share the feeling of the president that this is real and we will proceed as if it is real. No more debate on that issue. If anyone here cannot do that in good conscience and wants off the commission, leave now. Otherwise, get with the program and help tie down and eliminate this threat."

Commissioner Matthews was livid but did not leave. He knew how to strike back against the chairman and put him on the defensive. "I will call my good friend George Murphy at the Daily Times," he thought, "he will help put a stop to this unnecessary foolishness."

Chemosh smiled as he listened and turned to the others in the forces of darkness who were present, seeking to deceive the commission and protect the terrorists. "It is good to have at least one dark commissioner in the presence of all this light. He should be enough to delay the investigation when he goes public."

"Let's bring this to a close and break up into our working groups," Chairman Knight continued. "Focus on breaking the code, targets, status of deployment of operatives and timing. Run all agencies to determine any unusual activity in matters which require government approval. Check with the state agencies for similar information on matters which require licenses. Check with flight schools, rentals, etc. for any unusual foreign national activity. Assuming they have set an attack date, check with the airlines on dates in the future which already have an unusual number of reservations by foreign-born nationals. Go back five years and track foreign students from the Middle East, did they graduate, where they are now, and track their foreign travel over the past three years as much as we can. Barring any new developments, let's plan on meeting again Wednesday morning. Good hunting."

"Oh, one more thing," Chairman Knight added almost as an afterthought. "If anyone wants to stay and pray for a few minutes, I'm available. Obviously, there is no requirement or compulsion. This is strictly personal. I feel a real need to ask for wisdom and discernment for all of us in this effort as well as for protection over the nation." Most left feeling uncomfortable because they were not used to really asking for God's help, even though the vast majority professed to be believers. David Barnes stayed.

Embracing Together Tomorrow's Political Agenda

Down the street in the senate majority leader's office, the Together Tomorrow leadership was pushing their legislative agenda to a listening group of politicians, most of whom were running for reelection and needed the continued support of this seemingly unlimited source of funds. Former President Cox was making their pitch to the receptive audience.

"It is a new world out there," he began. "This administration has hijacked our resources for a totally unpopular and unnecessary war and turned the focus of the nation to fear. The future is not about fear. If you like occupying this office and want the White House back, we have to offer the people hope. America has to stop playing policeman to the world. We can't do it and the world hates us for it. All the last years have done is create a world of terrorists who want to kill us. There is a better way which will put us in power for decades to come.

"The Europeans have it right. They are united in spite of separate governments. They have a single currency, effectively open borders and a united economy. With the exception of England, who still follows the lead of the cowboy president, they have a better life than our citizens. We need to follow their example on this continent and form a united economy which will open new markets and opportunities, ultimately flooding the country with new voters who will vote right. Excuse me; I meant correct.

"We don't need 'border security.' We need open borders in a united economy from Mexico to Canada which would eliminate the need for people to come into our country illegally. Open the roads and have a continental driver's license to be issued by one of the three participating countries, but honored in all. Develop a single North American currency. Together we can improve opportunities for Americans by improving opportunities for all on this continent.

"Following the European model, we need to change our focus to economic issues. Leave the rest of the world alone, particularly the Middle East. What do we care about their form of government? They have always killed each other in religious wars. All we have accomplished is to make them want to kill us. Buy their oil, build their factories and sell, sell, sell. They will leave us alone if we leave them alone. That means we must have a more realistic attitude toward Israel. The United States has supported Israel no matter what. If we want peace, we need to reevaluate that commitment even as the rest of the world is doing. Israel is a political entity, not holy dirt. We must look to our own interests first.

"And one more thing that the Europeans have right which we have totally messed up. This religion thing is out of control. Look at the violence around the world – it's all tied to religion. No longer is religion about accepting others and loving them as they are. Now they want to change everything and force other people to be like them. The Europeans have concluded that religion is, for the most part, a negative and they have begun to institute legislation to deal with the hate religion engenders. We need to follow their example and stop these people before they seize control of our government and way of life. Free speech does not mean hate speech. We need legislation to stop the hate. That recent press conference where that old man blamed 9/11 on the so-called sin of the nation is an opportunity not to be missed. Bring him before Congress. Expose the hate. Use him to destroy the hold religion has on this nation before it is too late. Our cry must be, 'Freedom from religion!'

"My friends from Together Tomorrow are here to help those who are interested in advancing United North America (UNA) and in stopping religious abuse. America needs to change and become like the continent that gave it birth – and it needs to change now."

The speech – for it really was a speech – engendered standing applause and a wish that Cox could run again. The discussion quickly turned to how to make the agenda law and how to quickly take advantage of the Bookseller's statements to turn the country against all religion that would impact anyone beyond a single believer. "People can believe whatever they want," Cox added in response to a question, "but they cannot impose those beliefs on others. Religion is a private matter and it should stay private. The wall of separation should be absolute."

"He got it exactly right," Molech said to Cox's Keeper, who held him tightly. "I have never understood the Enemy's interest in prayer, but if we can make religion the enemy and humiliate those who call for prayer, we will be unstoppable."

Back in Williams

Preparations continued in Williams by groups with conflicting agendas. The Citizens Militia and police continued to recruit, expand patrols and prepare for Saturday's Security Fair. Tom Campy had shared with Sam Will and others in the leadership about his prayer time with Sally Johnson, suggesting that those who would, should begin to pray together. "The truth is that we need God to establish a wall of protection around our city and open our eyes to threats,"[147] he said. "I have this feeling that we will face much worse than the shooter – and soon."

The official response was not exactly positive as Sam Will replied,

"Don't take this religion thing too far or we will all be taken for fools like the old man at the press conference."

"Don't be offended Sam, but I don't believe that you can take religion too seriously and I also believe the old man was anything but a fool." Tom voice steadied, his eyes fixed on Sam as he said, "I'm the one who invited him to the press conference because I believed he was intended to be there and after I had heard what he said, I know he was."

"Time out," inserted Diane Conway, "there is room for both views. I, for one, like the idea of praying together. Nothing the police have done all these months has worked. Even if you didn't believe in God, He certainly couldn't do any worse than we have done for ourselves."

"Thanks, but not exactly what I had in mind," Tom responded in frustration.

In the old rent house off of Bell and 17th, the Sunday plan was now in place. One additional team member had been recruited from Doeg's group to be the driver. Another disguise was prepared and they waited anticipating the opportunity to strike at the infidels. It was still an adjustment to accept the fact that they were not to joyously give their lives in the effort. None of their training had prepared them mentally to survive and escape for another day.

Farsi had picked up the new messages from the website. He was in compliance with the request that they move quickly. The other message was troubling. Obviously, the delay was an issue with every one of the terrorists, but the idea that some would not be able to wait until they were assigned to attack, and, therefore, must be killed, was troubling. Killing infidels was glory, but killing brothers in the crusade was a whole different issue. He had never contemplated that before. In his teams, there was only one that concerned him and that was Doeg. Nothing yet indicated he could not wait, although he was openly restless and frustrated. He would bear watching.

Doeg listened to the request for a driver and passed it off to another on his team. He had plans for Saturday and might not even be here on Sunday. In his mind, he would be with his virgins in paradise. He would die, but not alone. Before he was finished, everyone in Williams would be afraid to put on a red jacket.

Meanwhile, Molech had completed his encore appearances to Susan

Stafford and Demetrius, deceiving them as either an angel of light or with a palpable darkness. The messages were received with relief and the two continued to separately plan and prepare. The engagement was now firmly set for Wednesday morning. By sending both, they might both die, but that didn't matter as long as Paul Phillips and the Bookseller were killed. Either together or individually, who cares, just dead, dead, dead. They might not experience the second death, but at least, they would experience the first – and soon – and would then be out of the way.

Jim Hunt found Chaplain Forest in his office and requested help getting an interview with the Bookseller for the Wednesday night special. Forrest laughed, "I will ask if he is led to appear. I can assure you that he won't unless he believes that is God's will. You have encountered no one like him before. There is nothing in this for him. He only wants to honor God and draw Christians into prayer and repentance so that America might survive and become a place of revival and awakening. I know that sounds radical, but God will not allow His people to continue to live in sin and be led away from Him. Judgment in the absence of a change of heart is sure.[148] It is as much a promise of God as is salvation for those who believe and commit to His Lordship."[149]

"That is why we want him to speak to America," Hunt responded. "America won't like hearing that, but they need to hear so that they can choose."

"I will ask," Chaplain Forrest promised, shocked by what he had just said. Perhaps he too was being changed.

CHAPTER 18

EYES BEGIN TO OPEN

Monday, February 4 – MD minus 111

HUSHAI WAS PLEASED with the American initiative, although he expected more questions than information. Dialog was what was important here and both sides made hard calls on how much of what they knew to share. Ittai had been instructed not to reveal the website or inquire about the two messages they had pulled off of it. If Iran was directed involved and knew that the US had discovered how communications are passed, that would end immediately. Same for the code, it was simply too great a risk to do more than ask questions.

"Hushai," Ittai began, "Satellite imagery confirms that the meeting has ended and the participants are on their way back here, probably to catch flights or travel to other airports and disburse. Any possibility we can get some help on who these people are and where they are going? Obviously, of particular importance would be information on travel by anyone in this group to the US."

"The simple answer, unfortunately, is, 'No,'" Hushai responded. "Other than El-Ahab, the Iranians don't know who these people are or where they came from. These people traveled here on phony passports and visas. They are not operatives, and thus, no one here has any history with them. It appeared that most had never been in Iran before. They were Eastern men clothed with Western culture and practices. There is no record to draw on to determine who they are, and the Iranian government is not going to act against them as long as their target is America."

"What can you tell me that they learned from their operative, Ahmad Habid, the man who should be dead?" Ittai asked.

"Tell the Americans that they were wise not to kill him now," Hushai answered. "He may be the only hope any of us has in finding out when the attack is planned. They allowed him in the meeting only long enough to outline what they wanted done to tie the American military down in the Middle East during the assault on their homeland. He agreed to nothing, but will plan a massive strike once he has a date. They didn't give him a date or any information on what they planned on doing in the US. He had some very unpleasant things to say about the white collar planners. He is not comfortable with men who have no blood on their hands and who are unwilling to risk themselves to kill their enemies.

"Here is the bottom line – the attacks have to be more than a month away because they know it will take that long to finalize plans and produce the IEDs and car bombs necessary to do the damage they desire. On the other hand, the attack date is not too far off if they called Habid in to tell him what they want him to do. They know he will begin to plan and work through logistics for the largest possible attack. The Iranians believe that the attack is probably ninety days out at the most and are preparing accordingly."

"Preparing what?" Ittai asked.

"What would you think?" Hushai responded. "They are preparing to take advantage of the vacuum which will be created if the terrorists succeed to launch a full-scale assault. They will destroy Israel, who will be without the help and logistical support of the Americans. They will use nuclear weapons if they have them by then. With America effectively negated as a threat, they will seek to unite other Arab countries in driving the Jews into the sea. It is a dream scenario for the current government. They know none of the other Western nations has the will or the military power to stand against them on behalf of Israel. It would be a complete nightmare for the world as Israel would use its nuclear weapons and the US would be in a position to similarly respond at least from ships and subs. I tremble to think what would happen here and around the world.

"The real problem is that the West doesn't understand what drives this sect and why they will never seek peace. Everything is based on the belief in the Hidden Imam and his prophesized reappearance. The West is often so blind. Hitler's *Mein Kampf* told the world exactly what he would do if he had power and the world was shocked when he did exactly what he said he would.

"In 1979 when Ayatollah Khomeini became the leader who established the Islamic Republic of Iran, it was written in Article Five of its constitution that the basis of the constitution and its government was the authority of the Hidden Imam. The constitution promises that the government will dissolve in his favor when the Hidden Imam reappears, yet the American news and government ignores this fundamental reality which drives Iranian policy and has divided Muslim believers for centuries."

"Help me here, Hushai. My knowledge of this teaching is very limited."

"It is not simply a teaching. It is a worldview that controls life and is the central reason for the conflict among Muslims. Its genesis was the battle for leadership after the death of Muhammad. Two groups emerged, one the Sunni, who accepted new leadership regardless of the leader's blood relation to Muhammad. The other, the Shi'a, believed that the true successor to Muhammad had to be a descendant of the cousin and son-in-law of the prophet. As such, these Imams inherited Muhammad's authority not only for civil rule but additionally his prerogative to interpret the Quran infallibly. At its core, the Shi'a's beliefs would result in absolute control of government and religion as one which is the Iranian model.

"Although there are divisions among the Shi'a, the group in control in Iran is among those who believe that there were twelve legitimate Imams, the last of which disappeared before 900 AD leaving no children. The belief is that he was hidden from the eyes of men by God in order to preserve his life and that he will be revealed to the world by God and will return to purify the faith and take the world for Islam. His return will be preceded by chaos, war, and bloodshed. He will come and lead a vast army to do battle with the forces of evil and after defeating evil will rule the world. This group also believes Jesus will return with him, not to rule, but rather to affirm his reign and assist in bringing peace to the world."

"Sounds a little like the Christian teaching on the Apocalypse," Hushai added, "but what does it have to do with the situation at hand?"

"Think about it for a minute. If you truly believe that there is only one legitimate earthly ruler, then all others are enemies as are their followers. The real danger here is that they believe they can speed the return of the Hidden Imam by creating the exact situation which prophesies say will exist when he returns – chaos, war, and bloodshed. If he is going to return in victory then you cannot be defeated, so you fear no one. The current government in Iran is actively preparing for the return of the Hidden Imam as policy and will do anything they believe will speed his return. They will fight those who oppose this teaching, which explains their actions in Iraq against the Sunni people. That is why America and the West generally are viewed as the Great Satan, the enemy of the Hidden Imam, the subject of the final battle for him to rule and Islam to control the world. Start the fight and he will come. That is what they believe and that is why they are so dangerous.

"I may live here, but I don't fully understand the implications of this teaching," Ittai continued. "You may know that I am a Christian, who walks through the Muslim practices so I can stay and do my job. It is difficult, but this is where God has placed me. The hardest part of all this is the deception under which I see these people live. Can you imagine believing that killing yourself and innocents brings their heavenly reward? Virgins to satisfy their wildest physical desires? Can you imagine a belief system that says chaos and war and bloodshed is good because it will bring a leader of peace? It's twisted and tragic. The more I see it, the more I ask, how can we contest it? How can we open these peoples' eyes to truth?"

"I have known that you are a Christian, for I too am a believer," Hushai answered. "They let me stay because I provide them information on the Americans. I am a necessary evil until they crush the Great Satan and then I'm gone. They will ultimately kill me like they will kill all infidels if they can.

"The answers to your questions are in God's hands. There is no policy your government can establish that will change the hearts of these people. You may be able to block their efforts for now, but something has to change fundamentally if there is to be hope here. The conflict and effort to control the earth have been ongoing for over a thousand years. The other day I was watching a cable news broadcast of a citizens group organizing to stop a shooter in a small American city. That broadcast ended with an old man speaking what I thought was the first true words of hope about the situation. He said we ought to pray and find out why God is allowing this. That is the real answer, for if God doesn't open eyes and change hearts, they will eventually prevail. If God does not protect America, your government can't."

They drove through the city in silence, contemplating the meaning of what had just been shared. Overwhelmed, emotions flooded their thoughts about these people and the terrorist groups assembling. A great sadness fell over them as they confronted the reality that all who lived and died in this blindness would not be experiencing their anticipated inheritance of many virgins, but in reality, would suffer the second death. The sadness was palpable and shared alongside them by the forces of light, which surrounded them as they turned to go back to the hotel.

Suddenly Hushai broke the silence, "Please, find a quiet place to pull over and let's pray. I feel an overwhelming sense of God's anguish and sadness over what he sees in this place – children taught to be killers, women treated like cattle, such worship of hatred and destruction. I want to pray for wisdom about the attacks, but more than that, I want to pray for these people that I know God loves. It is as if some force of darkness controls their minds and has blinded their eyes so they cannot see, and has shut their ears so they cannot hear. If only they could be freed to see and hear and understand the truth of God's love in Jesus Christ."

"My heart is one with yours, Hushai. There is more at work here than simply trying to stop the attacks. God has a much larger plan."

Ittia found that quiet place and they were together in prayer. Unseen and unknown, the car had been surrounded by the forces of light, creating an impenetrable barrier to the forces of darkness and causing the vehicle to be essentially invisible to human eyes. The presence surrounding the car was so great that the light which shone through the darkness, joined with the prayers of Ittai and Hushai, reaching the very throne room of God in Heaven. It shone through the spiritual world like the star that revealed the location of the birth of the Christ child,147 only this time the star was on the earth shining forth to the heavens, announcing the prayers of these two brothers joined by the forces of light. As the sun began to rise, there beside the two men appeared a third in the car. God had heard and remembered another time in this same part of the world when a faithful servant poured out his heart in prayer and He again sent Gabriel, an Archangel.[150] Ittai and Hushai trembled with fear as he spoke, "I am Gabriel. I stand in the presence of God and have been sent to give you these instructions for all your brothers.[151] Listen carefully. 'Stand together and pray,'" and he was gone.

Like the shepherds whose heavenly visitation announced the birth of Jesus, these two overcame their fear and rushed back to the hotel to share with other believers what they had seen and been told,[152] and to continue the search for information on the coming attacks. They knew that somehow this was all tied together in God's plan.

"Ittai," Hushai said as they parted. "Please find a way to get word of God's message to the old man in America. He needs to know and be encouraged."

"I will try," was Ittai's response and his mind raced to think of someone he could trust to deliver God's message.

Paul & Samantha Continue Their Search

Paul and Samantha sat in her living room trying to take in all that had happened since her Dad's funeral. It seemed like an eternity of change. Both were thankful they were not searching alone.

"Samantha, I am so sorry that your first encounter with the Bookseller was that outburst at Pastor Elkhorn. I have never seen him that angry. I was afraid you were going to get up and leave."

"I almost did. I was hurt and angry, but even in the midst of the outburst, there was one thing I could not escape. If I left, where could I go to get the answers? Everything I have heard about this man from you and seen in what he said at the news conference was consistent with the teachings we had read in the red letter books. He is radically passionate about God, but that passion seemed, at that moment, to center on a concern that we not be deceived about who God is. I think it was really an expression of his love for us."

"Help me understand, Sam, if you were aware of all those things, why the tears? I don't mean to invade your privacy, but I care about you deeply and I honestly just don't understand what you're feeling."

"You can ask me anything, Paul. I have nothing to hide from you. I think we're both considering the future of our relationship as well as our relationship with God. I want you to know what's on my heart as we walk through this together.

"I cried because I felt such a rush of sadness and disappointment that we may have gotten it wrong and I still may not be a Christian. We did everything that Pastor Elkhorn said to do and it was all wrong," she said, raising her hand to wipe a tear. "The Bookseller made it clear from Jesus' own words that God has to do something in us. It's not simply about us choosing God. He has to choose us and then change us. When we read that book called 'John' from which the Bookseller quoted, I really fell in love with Jesus and want to be His follower. The thought that I may have missed Him is heartbreaking to me. I really want Him; I want that change. I understand that I really need him. Does that make sense?"

"Yes, although the emotion I felt was more a fear of the second death and anger at Pastor Elkhorn. I am so sorry that we went there. I knew after my conversation with Professor Thompson that he didn't believe the Bible and I knew he taught at that church. I should have asked the Bookseller where to go to church."

"There was one really encouraging thing the Bookseller said," Samantha continued. "Did you hear? He said that God has chosen you to search and you are searching. I believe that He has chosen both of us and we are both searching. Don't you?"

"Absolutely," Paul responded. "The greatest joy of all this for me has been the search together and that was what the Bookseller said we should continue to do. I wrote down that reference to the verse he gave us. It was Jeremiah 29:13." Grabbing the Bible and going to the index to find the page number, Paul came to Jeremiah chapter 29. He found verse 13 and read, "You will seek Me and find Me when you seek Me with all your heart."

"What about that old is gone the new has come verse[153] and Jesus' statement that we must be born again? [154]Paul, do you think we have been changed? The dream showed you without the light inside and me in a fog, but that was a long time ago. It was before we began our search. How about now, are we different?"

"I have been thinking a lot about that," Paul responded. "We are different since the funeral. We have a desire to search for God. When that false dream came, God brought back the verses we had read to my memory and gave me peace that the dream was not truth. We both have a desire to please God and to know what He requires. Those are all new things. I am confident that God wants us and we want Him, but do we want Him with all our hearts? I don't know what that means really. I know we need to have faith in Jesus, but what does that mean? I still have so many questions."

"Me too, but I have a suggestion," Samantha answered. "Let's keep reading on in the Bible. Let's read the books after the red letter ones and see what they say. As we read, we can write down the questions we have and pray that God will show us the answers. When you meet with the Bookseller again, ask him to show you in the Bible what it means to have faith in Jesus. Write it down and bring it back and show me. We can do this together."

Paul turned in the Bible past the book of John to the book called Acts and began to read. Still unknown to Paul, the light within him burned brightly as he continued his search to learn more of the God who had already found him because he had sought God with all his heart.

Iranian Hardball

Security at Iranian airports was arbitrary and abusive. Under the direction of the Ministry of Intelligence and Security, the State Security Forces (SSF) had been given latitude to do whatever they deemed appropriate to protect the existing government from dissent or threats, real or perceived. Given the recent threat of war from an arm of al-Qaeda, it was now a matter of national security to know the actual targets of terrorists who trained or operated from Iranian territory. They could no longer be assumed to be friendly.

Security was on special alert in light of the way the terrorist planners had treated their own Ahman Habid. The terrorist leadership wanted his help but was unwilling to share specific information on their planned operation. Habid had noted their descriptions carefully and passed the information on to the SSF, who were now on the lookout for the leaders. They intended to get answers.

When Demas Assad, leader of the terrorist operatives in the United States, and the others arrived in a caravan at the airport, they were met by the SSF and taken to a secured area of the airport where they were directed to separate rooms to be interrogated. Assad was livid. "By whose authority do you detain these instruments of the Sheik who have come to complete plans for attacks to destroy our mutual enemy, America?"

The SSF commander's response was blunt, simple and effective, "One additional word from you that is not in response to a question and I will cut out your tongue." With that, he displayed a wicked knife that was still stained with some innocent's blood. The silence was deafening. Assad was a planner, not an operative, and he had no intention of sacrificing himself for the cause.

Assad's luggage and carry-on baggage were taken from him along with that of the others who had come in the caravan. As the baggage was searched, Assad's laptop was discovered in his carry-on bag. It was quickly removed to another room and given to a technician, who after some effort was able to sign in, access the programs and do a visual search. He found an index which included the agenda and a file entitled 'Final Solution.' He had been told what to look for, but because he didn't speak English well, he only knew that he had found what he was looking for. Inserting a connection to an external hard drive, he copied everything on the laptop for later analysis by the SSF. Then, looking carefully around the room to be sure the SSF personnel were focused elsewhere, he took a flash drive out of his pocket and quickly copied the "Final Solution" file. He returned the small drive to his pocket before anyone noticed and gave the external hard drive to the SSF official in charge. The computer and other luggage were returned to Assad and he went on his way, thankful to still have a tongue

CHAPTER 19

A GRISLY MYSTERY

Thursday, February 5 — MD minus 110 days

As the sun came up across America, sanitation workers in seven cities made gruesome discoveries of young dark skinned men's bodies thrown in with the garbage in dumpsters behind schools, shopping malls, and office buildings. The bodies all showed signs of been killed execution style; one was shot through the back of the head, hands still tied behind his back. As police units separately struggled to obtain identities, motives, and suspects, they found nothing. No state or federal agency had any record of fingerprints or dental records for any of the victims. There was no identification on the bodies. These men did not exist as a matter of record.

Throughout the day, medical examiners would determine that these were all young Arab men from unknown Middle Eastern countries. Slowly the routine murder investigations turned to the obvious concern of why these unidentifiable young Arab men were in the United States. When that threshold was reached, calls were made to Homeland Security, who began to patch together a pattern. The news caused those with knowledge of the agenda real concern. As feared, the operatives were already here.

Meanwhile in Williams and Washington

The morning was greeted in Williams by groups that gathered together in preparation for the day's anticipated activities. Officer Sally Johnson and Tom Campy had again gathered in her patrol car outside of Petersen Elementary School. There were now four, as others had joined – one more from the police force and one more from the Citizens Militia. They were as yet unaware of the discoveries of the executed men, even though one of the murders had occurred in a large adjoining city.

The Bookseller was up early, praying and seeking guidance for what was next. He had a real sense that God would yet use him and he wanted to be careful not to step out on his own. He was excited, but fearful for the nation and disappointed at the seeming lack of response to the call to pray. It seemed the nation was still asleep, particularly those who called themselves Christians. What would it take to awaken believers? He did not know but knew that whatever it was, God would allow it to happen if Christians did not change.

In Washington, Tom Knight and David Barnes had just completed a time of prayer with President Strong. Their prayers for wisdom and discernment to be enabled to understand the threat and to know how to respond, along with a cry for protection of the nation had been interrupted by a sense of sadness over the Middle East and a feeling of ultimate powerlessness. Feeling helpless, yet without shame or embarrassment, President Strong had humbled himself while praying by lying down on the floor prostrate over the Great Seal of the United States. He understood that he might be the most powerful man on the face of the earth, the leader of the only remaining superpower, but he could not overcome the darkness and hate encamped against America. He could launch a military or nuclear strike, but he could not change a heart. His cry for God's help came from a deep recognition of the need for divine intervention if there was to be any hope of stopping the never-ending assault of terror and hate. He knew that whatever generated that level of hate was beyond this world.

Later as he got up and sat across from the others on a couch, he said, "During our prayer I was reminded of what one of Israel's kings prayed in a moment of great crisis. King Jehoshaphat, who faced a massive army he did not believe he could defeat prayed, 'We do not know what to do, but our eyes are on You.'[155] That is how I feel, only worse because we do not even understand the extent of the threat. All I know in my heart is that it is there and every bit as real as the army Jehoshaphat faced."

"Not everyone would agree with you, Mr. President," Tom Knight added. "Yesterday at the end of the meeting, Commissioner Matthews took us all to task for overreacting to the perceived threat. He got pretty vocal in his objection that we have no concrete evidence and should back off. I wouldn't be surprised if he was the source of the George Murphy story in the *Daily Times* this morning, which asked where the press secretary has disappeared to and what is the secret commission he now heads. How do you want us to deal with that? Do you want me out front again as press secretary?"

"I will tell you exactly what I want you to do; ignore the story and keep working on the commission. The press doesn't run this administration. All they want to do is to criticize and take us down as part of the election campaign. I am not running and I don't care what they say about me or about what we are doing. Proceed with what we know is right and history will clean up the mess they are making to sell a few papers. When it is time, I will go public. Until then we have nothing to say in response to that story or any others. I want the response to be, 'No comment.' "

"Respectfully, Mr. President, that will just feed the fire. If we seek to avoid this, they will push all the harder for information. They will turn the investigative reporters loose and our opposition-led Congress will not be far behind."

"Tom, I don't care. We have to address the threat and cannot be diverted by this crowd or any other. Events will drive when we go public and I am frankly concerned that may have to be sooner rather than later. It is time to get real and quit playing the game. Politics is destroying our ability to govern this country. The poll-driven mentality which forces policy has been nothing less than a disaster. Long-term policy is impossible in a daily news cycle-driven environment. Politicians are too concerned about today's opinion and appearance to lead.

"John Kennedy used to retell a Chinese proverb which said, 'There go my people. I must find where they are going so I can lead them.' That is a perfect description of the media and poll-driven America of today, and I will not become a prisoner of the polls or the media. We will lead and they can follow where we are going or get out of the way while we persevere onward."

The discussion was broken up by a knock as National Security Advisor Troy Steed, Homeland Security Director Stephen Hollister, and CIA Director Crenshaw entered to give the daily security briefing. It was unusual for all three to come, which indicated there was significant news.

"Tom," the president continued. "I want you and David to stay for the briefing this time since it will impact the commission's work."

"Mr. President, there is news from Iran," Director Crenshaw began. "We have not gotten the detail we wanted, but we may have some better idea of timing and on who these people are. The Iranian operative was excluded from the planning for the attacks in America but was asked to prepare attacks in the Middle East against Western interests and to tie down the US military there in coordination with what they intend to do here in the States. Our best guess is something akin to the Tet Offensive[156] on as broad a front as possible to create chaos and as much damage as possible. There are no particulars because we believe that plan is only now being made.

"On the timing issue, the Iranians believe that the attacks on the US are ninety days out at the most. They base that on the knowledge of how much time it will take to prepare for such a massive attack in the Middle East. The terrorist planners would not give their man a timeline until closer to the date for the attack in the US. The Iranians are preparing their own mischief for Israel based on a ninety-day timeline which assumes that they believe the US would be unable to come to Israel's assistance either militarily or logistically. That affirms that the attacks in the US are intended to paralyze the country and make it impossible for us to respond elsewhere in the world to threats."

That comment was followed by sober silence as the six men in the Oval Office tried to take in what this could mean. The cogs turned rapidly in David Barnes' head as he processed the magnitude of the situation, finally thinking out loud he said, "The agenda, remember, 'Timing – MD'? Could 'MD' be Memorial Day? That's about ninety days from today. It would be a different approach from the past. They would not be planning an attack based on a Moslem historical event, but would be desecrating an American holiday. Wait a minute. Like the 9/11 attacks were on symbolically significant buildings, this time the attack would be on a day honoring American military. I think the Iranians may be right. The target date may be Memorial Day."

"Memorial Day, despicable, sounds just like them," inserted Troy Steed, "take our day to remember the sacrifices of our military for our country and turn it into the day of the greatest destruction since Pearl Harbor."

"Pearl Harbor is a good reminder of what we need to do and what we need for God to do," the president added thoughtfully. "Remember, our government had numerous warnings of the Japanese intentions which were ignored until it was too late. The only reason the whole of the West Coast was not opened to an unchallenged amphibious invasion was that our carriers were not at Pearl Harbor that Sunday morning. How many times in history has God saved us from ourselves? I sure hope that old man at the press conference was wrong and we are still living under at least some level of divine protection."

"Mr. President, you have to stay away from religion in dealing with this threat," Director Hollister warned. "You have already pushed it pretty far with your introduction of prayer at the commission. The congressional leadership will crucify you if you bring religion into this. With the temperament on the Hill, there is no telling what kind of firefight public statements invoking God would cause. The leadership in the Senate is trying to figure out how to make that old man a criminal under some new extension of the hate crimes law. It isn't worth the political capital that you are going to need to mobilize a response."

"You don't get it, do you," the president responded angrily. "I don't care about political capital. I care about protecting this nation and I cannot do that independent of God. Those children dressed up in suits playing games and dancing to the lobbyist tunes up on Capitol Hill can't see beyond their name in today's newspaper. I have had it with them! I intend to lead as I believe God would have me lead and they can follow or fight me. I believe that the people will follow if they see me seeking to follow God. End of discussion. Now, what new insights did we learn from the Iranians about these people?"

"Really more of the same," answered CIA Director Crenshaw. "They are described by the Iranian operative as 'white collar planners who have no blood on their hands, unwilling to risk themselves to kill the enemy.' He despises them, but will cooperate to hurt us in a coordinated attack."

"I cannot believe they don't know something," Troy Steed said incredulously. "The Iranians have their own issues with Al Qaeda and ISIS. There are not going to let this go and not find out what the terrorists intend to do. Remember, they have been threatened and they are going to want to know the exact nature of the attacks, the anticipate damage and the day and hour. They have their own agenda they would like to push if they know the US is incapacitated, and that agenda is spelled I-S-R-A-E-L."

"You are absolutely right," Crenshaw joined in. Our agents believe that is exactly what Iran will do if they really believe we will be incapable of a response other than nuclear."

Still thinking, David Barnes added, "That will be a measure for us as we get closer to MD. If we gather evidence that the Iranians are massing for an attack on Israel, either alone or in cooperation with other Middle Eastern nations, we'll know they believe we are going to be hit and rendered effectively unable to respond offensively."

"When do we tell Israel?" the president asked.

"Not until we are sure of what we face and what they will face," Crenshaw answered. "If Israel feels threatened, they will strike first with whatever level of force they believe is required to eliminate the threat. They will not be in the dark. They have a much more sophisticated intelligence network in Iran than we do. We can wait a month if Barnes is right about the date but no more."

"This raises the nuclear question to a whole new level," the president added. "We need to be sure what we are facing in 90 days is not nuclear and that the Iranians will not have nuclear weapons to use against Israel either. Steve and Tom, I want a report on my desk by Friday on what we are doing to monitor the possibility of nuclear devices coming into the country or already here in major population areas."

"Mr. President, the kind of attack which it appears we face does not lend itself to a nuclear weapon. If the intelligence is correct, they are not trying to kill masses of people, but destroy the ability to sustain our existence as a nation," David Barnes added.

"David, I understand the intelligence, but we don't get a second chance on this one so follow the nuclear possibility as well as whatever else makes sense. Have we gotten any closer to knowing the targets and how they intend to inflict such massive damage?" the president asked.

"All I can tell you right now, Mr. President, is that we are working on it," Chairman Knight answered. "Frankly, I feel stupid and afraid."

"Good," the president responded, "at least I'm not alone."

The phone rang and the White House operator announced an urgent call for Homeland Security Director Hollister. "Take it here," the president insisted.

One side of the conversation was enough to get everyone's attention. "What! How can that be? Seven young Arab men dead in seven different cities, all killed execution style and we have no information on who they are or where they came from or how they got here? Gather the forensic evidence as quickly as possible and release it to all our allies to see what they might know about these people. Absolutely no press, keep this top secret."

Turning to the group gathered in the Oval Office, Director Hollister reported what he had just learned of the seven young Arab men killed execution-style in seven different cities. "That confirms they are already among us as we feared, but I wonder why these men were killed," asked Chairman Knight.

"It would have to be discipline," Director Crenshaw answered. "Can you imagine the difficulty of keeping a large number of suicide operatives hidden and inconspicuous for months waiting to die killing their enemies who are all around them? They probably don't yet know the plan like how many of the 9/11 operatives did not know they were going to die. If this thing is really ninety days away, they obviously are having difficulty controlling their people and are trying to send a message to the others by executing the most unreasonable."

"How could they have coordinated this, all killed on the same day and even the same way?" asked Director Hollister.

"I think I have a partial answer," said David Barnes. "Let me grab my notes a minute. Yes, here it is. You remember those messages we pulled from the website? One was, 'Some Gs crave delay and are cautious. Give them life recklessly and in public. J-14.' "

"I don't know what 'G' means, but it must be a reference to their operatives. The rest of the message is clear through. They have simply reversed the meaning of the words. This leader, 'J-14' instructed the leaders of the cells to do that. Here is my translation, 'Some operatives (?) demand an immediate attack and have become reckless risking the mission. Kill them carefully and privately.' Remember that was sent from Iran while the planners' meeting was going on."

"I think you're right, David," the president said. "What about the other message from the website?"

"The other message was, '0-1 later. J-10.' Obviously, the 'J-10' is a different leader, which could mean either a geographic division of leadership or perhaps a different focus or plan. Maybe we are dealing with more than one kind of attack. The '0-1' is probably a reference to a place. The 'later' means that whatever is to happen in 0-1 is to happen soon. That was like a launch code. If we have this right, we are going to experience some kind of attack in a single city soon, whatever soon means."

"Look, I don't know whether David has it all right, but we cannot take a chance," the president instructed. "Tom, I need options on how to get this information in a useful form to local law enforcement so they can be prepared. We don't want to start a panic, but we have to respond. We have seven bodies which tell us this is more likely true than false. Get back to me in the early afternoon."

"Mr. President, one more thing," Director Crenshaw added reluctantly. "I wouldn't bother you with this, but it is important to our Iranian operatives for some reason and I want to be able to tell them we complied with their request. However, since it is so unusual I wanted your clearance."

"What is it?" the president asked curiously.

"They have sent a sealed message for the old man, the one who raised the issue at the end of the press conference in Williams. They saw a replay of that event on cable TV and have a message for him. I know it breaks all protocol, but I didn't feel I should open it and have no idea what the message is, but these men are key to everything we have learned to date and I believe that we should deliver the message as requested. I trust that if it was intelligence we needed, they would have already shared it with us. They have never done anything to make us question them and communication with the old man seems harmless."

"I agree. Don't open it and have the message delivered today," the president instructed. "I trust that old man's heart and our Iranian team. Should the old man want to send a response back, have it taken. I feel that communication between those three will benefit us, and nothing material will be withheld."

"Now, unfortunately, my schedule says I must meet with former President Cox and a crowd from the Senate that wants to create what they are calling the UNA out of Mexico, the US and Canada. They want something like another United Nations – and I am sure they have other things on their mind. I need to maintain my schedule and appear that things are business as usual. We don't want to make them suspicious. You all have plenty to do in response to what we've learned. Let's get to work."

CHAPTER 20

DISCOVERIES

Tuesday, February 5 – MD minus 110 days

UPON RETURNING TO his White House basement office, David Barnes fired up his computer and typed in "FS2.com" to view any recent postings. His eyes were drawn to new messages on the screen, again mostly gibberish except for one. There it was, the confirmation he both sought and feared. It read simply, "Evil – End for fun. J-14." Somehow he knew immediately that the opposite meaning was, "Good work – Begin though unpleasant." The same leader had sent the message. It was obviously a follow up to the earlier message which had ordered the executions. There would be more if needed.

Looking through the site more closely, he found another message which appeared to be a response to the second of the earlier messages that had been directed to a cell group in a specific location. It read, "J-10. 0-1. Never 2." That one wasn't so obvious, but the opportunity it presented was. Grabbing the phone, Barnes called Darrell Reed, the CIA's ultimate computer geek. "Darrell, we have two new ones on the FS2.com website. If you can find out from where they were posted, we might be able to find the location of the coordinator and one of the targets."

"You've got it," was the response. "I have the website up now, which two messages?" With the exchange that followed, the search began. David Barnes took a moment to pray silently that Darrell might have favor in his search and for wisdom regarding the meaning of the second message.

Blind Ambition

Back upstairs, President Strong and National Security Advisor Troy Steed sat across a conference table from former President Cox, Senate Majority Leader Howard and Chairman of the Senate Homeland Security Committee Crow. They pressed hard for their vision of an amalgamated Canada, US, and Mexico in some kind of economic and political union. The argument was for open borders and open markets, ultimately one currency and a unified system of regulations and standards which would be promulgated through a representative body of some nature. Again they pointed to the European model as the future, leading ultimately to an interrelated one world governing counsel through the United Nations. It was the same basic speech former President Cox had recently delivered in the Senate majority leader's office. "I wonder who they have in mind for the ultimate leader of this governing counsel," thought the president, seeing through some of the individual agendas.

"Look, Leonard," President Strong responded. You sat in the Oval Office for eight years and this idea was never advanced by anyone in your administration. Why are you so passionate now?"

"Mr. President," Cox answered. "This is an idea whose time has come. I should have seen it during my time in office, but I didn't. It is for you to be the bipartisan leader who advances this important vision for a better future for all of us in North America and ultimately the world."

"Do me a favor and drop the political spin," President Strong said, speaking with a passionate bluntness that surprised even him. "We all know that you, Leader Howard and Chairman Crow, are not here to make me a visionary. You are here to advance an agenda that gets people elected in your party which would include my successor. Hear me clearly, we all know I cannot run for reelection and although I would like to see my party back in majority control of Congress while maintaining the White House, that is not what will motivate me in these remaining months. What motivates me is what is good for the people of America, both now and in the future, if we can have a future in this world of violence and hate. Explain to me how this plan advances the security of the United States while improving economic opportunities for all out citizens and I will listen. I have no interest in the European model for America. We fought a revolution to break away from that once and I will not voluntarily take us back to what I consider being a failed model."

"Well, you may want to reconsider that," Leader Howard threatened. "I expect to have a bill on your desk within the next 30 days and if you veto that bill, we will crush your party in the general election. The people behind this bill have an unlimited source of funds and they will spend whatever it takes. If this does not happen in your term, it will happen after you are gone and we will have control of Congress and the White House for at least the next decade."

"Perhaps," the president responded thoughtfully, seeking to lower the tone of the debate, "but what about border security? No one has answered my question. I sent up a border security bill two years ago and you haven't even allowed hearings. Are you really going to argue that we should further open our already unsecured borders to terrorists and any weapon they can conceal or sneak across? Consider the danger to the American people."

"You have completely lost it," said Cox angrily. "This terrorism fight is like shadow boxing. Can't you get it through your thick skull that other than a couple of individual acts of rage on a military base, and a couple of crazies at a recruiting station and a Christmas party, there have been no – none – zero attacks on American soil since 9/11 and those were an aberration. If they hadn't been given American targets in Afghanistan and Iraq, there would be no worldwide terrorist networks. Leave them alone where they are, back off on the unconditional support of Israel, buy their oil, and we will all live in peace. It may seem trite to you, but the reality is that we need to go along to get along. This North American Union will resolve lots of future problems we are going to have with Mexico and could be a beginning for addressing Latin America's concerns. Wake up and stop trying to rule America with fear."

"You're the one who needs to wake up and stop trying to rule solely to get elected or stay elected," the president responded angrily. "The world in which we live is dangerous and includes many evil people who hate America and believe they are serving their god by killing us. They are not going away if we ignore them, and they are not going to stop planning and attempting even larger attacks against Americans here and elsewhere. They have no national headquarters where we could negotiate a peace or surrender, even if we were ready to waive a white flag. They are everywhere with a single purpose – kill the infidels and rule by Shariah law – and I might remind you that you too are an infidel by their definition. Now, Chairman Crow, Leader Howard, answer my question. Do I get the border security bill – yes or no?"

"You will not get a border security bill out of this Congress. We consider that to be inconsistent with our vision of a North American Union," responded Leader Howard.

"I appreciate your honesty," President Strong said soberly, "but I need to be sure I understand what you are saying. What you are telling me is that within 30 days you are going to put a bill on my desk, the effect of which would be that in less than 90 days from today, Mexican or Canadian trucks and other vehicles would have open access to American roads based solely on drivers licenses issued by officials in Canada or Mexico without any American involvement and without any American inspection at the border of the vehicles or their cargos. Did I get that right?"

"Absolutely, it is essential for the economic union. We must provide for the unrestricted free flow of goods across borders. We need to grow up and trust our North American partners to inspect loads and regulate licenses for vehicles crossing borders the same as for those vehicles operating in their countries," Leader Howard answered.

"You understand that this would create a security nightmare," the president responded.

"We don't see it that way," Cox replied, "and make no mistake about it, this will be a full court press. The Together Tomorrow PAC is unleashing ads all across the country next week. You can be on board or the target of the ads. It's your choice."

"Who are these Together Tomorrow people, not the out front crowd, but the real people who are calling the shots? Who is the real sponsor and who is the source of the unlimited funds? Why do they want us to open our borders with Mexico and Canada? You better know the answer to those questions before you tie your future and our nation to them," cautioned President Strong.

"You leave that to us. You make your political decisions and we will make ours," was Cox's blunt response.

"Yes, and one more question," the president inquired. "How much is the Together Tomorrow crowd paying you, Leonard, to trumpet their cause? Whatever it is, if you go public with this, that will come out and it will affect your credibility and the credibility of your argument."

Cox's legendary temper exploded into a tirade of threats and insults which President Strong finally cut off. "You forget where you are and to whom you are speaking. You may not like me, respect me or agree with me, but you will treat this office with the respect it deserves. One more outburst like that and I will have you forcibly removed, which you of all people should know I can and will.

"Listen for a minute; I don't pretend to have all the answers, but neither do you. I know that we are at risk now and I am praying for guidance on how to meet the terror threat. That old man in Williams was right. We shouldn't be arguing with one another; we should be praying together, seeking God's wisdom and discernment, asking for His protection over our nation."

"Mr. President, you raise another question we need to discuss," inserted Chairman Crow, who had been waiting for an opening. "We don't see religion as a neutral stance. If you consider the world in which we live, it is religion which makes it dangerous. People seeking to force their beliefs on others in the name of religion are the cause of violence. Our Constitution protects private religion, but that is it. People don't have the right to impose their religion on others or to force others to endure their religious propaganda. A man like the old man you reference is dangerous. He has caused disputes and debates across the entire country. Those who claim to be Christians are seeking to force their beliefs on the rest of the nation. They really are no different than the Muslim fanatics. The ultimate danger is the same. We believe that it is time for us to act against fanatic Christians like this old man."

"Exactly how do you propose to do that?" the president asked, shaking his head in disbelief.

"Our Committee will be reporting out an amendment to the Hate

Crimes Act making public religious motivation or incitement of others which could possibly lead to a violent or unlawful act a hate crime. We hope that will bring an end to religiously motivated hate speech. We intend to subpoena that old man from Williams as a prime example to the American public of why this legislation is required. His answers to direct questions about what he teaches and believes will reveal the truth of the hate in his heart toward those who disagree with him. We wanted you to know – as a courtesy."

President Strong sat silently still shaking his head as his emotions raced, and then suddenly the look on his face changed. He felt surrounded by an unnatural sense of complete peace. He had always known that the time would come when the American government would be used by enemies of religion to strike out against faith. He was surprised that it was coming this quickly and so overtly but was thankful that he was in a position where he would be able to stand against it. He felt strangely sorry for these blind politicos standing before him, speaking for the agenda of darkness. He remembered that Jesus had said, "Everyone who does evil hates the light and will not come into the light for fear that his deeds will be exposed."[157] That was what this was about, using the law to keep the real motivation for and the ultimate results of their deeds from being exposed.

"Mr. Chairman, I don't know how to respond," the president began. "You know I have thought from day one that the hate crimes legislation was a politically inspired bad idea. If someone intentionally commits a crime, they should be prosecuted for that crime to the full extent of the law regardless of their motivation. Is hate somehow worse than committing a crime for fun because the criminal enjoys hurting people? You have sent the message that some victims are more valuable than others for reasons that have nothing to do with the crime. That is demeaning and hurtful.

"Now to your amendment. To include religious motivation or speech as a hate crime would drop Sunday School into the same basket as terrorism. To make the legal standard 'could possibly lead to a violent or unlawful act' has only one purpose. Your perceived constituency wants to use the power of the federal government to end religion in America, specifically to stop Christian speaking and teaching that behavior the Bible describes as sin is morally wrong. Admit it. You want to make the religion of the Bible unlawful and now you want to find a way to punish an old man who calls on the Christians of the nation to pray. Do you see how ludicrous that is?"

"'Ludicrous' is not the word I would use," Chairman Crow responded. "A more realistic description is 'necessary.' We intend to protect the American people's freedom from religion."

"What you suggest is a hypocritical and dangerous policy," the president responded soberly. "You have the absolute freedom to believe or disbelieve what you want, but hear me carefully. There is a God in Heaven and if this nation declares war on Him and on those who have chosen to follow Him as you propose, that will be the day the end chapter on America is written. It will not play out immediately, but it will play out. Practice what you preach. Advocate what you believe, but don't try to legislate for or against religion. America is not endangered when people share what they believe. That only gives us choices. America is about choices, people considering different points of view and then deciding what they believe. Religion should be treated no differently than other First Amendment rights."

"Doesn't sound like we have anything we can agree on," observed former President Cox.

"Not on the proposals you seek to advance," the president replied. "I ask you to rethink carefully what you came here to advocate. These things are not in America's best interest, and if you go forward, events may soon make you appear the fool." And with that, he stood and left the room.

A Message Returned

Nothing surprised Carl Varvel anymore. His job for the CIA was simple: deliver sealed messages or die trying. His particular assignment on this day was to carry a sealed message and deliver it to a man named Samuel Evans White in Williams, Illinois. A plane had been put at his disposal and he had been flown to Chicago where he was met by local CIA personnel who drove him to Williams and stopped in front of some kind of rare bookstore located in a warehouse. As he approached the door, he saw the sign, 'READ LUKE 13:1-5' and he knew immediately who Samuel Evans White was. Varvel was about to meet the Bookseller.

Margaret answered his knock and he said, "Good afternoon. Is Samuel Evans White here? It is a matter of national security. I am Carl Varvel with the CIA," and he showed her his identification badge. "I have a message for Mr. White. It is urgent."

Margaret invited him in and left to find the Bookseller. Soon he appeared looking curious and surprised by the visitor. "I am Samuel Evans White. How can I help you?"

"Do you have any identification?" was the businesslike response. After reviewing the driver's license tendered carefully and satisfied himself that this was the intended recipient, Varvel had the Bookseller sign a receipt and handed him a sealed envelope labeled, 'EYES ONLY SAMUEL EVANS WHITE, TOP SECRET.'

"I have been instructed to wait for a response."

"Give me a few moments," he said leaving the room for a more private place to consider the message. Margaret joined him and asked, "Samuel what is this about? Why would the CIA be delivering a message to you?"

"I have no idea," was the response, "but I sense the hand of God's involvement in whatever this is. No one but God could make the CIA aware of me. Perhaps this is part of the answer to what we have been praying. Let's find out."

Unknown to the CIA was that 'EYES ONLY' had a different meaning to the Bookseller. He believed that the marriage covenant between himself and Margaret made them not only one flesh but one together before the Lord. As such, the message was for both of them. Opening the envelope, he read:

To the old man in Williams – the one who spoke after the press conference, greetings in the name of our Lord and Savior Jesus Christ.

We are brothers serving in Iran seeking to discover for your government details of a plot to attack the United States and, if successful, then Israel. We believe that what God has revealed to us is an affirmation of what He is saying to you and through you and others to all believers. The message was given by a heavenly being as we prayed. It was, we believe, an angel who said:

"I am Gabriel. I stand in the presence of God and have been sent to give you these instructions for all your brothers.

Listen carefully. Stand together and pray."

The message was unsigned.

The Bookseller was silent as tears came to his eyes. Soon he was sobbing, holding Margaret close as he sought to absorb the full meaning of what he had just read. He rejoiced through the tears in the affirmation of what now filled his heart. It was as if all the years of service and study had been in preparation for this time – and it had.

He breathed in deeply and exhaled with a long sigh, "This is it, Margaret. God is seeking to speak to His people and show Himself to the world. It will come down to one result, either God's people will hear and be changed, or the world will experience judgments in increasing magnitude until His people hear and change – or it will be the end. It is for a time like this we have prayed for all those decades, and we don't simply get to see it, we are a part of it. I cannot put into words the privilege of being a part of what God is seeking to accomplish. This is why I was born. May His will be done."

Taking a pen and paper, the Bookseller wrote his response.

My brothers – we will stand with you and pray, calling on all believers to join together and pray. Do not be afraid. Remember Hebrews 4:13. God is faithful.

The old man in Williams, Samuel Evans White

He folded the message, returned to the front and handed it to Carl Varvel who placed it in another "Top Secret Eyes Only" envelope, sealed it and left to begin the message's long return journey to Tehran.

CHAPTER 21

PREPARATIONS FOR THE MORROW

Tuesday, February 5 – MD minus 110

MOLECH APPROACHED THE night's duties with an increased sense of urgency. The dark wisp messengers who had come and gone with reports of events were troubling. Clearly the forces of darkness were advancing on all fronts to achieve the Dark Master's purposes, but just as clearly was the evidence of the Enemy's activity. Of particular concern was the slow, but growing response to the old man's call for prayer. It just wouldn't go away. Molech knew that there was real danger if the followers of the Enemy obeyed the instructions and stood together and prayed. There was a power generated by believers united together in real prayer that could not be overcome by the darkness.[158] The movement had to be stopped now.

What caused Molech the most concern was the great rejoicing among the forces of light. The issue remained in the balance, but the light within was drawing the truly faithful ones toward prayer.

Knowing that the center of activity at this moment was Williams, over that city Lucius, Niger and Manaen gathered with Barnabas and many others of the forces of light to consider the Spirit's activity and His instructions.

They knew how important it was to set aside their personal feelings and desires and to do only what they were instructed to do, exactly as they had been instructed when they were instructed. They drew strength from their unity even as the believers on earth did, and they rejoiced as they heard Lucius' report.

"Although there is not a widespread movement among God's people in America to pray together, the light within has called out the few truly faithful ones who are responding in obedience. This day began with the president in prayer with several like-minded brothers. He humbled himself and lay prostrate on the floor crying out Jehoshaphat's prayer of helplessness to the One who can help. His prayer was heard and his eyes have begun to be opened. He is being strengthened to stand. If he remains faithful, he can be used to advance the Father's purposes and perhaps this judgment will be withdrawn.

"In Iran two who were placed there to serve have been called and obeyed. They are unaware that the knowledge for responding to the Dark Master's plan has been given to a brother who knows not what he has or why. They have been led to speak with the Bookseller so that he will see the hand of God moving throughout the earth and be encouraged. There is much yet the Father desires to do through this servant, but there is much opposition and he is living unaware that he is in great physical danger. Without the Father's protection, he will be killed tomorrow.

"The Father has drawn Chaplain Forrest to repentance and back into His service. He is using Pastor Wilson, who has contacted archbishops in Rwanda and East Asia requesting a call to prayer for the churches affiliated with the Anglican Mission in the Americas. Those instructions were issued to their American fellowships and the churches in Africa and East Asia have joined together in prayer for America. There is much power being generated by their prayers, but believers in America must be awakened before it is too late. They will not avoid God's judgment because of the prayers of others. If they do not seek God and change, whatever circumstances are necessary will be allowed to awaken them to their sin and their need for God. It will become much worse for them than even the plan of the Dark Master if that is what is required."

On that sobering note hands were lifted as they cried out together,

"For the Light!" and then departed to their places of assignment wondering what the Father would allow in the coming days.

Argon's Chance

As he journeyed to begin the night's duties before him, Molech turned to Argon, who he had brought with him both to teach advanced tactics and to instruct what those under his command were to do tomorrow. "Understand the difficulty and importance of the task we have before us," Molech began. "This is a great opportunity to strike a mortal blow at the Enemy and is worth the risk assumed. The Dark Master has courageously chosen to openly rebel against the Enemy's limitations regarding the old man and the kid. There will be active and open opposition in the morning, so we must use everything at our command to defeat those two and stop the prayer movement begun by the old man. If we can kill him, his call for prayer for God's deliverance will appear foolish since God couldn't protect him. His death should end the threat and accelerate the accomplishment of the Dark Master's agenda to eliminate this false nation 'under God'. We cannot allow for failure, which is why the plan calls for two assassins."

"Exalted One," Argon replied, "We cannot fail with two such proven instruments?"

"Have you not heard of the recent execution of seven of the most faithful servants of the Dark Master by others in his service? These humans may be proven instruments, but they are so undependable. There had been ambitious plans for the seven, but these humans, even the faithful ones, cannot be controlled. Unless they are possessed, which is rare, they can only be influenced; and the more they become like the Dark Master, the more they lie and rebel against authority just like him. It is understandable but frustrating. That is why Legion is so valuable in influencing thousands to kill while committing suicide, believing that they are serving god and will be rewarding by satisfying their physical passions forever. They accomplish a mission and then are out of the way. It will work as long as the deception continues to provide an unlimited supply of killers willing to die.

"Argon, let me share more about tomorrow's plan and then we will influence our killers to complete their assignments. It probably will surprise you as much as it did me, but you are being considered for a new assignment and need to understand better how to master these human creatures. If things go well this next week, I have been told that you will be assigned to me as a mentor to learn how to lead those with the responsibilities over cities like yourself, so listen closely and learn.

"The Dark Master's plan for tomorrow is brilliant. The goal is to stop the prayer movement and to eliminate their perceived need to defend against future attacks. We can do that by killing the old man and by causing the shooter to be killed or captured. The plan does not allow for either assassin to survive. The one you found called Demetrius will die in a suicide bombing. The shooter, the one call Susan Stafford, should kill the kid and will be a backup assassin for the old man. However, in the process, she will be placed where she will be seen by others and unable to escape. If she is either killed or captured, the publicity and interest of the nation which the old man fed should end because the perceived threat will have ended. They will again let down their defenses. They have no idea what is coming on Sunday and later leading up to the Memorial Day, the elimination of America as a force in the world. They will go back to sleep, even as the plan for their destruction proceeds openly in their midst."

"Exalted One," Argon asked, "How can they be so foolish? Don't they understand that there exists a permanent state of war between the forces of light and darkness for their eternal future?"

"Actually, they do not," Molech answered. "That reality, along with our existence, has been hidden from all except a few with the light within, and fortunately, no one listens to them. They are considered fools, although the truth of the conflict is laid out clearly in the Enemy's book. Since they don't read the book, they don't know and most who do have been convinced that the book is a collection of stories and fables not to be taken seriously.

"In normal times, defeating prayer is easy. It can be almost completely eliminated or rendered ineffective without much effort at all. Unless the humans feel helpless, their natural response is always to deal with the issue themselves without asking for help. It is a matter of pride which we have worked so hard to develop over the centuries and ingrain into their very being. We have recently refined it so that now it forms a part of what they believe to be their 'religion.' I have to laugh at the way they have a passion for ignoring God and doing everything themselves, often in His name.

"Here is how it works. We have caused the culture in which they live to value self-reliance more than dependence on God or man. Kids are taught to respect the ones who did things for themselves, pulled themselves up by their bootstraps to overcome great adversity, and on and on. Here again, the schools help. Our deception has worked so well that the vast majority of them actually believe that there is a verse in the Enemy's book that reads, 'God helps those who help themselves.' What a joke, the man who can help himself doesn't need God and won't seek God, resulting in no prayer or relationship. This is an instrument we can use. I always impress on them that the 'verse' is found in Hezekiah 4:17."

"Wait a minute," Argon interrupted. "There is no Hezekiah in the Enemy's book. There are stories about a man named Hezekiah, but no chapter or book."

"True, Argon. You know that and I know that, but most church-going Americans believe that 'verse' is in there somewhere, and that deception alone keeps them away from real prayer or real relationship with the Enemy. With a little help, they soon develop a view that they can plan as they will and then ask God to bless their plan, or they can do what they want to do in Jesus' name and expect Him to be grateful for their efforts and to reward them. Both again are in direct conflict with what is said in the Enemy's book, but then they don't read it so we have a blank slate to work with. If we are careful, they will live their lives 'in service of god' and in reality do it in complete independence from God. Those people are our playground to advance the Dark Master's reign in the Enemy's name."

"Our difficulty comes when the humans begin to realize that the problems they face are beyond them. In those moments, they are vulnerable to pray and may begin to seek our all-powerful Enemy. We have to keep the focus on self-effort and off helplessness. We certainly have learned from our mistakes. About 150 years ago in New York, a man realized that his assignment from God was impossible and rather than giving up, the normal human response, he organized a prayer meeting that turned into what the Christians call the 'Second Great Awakening.' We call it the 'Great Mistake' because it could have been stopped if we had moved quicker to discourage those who sought to pray and attacked the leadership as failures because they didn't know what to do. It was a nothing event that exploded before we knew what had happened. We will not make that mistake again. That is why tomorrow is so important. We will take out the leadership and discourage the masses from prayer, and it will be over. Come, let's instruct our instruments. Watch carefully. If you are to lead, you need to learn how to use these tactics in extreme situations."

Molech's Deception

As they entered the garage apartment, Molech centered himself high over Susan Stafford, assuming the visible form of an angel of light. Once again, Susan was almost blinded by the brilliance of the unnatural glow and terrified by the voice not of this world. "My child, the time has come for you to execute god's judgment on the one who seeks to lead masses to suffer the eternal judgment of the second death. He must be stopped before he can succeed in his mission of deception.

"Tomorrow as the sun rises, park down from the warehouse which houses the rare bookstore on President's Street just across the tracks. Prepare there and wait. At 8:00 a.m., a young man will come and enter the warehouse. After some time, he will come out with an old man walking toward you. Be sure to kill him, and then if you can, shoot the old man as well. He too seeks to mislead and distort truth. Do not be afraid and do not doubt for I will be with you to guide and protect you."

As suddenly as it had become light, it became dark. The shooter felt again in her element as she prepared to obey. She didn't like the idea of remaining in one place for such an extended period of time or that it was such a public place, but what risk could there be in the presence of an angel, seeking to obey his command?

Argon had never seen the angel of light deception before and was amazed. I must acquire that power, he thought as Molech entered the room where Demetrius sat waiting for further guidance. The room again became dark, a darkness so unnatural and deep it could be felt. Again out of the darkness came a voice unlike that of any human, "Demetrius, the time is now to honor Allah with your sacrifice by killing the old man, the infidel they call the Bookseller. He will be leaving the rare bookstore in the warehouse on President's Street across the tracks in Williams around

8:30 AM tomorrow morning. Approach him on foot from the tracks. Wait there until you see him. Detonate your explosive only when you are sure to destroy him. Your reward awaits your obedience."

The palpable darkness was gone as quickly as it had come. Demetrius rejoiced that his life purpose would soon be accomplished and he would live in eternal pleasure. He had no doubts or fears, for he had never encountered truth. The deception had been complete from birth.

Watching Molech's deception, Barnabas and Lucius wished they had been instructed to confront the lie with the truth, but they had received no such instructions. The forces of light were not free to act independently. They had to wait for instructions and then obey immediately for the Father's purposes to be accomplished through them. In the absence of instructions, they had to wait. Sometimes that was hard, but they knew they served a Holy God and that His ways and timing were always best. So they watched and waited for instructions.

"Lucius, what does Satan think he is doing by confronting God's express limitations over the life of Paul Phillips and Samuel Evans White. He heard the Father speak. What could motivate him to challenge God again?"

"Barnabas, sometimes you surprise me. In all these centuries of watching him at work have you missed his motivation? From the rebellion in Heaven until now, Satan is driven by envy and hate. He wants to be god and hates the Father, who is God, and all who serve Him as God. His language is lies, to such an extent that he deceives himself into believing that when God speaks, there remains a way around what He says. Satan will try to kill them both tomorrow. The only question that remains unanswered is what the Father will allow."

It's Williams

Darrell Reed had been mightily at work seeking to discover from where the two new messages had been posted on the FS2.com website. He was successful on the "J-10.0-1. Never 2" posting, but wondered what could it possibly mean. Understanding that translation of gibberish was not the job description of a computer geek, he called David Barnes to pass on what he had learned thus far.

"Hey David, geek here, I have one of the two thus far. The 'J-10.0-1. Never 2' message was posted from Williams, Illinois. Now tell me what it means."

"You are incredible," was Barnes response. "Brilliant. All I know for sure about the message is that it is a response to an earlier message disclosing a schedule for some terrorist act in Williams. I have to get off the phone now and pass this on. Thanks again and good hunting on finding the source of the other message."

Stopping first to thank God for what had been revealed, Barnes then called Tom Knight with the news. "Tom, we have the location for what appears to be the initial action. It's Williams, Illinois. That's where the message was posted so that is what '0-1' means. Williams must have been designated '1' because it is the first place for an attack of some nature. I believe that the rest of the message deals with timing for the attack. I think it is either in two days or five days. I don't know which, but I would think five because it would be more of an opposite. Seven days in a week minus two or five. That compared with simply adding two. If it meant to add two, then it would have been negative two not "Never 2." I may be wrong, but if I'm right, that means either Thursday or Sunday."

"Thanks, I'll take it from here," Chairman Knight responded. "I will want you at the meeting to answer questions and give us your views. Make sure they keep looking for the location from which the other message was posted. Perhaps then we can find the designated leader of the 'MD' operation."

"Will do," Barnes responded. "Just have someone let me know where to be and when."

Phones rang throughout Washington DC waking key officials for a middle of the night White House meeting. Those gathered in the situation room with Chairman Knight included the president, the chairman of the Joint Chiefs, the directors of the FBI, CIA and Homeland Security, the national security advisor along with designated advisors and David Barnes. The president opened the meeting with a brief prayer and then turned the meeting over to Chairman Knight, who briefed the group on the latest intelligence regarding Williams.

"What is the exact nature of the threat?" asked General Hodge.

"We don't know," Knight answered.

"Well then what do you want from us?"

At this point, the president stepped in. "I will tell you what I want from all of you. Tomorrow morning by 10:00a.m., I want your recommendations on my desk for how we prepare to prevent an attack on Williams if possible, but certainly how to respond to some kind of terrorist attack as early as Thursday. How do we advise the city and the state's leadership? What resources should be deployed under what command structure? What are the rules of engagement? What, if anything, should we tell the public and when?

"I need your collective judgment. Ignore the political consequences of our actions. We are in an election cycle, which means that whatever we do will be used by those seeking office, but that is not an issue. The only issue is the security and safety of our people. Keep this absolutely on a need-to-know basis. We don't want the terrorists to know we have found their means of communication. I need a target assessment in Williams. What are they after? Why of all places Williams?"

The president dismissed himself and the discussions began in earnest.

CHAPTER 22

BEFORE THE STORM

Wednesday, February 6 – MD Minus 109

S HE DIDN'T LIKE it, but she obeyed and parked her car in a very public place across the street directly north of the warehouse as the sun rose. She set up in the trunk, raised the license plate and sighted a clean shot to the sidewalk near the bookstore entrance where the targeted young man was expected to be in a couple of hours. Lowering the plate, she waited, wondering why she had been chosen and thankful to know that what she did today would protect others from the fate of the man she killed at the park and ride. The horror of that moment just would not go away. She remembered clearly the look of terror on the dead man's face, the sound of his screams as he was judged and condemned to what must be Hell – to an eternity of suffering and punishment – the unimaginable. This would be one kill she could celebrate.

It was not long before she heard the sound of someone walking past her car toward the warehouse. Soon other sounds began to invade the quiet as a camera crew set up directly across from the warehouse, hoping to catch some shots to use on tonight's special. They still didn't have an interview set up with the old man, but Chaplain Forrest had agreed to ask and that was him at the door to the warehouse entering now. There was hope, thought Producer Hunt, "We may yet get an exclusive."

One of many trains raced by as the traffic picked up. The campus was beginning to come to life as sleepy students headed to the dining hall for a quick cup of coffee or breakfast before early classes. Too much activity, she thought, but then an angel should be able to protect her. After all, she thought, this was a mission for god.

Elsewhere, Demetrius had awakened and was preparing for his glorious entrance into Allah's presence, believing he would soon achieve his reward. He worked quickly and quietly, knowing that discovery by any of his fellows would be disastrous. They were unaware of his special assignment and would not understand. His hatred for the infidel's public insults was so great that he would kill his companions if they tried to restrain his mission. The old man must die. Soon he had his explosive vest in place, covered by a winter jacket, and began the long journey to the warehouse on President's Street and entry into his reward.

High above the city, the two opposing groups met briefly to consider the coming day's anticipated events. Molech was pleased with the progress of the chosen instruments and excited at the chance to rid the earth of the Bookseller and his protégé. The plan was working even better than expected.

"Look Argon," Molech observed, "A camera crew is present for the attacks. Can you imagine what that will be like when broadcast across the country in living color?" He sneered. "No one will cry out to the Enemy for protection after they see this. It is simply too good. They should get a clear view of the shooter's car, which will guarantee that she will be captured and the reason for all the fear of violence will end. Soon the fools will sleep again until the real attack comes, and then it will be too late. It will be over for America."

"Listen carefully," Molech directed. "Be sure that the Keepers for Susan and Demetrius do their jobs. Have them continue to pour the Dark Master's influence into them so that they have no second thoughts and will complete their missions. Use the Tempters named Hate and Lust on Demetrius and use Guilt and Fear on Susan so they will be motivated to perform exactly as required. We must keep our hold on them such that the forces of light cannot at the last moment thwart the plan."

"Send messengers to Keepers throughout the city to prepare those under our influence to respond in accordance. Others are doing so around the earth even as we speak. We want the old man ridiculed and the shooter vilified. If we are successful, people will consider the old man a fool for what he said – stupid for challenging the religion of hate. The fear people already have of speaking out against it will be magnified, which assures the movement will grow with little real opposition."

"Regarding the shooter, we must use our influence to make her a picture of evil incarnate. Cause them to hate her and to no longer be afraid. Cause them to want to celebrate and take their collective guard down. Create a lack of interest in the Citizens Militia so we can get on with preparations for the real attack. What a glorious day is coming!"

Elsewhere, a sober but expectant group of the forces of light gathered. "Barnabas, I have received no further instructions," Lucius shared. "It is clear that the Father intends to allow the Dark Master to attempt to execute his plan to publicly kill the Bookseller and Paul Phillips."

"Brothers, listen closely," Lucius said, addressing all who were present. "Do not fret or be concerned with what you see before you. It is only the physical. You know that reality exists only in the invisible.[159] The Father remains sovereign,[160] and when He chooses to reveal what He will allow, it will come to pass exactly as He has determined. Listen for the Spirit's commands, obey immediately and completely. The day is the Lord's. For the Light!" and lifting their hands toward Heaven, they separated to await the Father's will.

Interview Accepted – with Conditions

Before they prayed, the Bookseller shared with Chaplain Forrest the message from the unknown Iranian brothers and how it was delivered. "I always evaluate what anyone tells me they have experienced in light of what has been revealed in scripture," the Bookseller began. "I look even more critically when someone says they have a message for me from God. I know that if God wants to speak to me, He communicates through the Holy Spirit within and the message is always consistent with the Bible. I have found, however, that sometimes He uses other believers to confirm what He has already been saying to me. This message and the circumstances surrounding its delivery line up with both. I believe that it was clearly God speaking with a message for all believers."

"Yes, I agree," Chaplain Forrest responded. "Scripture tells of an angel appearing to the Apostle Paul to tell him that all aboard a ship on which he was being taken as a prisoner to Rome would survive a storm if they stayed on the boat.[161] God has often used angels to communicate with believers for themselves and others."

"Gabriel was the angel God sent to Mary to tell her that she was chosen to give birth to Jesus and to Zechariah to tell him of the child who would be John the Baptist,"[162] the Bookseller added. "The message of the angel is exactly what God has been telling me to say, 'Stand together and pray.' Nothing is more biblical than calling God's people together to stand before Him and pray."[163]

"Perhaps God has provided another opportunity for you to do just that," Chaplain Forrest observed.

"What do you mean?" the Bookseller asked.

"I know you don't watch much television so you probably don't know that tonight ITN, the Independent Television Network, will be broadcasting a special on the situation here in Williams. They have spent the last few days filming interviews with the victims' families, the police, the Citizens Militia, pastors responding to your comments at the news conference, citizens and politicians. They want to interview you as part of the production. Samuel, I trust them. The lead producer is a believer. I sense God's involvement in this. He has provided you with this opportunity which further affirms the truth of the angel's message. You need to do this."

"Candidly, Forrest, I have been watching for God to provide another opportunity to share His message. It has been made clear to me that God is not yet finished with me. There is more for me to do, but I cannot allow a situation where what I said could be changed by editing in any way. Tell your producer friend that if he will come here, he can interview me live during the broadcast, provided that he agrees to broadcast everything I say and not market it to other networks. They can ask me anything they want as long as they broadcast the complete answer at the same time as they broadcast the question. Both live," he repeated with emphasis.

"I'll bet they haven't encountered conditions like that before," Chaplain Forrest responded with a smile.

"Perhaps not," the Bookseller answered, "but if God is in this, they will accept the conditions. If not, God will deliver His message another way or use another messenger. Enough talk, let's pray. Paul will be here shortly."

Surrender

Paul's night had not been uninterrupted. Once again, the Curtain had been opened and he dreamed. He saw in the sky what seemed to be thousands upon thousands, and ten thousand times ten thousand from every nation, tribe, people and language wearing white robes and crying out together in a loud voice, "Stand with us and pray for your brothers. Ask the Father to cleanse and purify His own and to restrain the hand that seeks to destroy you all." Their faces were human, but equally not human in that they shone like the sun and their robes were as white as the light. They spoke with passion and with tears, much like Jesus when He cried over Jerusalem as He entered for the last time to give Himself on the cross.[164]

Paul awoke with a burden to pray even as he had dreamed, after which he rushed to get ready to go to see the Bookseller, wondering what he had seen and what it meant. He arrived at the warehouse just as Chaplain Forrest was leaving. "See you in an hour or so at my office," he said. "Pastor Wilson will be there to join together in prayer. I am disappointed that there is only one Pastor who accepted my invitation, but it is a beginning."

As Paul entered the warehouse, Chaplain Forrest crossed the street to speak briefly with Producer Hunt, who was setting up a camera crew to get some background video of the warehouse. "Good news, Mr. Hunt. The Bookseller will consent to an interview if, and only if, you agree to do it live and to broadcast everything he says, no edits and no sales to other networks.

"Totally unreasonable as I expected," Hunt replied with a smile of glee. "We agree. Do you think he would mind if we took some video of him this morning to use for promotions today?"

"I honestly doubt he would make time for that," Chaplain Forrest responded. "He wants to say what he believes God wants him to say, but he doesn't want to in any way promote himself. It is the message that matters to him. I do have a suggestion that isn't ideal but should work. If you keep your crew here for an hour or so, you will be able to catch some video of him coming out of his office walking to mine where we are meeting with others to pray. That is the best I can do."

"If this man were only a politico, we would have to beat him away from the camera with a stick. Alright, not what I had hoped for, but it will have to do," he said reaching for his cell phone to share the news with Carl Stern. A live exclusive interview with the Bookseller should assure a massive audience. People were still curious about what he said and what it meant. Now the hard part, what questions should they ask?

As Chaplain Forrest walked away toward his office in the Campus Chapel, his eye caught what seemed to be the movement of a license plate on a car parked down and across from the warehouse. What could that have been, he thought and just as quickly dismissed it as an overactive imagination. He could see no one in the car or near the car.

Across the tracks, Demetrius sat hidden in a group of trees, watching for the old man to leave the warehouse, ready for his glorious departure to his reward.

Prepared for Physical Death

"I had another dream," Paul said to the Bookseller. "The sky was filled with masses of beings that appeared like people, clothed in glorious white robes like the sun and with radiant faces. They were all saying, 'Stand with us and pray for your brothers. Ask the Father to cleanse and purify His own, and to restrain the hand that seeks to destroy you all.' Is this biblical? Is this from God?"

The Bookseller almost could not contain his excitement. "You are asking the right questions and you already know the answers. Both the experience and the message are biblical and completely consistent with what God continues to affirm to believers in different ways. The group you saw in your dream is what the writer of the Book of Hebrews calls, 'A great cloud of witnesses.'[165] He wrote that we should run our race, a reference to our life as a believer, with perseverance because we are surrounded by a great cloud of witnesses. Those witnesses are believers who lived before us who cry out to the Lord for us. They were pictured in your dream, much like Moses and Elijah when they appeared with Jesus on what we call the Mount of Transfiguration.[166] God's message is the same; we must pray together and stand before Him and be changed, or we face a great disaster at the hands of our enemies. Allowing the disaster will be the judgment of God if we ignore His message."[167]

"The people I saw were passionate, and as they spoke they were crying," Paul added.

"We forget about the judgments through which many of those who went before us suffered as a result of their sin and rebellion," the Bookseller added. "Scripture is filled with examples of God's people turning their backs on Him when they become safe and prosperous. Soon they are satisfied in their abundance and begin to believe they no longer need God, so they ignore the teachings of scripture and live as they wish without God. This generation is no different. We are willful and have made our wants and desires our gods. We pursue them above everything else. Those who went before know that the Father will do or allow whatever it takes to cause His people to turn back to Him.[168] Having experienced God's judgment, they cry out for us to be awakened before it is too late. They don't want us to suffer as many of them suffered unnecessarily. Their passion must mean time is short."

"What they said is exactly what you said at the press conference," Paul responded. "It's like a Heavenly confirmation of the message."

"Yes," the Bookseller continued, "and that is not the only confirmation God has sent. I need to tell you of a message I received from two brothers in Iran, and how it was delivered to them. There is absolutely no doubt that what you heard in your dream is God's message for believers now."

As he finished telling the story of the angelic visitation, suddenly Paul interrupted. "Wait a minute. That message, the one from the great cloud of witnesses, was that for me too? They said, 'Stand with us and pray for your brothers.' Does that mean I am a brother? Have I been born again?" Even as there had been in the cry of the great cloud of witnesses, there was real passion in Paul's voice.

The Bookseller paused and prayed silently for wisdom before answering, "We need to be cautious in our understanding of dreams, for the Bible contains examples where unbelievers were used to carry messages for believers in dreams. One obvious example is the dreams of Pharaoh, which Joseph interpreted to reveal seven years of plenty which would be followed by seven years of famine.[169] Those dreams were a message from God which ultimately saved the lives of those God had chosen to be His people,[170] but it did not mean that Pharaoh was a worshiper of the true God. You have been reading in the Book of Acts about the activity of believers after Jesus return to Heaven. Let's look there first to see what the Apostles said was required to be saved, and then let's look for what the Bible identifies as the fruit of the new birth and see if it is evident in your life. Then we can know for sure.

"When Paul preaches, he declares Jesus to be both 'Lord and Christ.'[171] Peter affirms Jesus' death on the cross and His resurrection from the dead. He describes Jesus as 'the author of life' and declares that 'salvation is found in no one else.'[172] For the believer, Jesus' death on the cross is a very personal event, for we all have come face to face with the reality that it was our sin and rebellion against God which caused all His pain. There is no one else to blame, no place for pride; we were as criminals facing a much-deserved execution who were not simply pardoned, but Jesus suffered and was executed in our place.[173]

"I know you accept that intellectually, many do, but the new birth is not an intellectual exercise. It is an act of the Holy Spirit in response to a heart which desires to be changed to be made like Jesus. This desire to be changed is reflected in the act of repentance. Remember, that was the message Jesus preached. He said, 'Repent for the kingdom of heaven is near.'[174]

"Repentance is not simply admitting a wrong and asking to be forgiven. Repentance is crying out to God from a heart that wants to be changed so that you come to hate the wrong and the offense it caused to God. Repentance is a way of life for one who has been born again, for God places His desires in their heart and mind.[175] You will know you have been given a new heart when you recognize that new desire to know God's word and to obey Him because you love Him.[176] The desire to know and obey God can only come from the new heart and new spirit which God places within as part of the new birth.

"An old preacher looking back on the time when he was born again explained what had happened to him like this, 'I didn't understand much of the detail, but I did know one thing. I knew I was under new management.' That is the clearest evidence of the new birth, recognition that you are under new management and you rejoice in that fact and seek to obey. Suddenly you want to follow the Lord and are willing to venture you're all in service of Him.

"Scripture supports this. Paul wrote, 'If you confess with your mouth, Jesus is Lord, and believe in your heart that God raised Him from the dead, you will be saved'[177] Romans 10:9. Lord means master, the one in absolute control. To become a believer means surrendering yourself to the will of God, something that is only possible when you have been given a new heart and a new spirit as part of the new birth. If you have that desire, you have been born again for only God could give you that."

"It is strange. Mr. White," Paul responded, "but I know I have been changed. For some days now I have been filled with a compulsion to know more about God. That feeling has changed or matured or something so that now I want to know God. It is not enough to know about Him, and I do have a desire to follow Him. I want to know what He says and do it because I know in my heart that Jesus died in my place for my sins, and then rose from the dead."

"My brother, like all of us, your search will continue as you grow in relationship with Jesus, but it will be easier now for it is illuminated by the light within, the Holy Spirit," the Bookseller said with joy. "I have been listening and watching you closely. I have seen clearly the evidence of the new heart and spirit within you, and now you have confessed that for yourself with your mouth. I can call you brother because I believe that God has made you my brother in Christ. Yes, I believe you have been born again."

As they hugged and rejoiced together, thanking God for His work in Paul, the Bookseller issued an invitation. "I am leaving now to go to meet a few brothers in Chaplain Forrest's office to pray. Join us."

"I would love to," Paul responded, excited at the invitation.

As they were walking toward the door, suddenly the Bookseller stopped and reached out his arm to stop Paul. "Before we leave this place I feel a sudden compulsion to pray the Lord's Prayer together. I don't know why, but we must do this," and he knelt. Paul followed his example and the Bookseller led as they prayed out loud.

Our Father in Heaven, hallowed be Your name, Your kingdom come, Your will be done on Earth as it is in Heaven. Give us this day our daily bread. Forgive us our debts as we have forgiven our debtors. And lead us not into temptation, but deliver us from the evil one, for Yours is the kingdom and the power and the glory forever. Amen.[178]

Outside a license plate was lifted and a rifle made ready. Demetrius, his hand on the triggering device, had crossed the tracks and was ready to rapidly approach the old man when he appeared. The ITN camera crew was waiting to begin filming the moment the Bookseller appeared at the door. The forces of darkness had gathered with glee to witness the executions by their chosen instruments. The forces of light were also present, still sober and still awaiting instructions, wondering what God would allow, unaware of the Bookseller's prayer.

CHAPTER 23

DECEPTION SUCCEEDS AGAIN

Wednesday, February 6 – MD Minus 109

ELSEWHERE IN WILLIAMS, another early morning meeting was nearing its conclusion. Tom Campy had been excited at the possibility of including the young Arab school teacher as a member of the Citizens Militia. It would be a good thing, he thought, to put a positive face on Arabs in America, to show once and for all that they are not all terrorists. It seemed particularly important after the grisly discovery in seven cities of undocumented young Arab men killed execution-style. The news had been filled with reports about the discoveries. The consensus of the "talking heads" was that this was evidence that there were terrorists already in the United States preparing for an attack of some nature. The government had been strangely silent, referring only to an on-going investigation.

Tom had traded off his morning high school assignment with another Citizens Militia member to conduct this interview himself. Officer Sally Johnson, his prayer partner, joined him, but they didn't share the same enthusiasm for the candidate. Sally had accepted Tom's invitation because she didn't want a mistake made and a potentially armed threat sanctioned.

Abdul Farsi had already passed the police background investigation, but she simply didn't have peace about this and couldn't say why.

"Mr. Campy, Officer Johnson," Farsi continued, "You need to understand how this threat makes me feel. As a school teacher, I work with children every day who are afraid. This most recent event, the discovery of the bodies of seven Arabs now believed to be terrorists, has only magnified that fear. They need to be reassured by the physical presence of Citizens Militia volunteers. They need to know that if someone tries to harm them, they will be protected, whether it is from the shooter or a terrorist. I understand from the news that one of the seven bodies was discovered near Chicago, which raises additional concerns. The children must be protected," he repeated with convincing emotion.

"I am not going to lie to you," Farsi continued, "of equal concern to me is the safety of moderate Muslim Arab brothers who have come to America legally for an education and who, like me, have grown to love the country and have chosen to legally stay. There are thousands of us across the country contributing in many ways. We are a threat to no one, but racial profiling puts us at risk of official discrimination and public isolation. If I can help show the people of Williams that we are on their side against these threats, it will not only help them feel more secure but perhaps will help them to view my Arab brothers differently."

"I completely understand and agree," was Tom Campy's response. "I talked with the parents of several of your students and they have nothing but positive things to say about you and your influence over their children. America is a nation of immigrants. We need to learn from you as well as you learning from us. I would like to have the opportunity to hear more about your faith and way of life, and to share mine with you."

Farsi swallowed hard and responded, "I would like that. It would be good for you to understand the peaceful teachings of our faith and I would like to understand yours. Frankly, the conflict between what Jesus taught and how he lived with how many Christians live today is troubling to us. You may not know that Jesus is also one of our prophets."

"Jesus is much more than a prophet to us, but then that is a subject for another day," Campy answered.

All this time, Sally Johnson remained strangely silent. Farsi noted her silence with some concern, wondering why these Western cultures allowed women to be so out of their place. The day would come when that too would change, he vowed silently to himself.

"Mr. Farsi, complete your training and you can join the Citizen's Militia," Tom announced. "You can do that in a day or a couple of nights. If possible, I would like for you to complete your training over the next few days so you can be a part of the Security Fair on Saturday. It would be good for the public to see you, a young Arab man, standing in uniform to protect them. Here is the number for you to call to schedule your training. I have also written my cell phone number on the card so you can call me when it is completed and we can discuss your assignment."

Tom handed Farsi the card and he left immediately to schedule his training. He had already arranged a substitute teacher for several days as needed. He wanted to hurry and become official in time to find out the deployment plans for Sunday.

"You certainly were uncharacteristically quiet," Tom addressed Sally carefully. "What's going on? You agree, don't you, that having a young Arab male as a protector would send a positive message to the community?"

"Well, I have two responses to that," Sally replied. "The Citizens Militia was established to protect the citizens, not politicize them. I am concerned with anyone who has more than one agenda as their reason for being in the group. The purpose of this organization is not to reassure the citizens that young Arab males are safe, it is to make all citizens safe. Where did we ever get off on all this racial correctness? My view is simple, if you are an American – you are an American, whether you are black, white, Arab, Asian, Hispanic, Native or European. Similarly, if you are in this organization, you are in this organization because you are here to serve the purposes of the organization and not make a political statement. It is like being a follower of Jesus; nothing matters except whether you follow Jesus.

"Tom, I know what you are trying to do for appearance, and the argument has some appeal, but I am not sure about this particular young Arab man. You let him in with a divided agenda and we didn't even pray before or after his interview. I thought we had agreed to pray about everything connected with this effort."

"Wait a minute," Tom replied defensively. "He has no police record anywhere in the United States and he has already been chosen to teach

American kids. The parents support him. The ones we called were very positive. Is this woman's intuition or are you effectively racial profiling and decided that no young Arab males are safe?"

"Neither," Sally answered. "Having no police record means little when you consider that the seven Arab men who were just killed execution style don't exist as a matter of record anywhere. I simply don't have peace about this man or the way he was selected. We should have prayed. A clean record does not indicate a clean heart. Only God can judge the thoughts and attitudes of the heart.[179] Good references can mean nothing more than this man is a good actor when he knows he is on stage. His responses seemed canned to me. He was saying what he thought you wanted to hear.

"Tom, listen to me. What do we really know about this man beyond the fact that he came here on a student visa to study, got a degree and stayed as a teacher – a critical career for which special provision is made under our laws to allow for permanent residency? That could have just as easily been a plan to establish a base here as it could be a career path. I am not comfortable with him. I sense something else is going on."

"Well I simply don't agree," Tom responded. "This man wants to defend children like those he teaches and at the same time, he wants to make a public statement in support of moderate Arabs. There is nothing wrong with that. Our government has been criticizing moderate Muslims since 9/11 for not speaking out against terrorism. This man will speak out openly against them by his participation with us."

"I sincerely hope you are right, but I don't share your optimism about his agenda or motivation," Sally concluded. "Watch him carefully, clean record and all."

Simultaneously in Washington

In Washington DC, one meeting continued while another commenced. In the situation room of the White House, the debate had been fierce because the extent of the threat was still unknown and the intelligence seemly went against the history of the known enemy.

"Why Williams?" CIA Director Crenshaw asked. "Williams is nothing more than a little college town near a big city. There is no target in

Williams worthy of an attack based on their past attempts. There is no symbol of America there, no place where a great multitude will gather so that they could kill lots of people, and there have been no threats or warnings. It doesn't make sense. What are we defending against?"

"It can't really be Williams," replied Director of Homeland Security Hollister. "It has to be Chicago, where the people are and where there are obvious targets. The terrorists must intend to launch a 9/11 type attack there and are housing the terrorists in Williams. Is there a major sporting event going on Thursday or Sunday in Chicago?"

"Yes there is," answered Chairman Knight. "There's the Chicago Bulls' game but I think we are off the mark. If we are right in our translation of the messages that have been intercepted, this will not be a 9/11 kind of attack. This is different. The big attack is set for several months down the road and it is not a 9/11 plan. This has been backed up by intelligence on the ground. I don't know what the current threat is, but I expect it is something we have not encountered before on American soil. I think they are testing in a small American city a new campaign of terror like the Infatida Israel has faced. We are going to see an attack which is the predicate to a national campaign of car bombings and other indiscriminate killings to terrify the public and hope for a political response like they got with the train bombings in Spain. Then the big attack would not be necessary. We would just give up and abandon the Middle East."

"Gentlemen," Nation Security Advisor Troy Steed announced, "we need to prepare for both possibilities in a way that does not compromise our ability to continue to intercept their communications and does not terrify our citizens, but we have to be on the ground ready to respond by the end of today. Tomorrow is Thursday. We have to have a coordinated response team present and prepared to deal with the threat whatever it is."

The debate continued until a consensus was finally reached and the list of recommendations was prepared for the president's review. The group entered the Oval Office just as Paul Phillips had entered the warehouse in Williams to meet with the Bookseller. "Mr. President," Tom Phillips began, "we cannot define or isolate the threat. We don't know the target, the weapons or the timing beyond tomorrow or Sunday. If the real target is Chicago, there are substantial buildings to hit and if killing masses is the goal, there are Bulls' games tomorrow and Sunday. If it is Williams, there is the college and a religious museum of some nature to target, but no mass events on Thursday or Sunday."

"Then we must be ready for anything," the president responded. "What do you recommend?"

"Mr. President," General Hedge, Chairman of the Joint Chiefs, began, "we recommend that we deploy the Alpha Force to Chicago under a type 3 protocol. That would include rapid response capability, AWAC detection and control, local shoot down and force response authority, fighters on runways hot and ready, anti-aircraft teams, radiation detection and response teams, bomb detection and disposal teams and a military medical response team. That should provide us the flexibility to respond to diverse local attacks, but it will not prevent an attack unless we can detect the specific threat."

"What can we do about prevention and detection," the president asked. "I don't want to sit here and wait for people to die before we do something."

"We are not without options for detection even this late, Mr. President," answered Homeland Security Director Hollister "The problem we face is how to mobilize local authorities and our citizens without creating unnecessary panic or alerting the terrorists that we have found their method of communication. If we lose the ability to intercept some communications regarding the planning for MD, we will have suffered a far worse defeat than any single terrorist attack could inflict."

"What do you suggest?" the president said sternly.

"We have been through this since you dismissed us last night and have debated it from every possible angle. Our conclusion is that we contact state and local officials in Illinois and advise them that we have an unconfirmed terror threat for a possible attack in Chicago or Williams over a ten-day window commencing tomorrow. We will insist on federal coordination and that they not advise the public of the existence of the threat. Particularly in Williams, the response to the threat needs to be limited to the police. We don't want the citizens group to know about the threat or be involved. We really don't know who these people are and they haven't proved themselves yet."

"We will raise the terror alert at the airports and increase security at all charter or business jet facilities. We are going to have undercover security personnel at the Bulls' games and bomb sniffing dogs at all points of entry. Precautions will be taken to deny access to the facility in the event that the attack is planned to utilize car bombs. The unmarked radiation detection vans will be driven through Chicago and Williams 24/7. Our cover will be that this is a preparedness test to check deployment and coordination of federal forces with state and local officials in a simulated terror threat. That should downplay the danger and not alert our enemies that we have access to their communications. One additional part of the plan will require your help, Mr. President."

"Whatever you need," the president immediately responded.

"To have any chance of detection and prevention, we need the public to be involved. Their eyes and ears are the only chance we have to find these people in a hurry. We don't want to simply target the Williams area because that will give away our knowledge of their communications. We are recommending that you make an announcement requesting citizen involvement in reporting any suspicious activity or people to local or federal officials. We can tie it to the discovery of the seven unidentified young Arab males killed execution style. Obviously, something is going on and the media has played this hard as evidence of possible terrorists among us. Our response has been that we are investigating. Now would be a perfect time to report conclusions and use the opportunity to emphasize the importance of citizens' involvement across the nation. That would help us address the Williams event now, but more importantly, it can start the ball rolling toward addressing the planned MD attacks nationwide."

"I like it," the president responded. "I will need some help making sure I say enough but not too much. We need to do this today if tomorrow is a possible attack day."

"Mr. President, I hate to bring this up, but what about the congressional leadership. Should we tell them what we have learned and are doing?" National Security Advisor Steed asked.

"Absolutely not," was the president's immediate response. "The congressional leadership is not on the same page with us about the terrorist threat to America. They don't believe there is one and we have no facts, only conclusions drawn from gibberish and an assumed location because gibberish was posted from Williams. We will not give them the ammunition they need to destroy our efforts to prepare for MD. If something happens, we will consult then. For now, we are doing nothing that requires consultation and candidly, they have nothing constructive to say on the subject. No consulting with Congress – no media involvement other than my announcement – that is it, paragraph, period – the end."

"One more thing Tom, do not involve the commission in this. We already know we have a leak in Commissioner Matthews. I don't want to read about our discussions on Williams in the Times Dailey. Keep the commission focused on MD.

"General Hedge, issue the deployment order for the Alpha Force to Chicago under a type 3 protocol and the other forces as you described immediately. They must be there and ready to respond by the end of the day. Director Hollister, mobilize the Homeland Security plan to coordinate with the state and local officials. Make sure they understand that this is not a confirmed threat, but that we are responding to it as if it was to test our joint force capability and they should respond as if there was credible evidence of attack. Tom, I will also need your help with the announcement. I want to make the statement by noon Chicago time."

As the group left to issue orders and confirm deployment, the president asked Tom Knight and David Barnes to stay for a moment. "Mr. President, I don't mean to sound foolish, but I guess I am. What is the Alpha Force and what is a type 3 protocol?" asked David Barnes.

"Without getting into too much detail," the president responded, "about five years ago I ordered the Joint Chiefs to develop a plan to prevent and respond to terrorist threats in the homeland. Since then the Alpha Force was developed and trained in coordination with our friends in Israel, who are really the experts at living under the constant threat of terrorism. The group has worked with the IDF, Mossad and Shin Bet to learn from the best to be the best. We have made a lot of progress at preparation for a single attack or a concerted series of single attacks. Unfortunately, nothing in our preparation considered some type of attack which would negate America as a force in the world, such as is apparently the MD plan. Our preparation does, however, give us the ability to deal with the current threat. Type 3 protocol is the rules of engagement and command structure for a type of perceived threat."

"I wish the public was aware of what you have been doing to try and protect them," Barnes responded.

"That is not important. What is important is that I do everything I can," the president answered. "Now before Tom and I get down to working on the statement, David, your marching orders are to follow up on the search for the location from which the presumed leader of MD posted that last message. If we can get geography on him, perhaps we can find him. If what we have learned from our Iranian sources is correct, he does not seem like the type who would stand up well to serious interrogation."

"Now, before you leave, let's pray. We need God's wisdom and frankly, a break somewhere to find the threat."

A New Political Strategy to Force Open Borders

They gathered in the Senate majority leader's office to do the bidding of the Together Tomorrow crowd. None of those who met this morning understood why the push for the North American Union was so important to this group or why the insistence on the short fuse to force the open borders provision. All they knew was that politics was about impressions and money. Together Tomorrow had the money and they must somehow take their agenda and create the impression that it is essential for America's future.

"This is on its face an impossible task with a hard-headed president like Strong," Majority Leader Howard complained. "He will veto any bill we bring him within the timeline we have been given unless the American public and his own party force the issue."

"This man is strong in his beliefs, but he is also a politician in a political party that is in trouble," former President Cox observed. "Like all politicians, he will compromise his beliefs if necessary to survive an election or preserve a legacy. He isn't running, but his party is and he cares about his party. More importantly, he cares about his legacy. He presents himself as the man who is strong in the war on terror. We have to somehow position the Together Tomorrow agenda as the ultimate essential policy to fight terror. If we can sell that, he has to come around or be opposing who he is. His party will force the issue and might even help override a veto."

"No wonder you were elected twice and could have been a third or fourth time if it wasn't for the Twenty-second Amendment," Majority Leader Howard observed almost worshipfully. "You are a political genius.

That is the strategy we will use. Get the Madison Avenue pros and consultants to work on a theme and set of talking points. We will take the terrorism issue away from President Strong."

"Be careful that we don't lose the peace crowd," Chairman Crow warned. "We have to pose this so that it appears strong against terrorism but promotes peace. If we are careful, we can appeal to both groups while attacking the religious conservative crowd that opposes us and our agenda. We can use the North America Union campaign as a vehicle to address the causes of terrorism which are economic inequality and religious intolerance."

"That should definitely work and if successful, put those Stone Age religious bigots back in their caves where they belong," former President Cox replied angrily, remembering the attempt at his impeachment.

"I have already started my part of the effort," Chairman Crow noted. "Late yesterday the Homeland Security Committee met to consider an amendment to the Hate Crimes Act adding religion as the motivation for the commitment of a crime or the act of encouraging another to commit a crime with a religious motivation as a designated hate crime. That will take us far down the road to protecting the peoples' right to freedom from religion and get these religious radicals off our backs. We have already set hearings and voted to subpoena the old man from Williams. That subpoena should be served this morning even as we speak. When we finish chewing him up in public, even President Strong will support the bill."

"If this campaign is to commence Monday, we need to get the whole caucus on board soon," observed Majority Leader Howard. "We need to be prepared to outline the program to our troops by Friday at the latest."

"We will be ready," Cox replied, knowing that the unlimited checkbook would provide all they needed to recruit their political army.

CHAPTER 24

UNEXPECTED CONSEQUENCES

Wednesday, February 6 – MD minus 109 days

THERE HAD BEEN a scream in the invisible darkness the moment the Bookseller and Paul Phillips knelt to pray the Lord's Prayer. No single prayer ever raised carries such power.[180] It acknowledges God as Father, that He resides in Heaven and that He is holy. The prayer calls for His Kingdom to come and His will to be done on earth as it is in Heaven. The forces of darkness understand the meaning of those words unlike any human for they once resided in Heaven until they were cast out due to their rebellion. Driven forcibly from Heaven and thrown down to earth, they continued to defy God's will on the earth with the battle raging on among those humans who still occupy it.[181]

The prayer acknowledges God's provision and calls for the believer to forgive as he has been forgiven. What was of greatest concern this day to Molech, Argon and the other in the forces of darkness, however, was what came next in the prayer, "Lead us not into temptation, but deliver us from the evil one." They hated those words with a vehemence greater even than the request for the Father's will be done. They hate those words because the prayer calls them what they are – evil – and it calls on the Father to deliver the one who prayed. Those words always reminded the forces of darkness that God remained sovereign and nothing they had planned could come to pass unless He allowed it.

Curses and cries arose throughout the invisible realms as the forces of darkness stopped to see if their Holy Enemy would answer and how. As the final declaration of God's Kingdom, power and glory were raised by the two kneeling men, Molech screamed instructions to Keepers and Tempters and others to awaken them to their assigned duties. The forces of darkness moved with desperate haste to consummate the executions.

As the two men stood, Paul asked, "Mr. White why is it necessary to kneel when you pray?"

"It is not necessary, Paul," the Bookseller replied. "Jesus sometimes prayed standing with His eyes lifted to Heaven,[182] but there are times when I kneel simply to acknowledge that God is God. It is a sign of respect, forcing myself to be humble before God, remembering that it is I who serve Him, not He who serves me. Right now I feel the need of His presence and involvement more than at any time in my life so my heart demands that I kneel to show my love for Him and my submission to Him."

The desire to see all believers united in prayer, crying out to the Father even as Paul had described the great cloud of witnesses, was forefront in the Bookseller's heart and mind as he opened the door and they stepped out into the sunlight for a brisk walk to Chaplain Forrest's office. He noted some unusual activity this morning. A camera crew was directly in front of him across the street, obviously hustling to film them as they walked. This must be the ITN group that Chaplain Forrest told him about, he thought.

He saw movement behind them coming quickly from the direction of the tracks and an odd looking man running toward them from the corner across the street, waving a paper in his hand and yelling his name. There were students walking toward the campus for morning classes. It seemed chaotic.

Jim Hunt was frustrated. They were ready, but here came the Bookseller with no advance warning. Scrambling to get the best angle possible, he directed the camera crew into action. This was really difficult because of the people around him. He knew about the kid, but where did those Citizens Militia people come from? The Bookseller must have 24-hour protection because of the threats, he thought.

Demetrious saw the old man and Paul as they left the warehouse and began immediately to approach them from behind. There was nothing between him and the old man, and he saw nothing in front of them. He walked quickly to catch up without running and drawing attention. There were many more people in the area than he had expected. He saw the camera crew and students walking toward the campus on the other side of the street. Good, he thought, many would die this day with the old man and he would enter his reward having killed more infidels than he had hoped. He approached without fear, smiling.

Susan was frustrated by all the activity. It was difficult to focus and those two huge Citizens Militia representatives made aiming all the more difficult. Her eyes caught the movement of the camera crew and in an instant, she was terrified. Escape was impossible she thought until the quiet was broken by that unearthly sound which was directing her this day. "Kill the boy now and then the old man." She aimed carefully over the shoulder of one of the red-jacketed men and fired a single shot at the head of the only young man she could see. As it struck him, his head exploded and there was instantaneously a brilliant flash of light which temporarily blinded all who were between her and the railroad tracks.

For a moment, her eyes would not focus and that voice again screamed, "Kill the old man." She looked and could see only one man sort of wandering near the curb in front of the warehouse, unable to see clearly she fired at his chest, knowing that her eyesight could not be trusted for a second head shot. He grasped his chest and fell in a pool of blood. The Citizens Militia representatives looked right at her, but did nothing and then they were gone. They vanished without a sound.

Panicked now, she carried out her plan of escape, quickly getting to the driver's seat and leaving. The silence of the hybrid in motion would leave nothing for the temporarily blind crowd to remember. She drove only three blocks, parked on the street and entered a coffee shop where she ordered a small cup of today's special and sat while the world outside awakened from sleep.

Within moments, police cars raced past the coffee shop accompanied by other emergency medical vehicles. That, she thought, was a waste of time. She knew she had hit both targets and they could not have survived. She remained surfing the internet on her laptop for an hour and then went home, confident that the angel of light would be pleased. She had obeyed and he had protected her. The world would be spared the deception of the two targets. People would never know that she had spared them from the second death.

Truth and Consequences

There was total confusion in front of the warehouse. Detective Pete Samson was trying to get a handle on what had happened and it seemed all he got was contradictory witness statements. About all people agreed on was that there were two dead bodies, the shots came from the direction of the campus and no one could see the shooter because everyone had been temporarily blinded by a great flash of light.

Addressing the questions to Jim Hunt and his crew, Detective Samson asked, "All right, let's go through this one more time. The Samuel White and Paul Phillips came out of the warehouse. They walked to the sidewalk and turned to head in the direction of the campus. What happened then?"

"As they came out of the building, they were joined by two enormous members of the Citizens Militia, red jackets and all," answered Producer Hunt. "They seemed to just appear out of nowhere. They walked in front of them as they headed toward the campus. I saw a man running across the street yelling the Bookseller's name. A shot rang out and it was as if the sun itself exploded and I couldn't see. I went to the ground as carefully as I could to lay flat on the sidewalk to avoid being hit. Another shot rang out and I heard nothing except the ghastly sound of someone moaning as they fell to the ground hard.

"As soon as I began to be able to see, I turned and looked in the direction the shots came from and saw nothing of the shooter. The street was empty except for people obviously blinded even as we had been. There were others running toward the sound of the shots from the campus. They must have not been present when the shots were fired because they could see. I grabbed my cell phone and called 911. Only then did I see the carnage across the street. They were obviously dead. There was nothing more I could do for them."

"Where were the members of the Citizens Militia?" Detective Samson asked. "Did they return fire at the shooter or pursue him?"

"They were gone," Hunt answered. "I know that makes no sense, but it is true. I saw them there when the first shot was fired and when my eyesight returned after the second shot they were gone. Ask Phil and Roy, my camera crew. They were here with me. We were trying to get some video of the Bookseller to use tonight in the special on Williams. They saw the same thing I did."

"Wait a minute. Did you say a camera crew? Did you film any of this," Samson asked excitedly.

"I don't know what we got, but we were filming through the whole event," Phil responded. "I left the camera running even when I couldn't see and fell to the ground. We are trained to never turn off the camera in a firefight and that is what this seemed like for the moment."

"I want to see the film right now," Samson demanded.

Phil and Roy set up the video in the van and they watched in confusion. "This cannot be right," Hunt declared even as the film continued. "Where are the Citizens Militia people? I saw them. I'm not crazy. You two, didn't you see them?"

"Absolutely," Phil responded. "I saw them through the viewer as I was filming. There were two men in red jackets walking in front of the Bookseller and the young man. They were there."

"Well," Samson answered, "they are not on the film and the Bookseller and Paul Phillips said they didn't see anyone in front of them. This is a great story. Here we have one dead young Arab male, obviously a terrorist, complete with an explosive vest – and a dead process server. A camera crew from a national network says that the Bookseller and his young friend were protected by two enormous members of the Citizens Militia, but the video taken during the event doesn't show them. The video shows Mr. White and Paul Phillips walking directly toward the shooter completely vulnerable. The shooter doesn't shoot them but shoots a terrorist seemingly sent to kill them and a process server seeking to serve a congressional subpoena. What is this, the shooter is now the protector?"

Barnabas smiled as he watched from above, amazed again at how the Father could take what was intended for evil and use it for good. It had been instantaneous, but then it is always instantaneous. The Spirit's instruction had been heard and obeyed. Simeon and Apollos, Guardians for Paul and the Bookseller, were transformed into the appearance of members of the Citizens Militia, able to be seen only by the shooter and the television crew. The explosion of light had been Barnabas' assignment. After the second shot the Guardians vanished from human sight, their immediate purpose accomplished.

In a combination of anger and terror, Molech gasped at what he had seen played out before him. The Dark Master's personal instruction for the effort to kill the Bookseller had been undertaken, and it had failed. The Enemy had won a clear victory and in the process, the larger plan had been endangered. The shooter was still out there and the whole failure would saturate the airwaves leading up to the ITN special to be broadcast tonight. The Bookseller would again have a worldwide audience to speak for the Enemy. It was a total disaster. Someone would suffer the wrath of the Dark Master.

Scrambling for survival, Molech grabbed Argon by the throat screaming, "You fool. It's you – you caused this disaster by picking that Demetrius character. Had he performed, they would all be dead, but what you did was get him killed and allow the shooter to escape. I would kill you if I could. I can't, but I can do this," and throwing him to the ground and putting his finger in Argon's face, Molech yelled with an unearthly screech, "You, Argon, are demoted to messenger," and with that, Argon's body shrank seemingly into itself, becoming a mere dark wisp-like the multitudes around them. Molech left to appear before the Dark Master to explain Argon's failure.

The President Hears

Word spread quickly in both public and governmental circles, the Williams shooter had struck again. This time, there were two victims, one an apparent terrorist attempting to kill the Bookseller, the other a private process server in the wrong place at the wrong time. Reactions were predictably contradictory.

Troy Steed, the national security advisor, broke in on the president and Tom Knight as they were working on the draft statement seeking citizen involvement. "There has been another shooting in Williams. A terrorist wearing an explosive device was killed as he was apparently attempting to kill the old man who closed the press conference last week. Could this be the Williams' attack described in the message Barnes found on the FS2.com website?"

"No way," the president responded. "The threat we have been preparing to encounter is not simply an attempt to kill the old man. That had to be either the act of a rogue, like those killed execution style recently or a domestic cell which couldn't stomach what he said and wanted to strike fear in the hearts of others who dare to publicly oppose their beliefs."

Pausing to consider what this might mean, the president added, "You know, that is a big difference between the Christian faith and the radical Muslims and what makes them so dangerous. A Christian may try to persuade you to believe as they do, but they don't threaten to kill you if you disagree. They may call your conduct a sin, but they don't cut off your hand or arm or even your head if you live in ways they consider to be wrong or publicly oppose them. They don't seek to advance their religion by fear."

"Some might disagree with that assessment and remind you of the Crusades and other atrocities committed in the name of Jesus over the centuries," Steed commented.

"Yes, without a doubt over the centuries some have brutally killed unbelievers in the name of Jesus, but there is a difference," the president responded. "Nothing in what Jesus said or taught encourages or commands that behavior. Those who have acted that way do so in direct disobedience of the teachings and life of Jesus. No so for those following the teachings of the Muslim book. It forms the basis for the actions of the radicals. They are arguably commanded to kill unbelievers who will not submit to their religion."[183]

"I am thankful that they didn't kill the Bookseller. He is unafraid to speak what the Bible teaches in love to both Christians and non-Christians alike. We need his voice out there to balance radicals on all sides. I understand he is to be interviewed on the ITN special tonight. I for one will be watching to see what he says about this."

"Yes, me too, I will be watching, but in the meantime, we have a draft statement to finish and deliver," Tom Knight interrupted. "We need to add information regarding the additional dead terrorist in Williams. It is not a good sign that they have been able to bring explosive vests into the country. This threat is only becoming more real."

"Troy," the president instructed, "find out all the additional detail on the attack from the state authorities you can, but don't change the deployment plans. We need to be ready for what's next in Williams."

"Yes, Mr. President," Steed responded as he left to obey.

Panic in Cambridge

Abdul Farsi's had just completed his qualification training for the Citizen's Militia and was walking from the police firing range when his cell phone rang. He did not recognize the number, but he knew the area code – 617. That is where the plan had been initiated some five years ago. As soon as he was sure no one was close enough to overhear, he answered, "Farsi here, who is this?"

He recognized the voice immediately. It was Demas Assad, the stateside leader of MD. "Farsi what the hell is going on there? You are not authorized to launch random attacks. The whole plan is at risk because of the foolish attempt to kill the old man."

"I don't know what you are talking about. Why are you of all people calling me? What old man and what attack?" Farsi responded in confusion.

"That fool who interrupted the press conference last week in Williams. Someone described as a terrorist tried to kill him and only got himself killed by the shooter. It is absolutely insane. He was shot in the head so no one will ever know who he was, but he had an explosive vest which tells the authorities we have them in the country. This is going to make everything harder and more risky."

"Slow down," Farsi said. "I will investigate and get back to you via the website. We can't risk cell phone communication. Please don't call me again unless it is an absolute emergency."

"This is an emergency," Assad answered. "If we cannot control our people, we are going to have to move MD up or drop the plan altogether."

"Be realistic Demas," Farsi responded. "It is hard to keep hate in a bottle. You knew that when you joined in a massive effort to cripple the United States. This is not about nineteen people hijacking airplanes; this is about a thousand operatives in a coordinated series of night attacks and other thousands in killing squads. We can still move enough new people in before the attacks to replace those we lose, particularly if that North

American Union proposal is forced through. In that case, we can move them up from Mexico in a day. Tell Phygelus we are still on for Sunday. We will see how they defend against real terrorism in their backyard."

The World and the Majority Party Respond

In Africa, Asia and elsewhere around the world where believers had begun to gather together to pray for America, there was great rejoicing at God's miraculous provision in protecting the Bookseller. There was also a sense of anticipation of the ITN broadcast which would be shown worldwide. They wanted more details on what really happened in Williams, but most of all they wanted to hear what God would say through the Bookseller.

In Tehran, the flag was up, but Ittai and Hushai had agreed to wait until after the ITN broadcast to meet. There was a sense of excitement and foreboding over developments in Iran and Russia. Israel must be warned soon.

Ittai carried with him the Bookseller's answer, "My brothers – we will stand with you and pray, calling on all believers to join together and pray. Do not be afraid. Remember Hebrews 4:13. God is faithful." He had looked up Hebrews 4:13 and was greatly encourage at what he perceived to be the message. It read, "Nothing in all creation is hidden from God's sight. Everything is uncovered and laid bare before the eyes of Him to whom we must give account." God knows and remains sovereign. There is hope. He will reveal truth.

In Washington, Chairman Crow was livid. "This is a disaster. Now that a terrorist has tried to kill the old man, the whole country will watch his interview tonight. They are saying on the news that he was protected by angels, invisible to all but the killer and a few others. What are we going to do with this?"

"I tell you exactly what we are going to do," former President Cox replied with particular coldness in his voice. "We are going to monitor what the old man says to find what we can use to our advantage. Then we are going to go public with a spin on this that argues for immediate implementation of the Together Tomorrow agenda as the necessary tool to confront terrorism. We will take a negative and make it a positive. That is the essence of politics. Remember, this is not about facts but the perception of what those facts mean. We can use this. We just have to be careful and smart."

THE CURTAIN

CHOICES

BOOK II

DAVID T. MADDOX

CHAPTER 1

THE ANNOUNCEMENT – THE RESPONSE

Wednesday, February 6 – MD minus 109 days

I T HAD BEEN over a decade since there had been a sense of holy awe in the chaplain's office on the Williams College campus, but the presence of the Lord was very real to the four men as they shared and prayed together there this day. The events of the past few hours only made them more passionate to obey the four-word command given by Gabriel to their Iranian brothers, "Stand together and pray."

"I sent a message back to them acknowledging God's command and hoping to encourage them in their search. I told them we would stand with them and pray and call on all believers to join together and pray." Looking around the room and knowing that Chaplain Forrest contacted all the pastors of true churches in Williams, the Bookseller observed, "It is clear that message hasn't yet been received by the local church leadership."

"Today may change that and you will have an opportunity to obey the command tonight when you are interviewed for the ITN special," Chaplain Forrest commented. "Pastor Wilson's church is meeting to pray tonight. Not all the leaders have closed ears."

"Yes," responded Pastor Wilson, "and I contacted the archbishops in Rwanda and East Asia and they have issued a call to prayer for the churches affiliated with the Anglican Mission in America. They also issued a call to pray for America to their churches in Africa and East Asia. Much faithful prayer is being raised around the world, but sadly little here in America, the subject of that prayer."

"Chaplain Forrest, would you be willing to open the chapel over the noon hour and at night for prayer? I would be willing to join with others to lead prayer for our nation," Paul Phillips suggested even surprising himself. "Perhaps other students would join with believers in the community and pray together."

Turning to the Bookseller, Paul asked, "Mr. White, maybe you could come the first evening and share and answer questions. After what happened today, people would come to hear. Maybe you could even say something about it in your interview tonight and we could start tomorrow."

"Yes, yes, yes!" Chaplain Forrest responded with enthusiasm. "The chapel will finally become a house of prayer as Jesus said the church would be."[184]

"This is important," the Bookseller interrupted. "Do you see what God is doing? The formal leadership of the local church has not responded to God's call, so He is going beyond them to find others with a heart to obey Him now. That has always been God's way. If those called to lead will not lead His people as He commands, He will first give them a chance to repent and obey, and if they refuse, He calls others. God's plan waits for no man or institution and is dependent on none. His will be done."

There was silence as those present considered the words spoken by the Bookseller. The message seemed clear that they must go beyond formal church leadership and perhaps into homes to reach believers led to pray by the Holy Spirit, the light inside of them.

"You are right, Mr. White," Pastor Wilson said breaking the silence. "Remember, Jesus told the parable of the tenants against the religious leaders of His day that refused to walk in obedience. His closing statement to them has always been a cold warning I have never forgotten. He said, 'I tell you that the kingdom of God will be taken away from you and given to a people who will produce its fruit.'[185] I fear we may be there or getting close in America. That is part of the reason for the Anglican Mission in America."

"Don't forget Jesus crying over the city of Jerusalem," Chaplain Forrest added. "In seventy years the whole city and nation would be crushed by the Romans 'because,' Jesus said, 'you did not recognize the time of God's coming to you.'[186] Clearly, God has come with His message and we must respond or expect no better from the terrorists than Israel suffered at the hands of the Romans in 70 AD."

"I do not know whether the formal leadership can be awakened," the Bookseller answered with a deep sadness and concern in his eyes. "Only God knows, but the command is to call all believers to join together and pray. All we can do is obey, pray and appealing to the leaders to lead in prayer. The rest is in God's hands."

The President Speaks to the Nation

Tom Knight stepped to the podium to make the formal introduction, "Ladies and gentlemen, the President of the United States." Those in the press room at the White House stood and became quiet as President Strong approached the microphones.

"Thank you, ladies and gentlemen; please be seated."

"My fellow Americans, I have asked the networks for time this morning to bring a report on recent events which concern all of us and to ask for your help. Earlier this week we were awakened with reports from seven cities of the discovery of seven young Arab men who had been killed, their bodies discovered in dumpsters. As you have heard in the news reports, these seven men carried no identification and the forensic studies here and abroad have revealed nothing to date about their identities or country of origin. They are non-persons who arrived unknown and have died unknown, here illegally for an unknown purpose."

"This morning in Williams, Illinois another unidentified young Arab man was killed as he attempted to detonate an explosive vest. Again the body carried no identification and forensic evidence has thus far given no information on his identity or country of origin. Thus, we have another non-person who arrived unknown and died unknown."

"It is important that we all face, without alarm or fear, the reality that some group is seeking to infiltrate our nation with non-persons and equipment that can be used in some form of terrorist attacks.

"The full resources of this government are being employed worldwide to find and eliminate this threat. While I cannot discuss the specifics of what is being done, as our enemies monitor our broadcast communications even as we seek to monitor theirs, but I can assure you the effort is as complete as possible. Your government cannot, however, succeed without your help and without Congress addressing border security immediately. We need the eyes and ears of every American watching their neighborhoods, workplaces and cities to advise law enforcement and Homeland Security of any unusual activity or the presence of any unusual person. We are not on a 'witch hunt' against people of Arab nationality or any other national group or religion, for terrorists are not limited to any nationality and we know that all Muslims are not terrorists. We do, however, need to all to join together to stand against those who seek to do us harm in our own nation, and we need to close the open door on our border.

"We are obviously concerned, but not alarmed. We know that if we come together as Americans, we can protect one another and make it impossible for non-persons with evil intentions to walk freely among us, seeking to do us harm. Please take these efforts seriously as your duty to your fellow citizens."

He paused, sighed and then continued in a quieter voice, "Unfortunately, we must expect that a day may come when somewhere in the United States, an attack will be launched, perhaps several or even many. We will be prepared to respond, and if we work together, most threats can be eliminated. But it would be dishonest to tell you that we can prevent every killer sent to the US from carrying out a hate-filled mission.

"Last weekend an old man in Williams, Illinois stepped up to a microphone at the end of a press conference and asked that believers in America pray together for God's deliverance and for the wisdom to understand why God has allowed the terrorist threat to happen. This old man was a target of the terrorist killed this morning in Williams. They obviously didn't like what he said and sought to silence him by killing him. That is their way. It is not ours.

"I would like to close this morning by modifying what Mr. White said and ask all Americans to join with me in prayer for God's wisdom and deliverance from this threat. Thank you."

He took no questions as he walked soberly back to the Oval Office.

An Unexpected Reaction

The White House press corps was stunned. There was something about the way the president had spoken with frankness and honesty that traversed politics and agendas. Here was the leader of the free world, standing before his people humbly and honestly seeking their help in facing a common danger. The mood changed instantly and the desire to criticize was replaced with a desire to be a part of this effort to encourage the people to stand together against an unknown threat. Their reports and commentary began to reflect the changed attitude.

In New York, George Murphy, a reporter at the *Times Daily* began to reconsider the leak from Commissioner Matthews regarding Press Secretary Knight's secret work at a presidential commission. Something was obviously going on within the government to address what the president considered to be a very real threat. This morning's statement was part of a much larger effort of some nature. There was a story there to be mined.

The networks scrambled to determine how to deal with the new candor about a possible threat. At ITN, work on tonight's production continued to change as the news required shift after shift in focus. There was now unconfirmed word of a military deployment of some nature to the Chicago area. How did all this fit into the reality of a shooter still at large and another dead terrorist? Why had they targeted the Bookseller and why would the shooter protect him?

Around the country, law enforcement organized to receive and process thousands of phone calls that began to be made shortly after the president concluded his statement. People who had seen things that troubled them finally had permission to step forward and share their concerns with the authorities. Most of the initial calls seemed insignificant, but all were cataloged, briefed and forwarded to Homeland Security for analysis even as they were being investigated at the point of origin.

As reports on the president's statement were combined with local announcements by other political leaders to join together in this effort, citizens began to think back over things they had seen and wondered about previously. In Carmen, Arizona teenager Juan Martinez decided to change his way to school back so that he would ride his bike in front of the old Craig place and see what was going on with the over the road trucks from Mexico. Retired truck driver Sam Will, who headed the Citizen's Militia in Williams, decided to follow up on stories he was hearing from some of his old trucking buddies about an operation called Brother's Trucking. Even Chaplain Forrest was rethinking what he had seen of the car with the strange moving license plate before the shooting in front of the warehouse. He had been wondering why the car did not show up on the ITN video taken of the shooting.

The call for prayer had not gone unnoticed here or in the invisible realm. It reinforced what the Spirit had been saying to those with the light inside and created a sense of need among many who remained under the influence of the forces of darkness. The battle was joined as God enabled the blind to see and the deaf to hear and become searchers. Keepers and Guardians waged war over every soul as God called many to Himself. All who watched had seen the president admit he needed God's help. If he did, then perhaps they did too.

The president's statement had reinforced the importance of the coming Security Fair in Williams. For some unknown reason, their little town was center stage before all of America. The ITN commitment to continue the series they were doing, combined with the reality of the attempt on the Bookseller's life by a terrorist, made the threat real in this place. Officer Sally Johnson had been advised of the raised terror threat in Williams and she had been planning how to incorporate the Citizens Militia into the police deployment without telling them of the threat. She understood why that information needed to be kept confidential within law enforcement, but it was hard for her personally to withhold that information from Tom Campy, whom she had come to like and trust.

A Different Response

The reaction to the president's statement was not universally favorable. In the Senate majority leader's office, the legendary temper of former President Cox once again erupted and he threw a book through the television screen, accompanied by a stream of profanities as he stomped around the room like a spoiled child throwing a tantrum. The field had been taken from them in a moment. They would have to completely reorganize the effort and redirect it to counteract the president.

"That man is impossible and worse of all, he believes that garbage," the former president screamed, continuing his rant.

"Calm down, Leonard," Majority Leader Howard interrupted. "Remember your own advice. All we have to do is turn the perception and join in the fight against terrorism. We make the Together Tomorrow agenda the way to fight terrorism and he has to join us. When we met with him, he warned us not to ignore the terrorist threat. He knows something is going on and we need to take advantage of that and take the initiative away from him. Rather than following him, let's lead. He has admitted he doesn't have the answer and needs God to tell him what to do. Let's provide the answer and the American people will follow us and ignore his 'God language.' A president is supposed to have the answer. He has shown weakness. We need to take advantage."

"What specifically are you thinking?" Cox asked.

"Let's call our own press conference and not only make a statement but also, let's take questions and appear open. Let's acknowledge the president's call for citizen involvement and offer congressional cooperation in the effort to confront the threat. Remember George Murphy's article in the *Times Daily* regarding the press secretary's involvement in some secret presidential commission? Let's call Tom Knight to appear along with others from the intelligence community before the Senate Intelligence Committee in closed session to report on the crisis. We can find out what is going on and arrange a few convenient leaks as needed to take the initiative away from the president."

"Well, if we are going to take him on, let's take him on," Chairman Crow added. This is the opportunity we have needed to present the agenda as an antiterrorism package. None of us believe fighting terrorism does anything other than create more terrorists, but we can pitch this as self-defense on the homeland which even the peace movement would have to agree with. We can blame the current policy for creating the problem and we will have the answer the president doesn't seem capable of providing. That will make him a lame duck even in his own party."

"You are absolutely right!" Cox said excitedly. "Sorry, it's hard to be on the outside when a couple of years ago his office was my office. I resent this mouse of a president and his calls for prayer. That bunch wraps themselves in religion, claiming a divine right to lead. We have got to get religion completely off the public stage. We have made a lot of progress, but the job is far from complete. The cry must remain, 'Freedom from religion!'"

"It's not that difficult," Majority Leader Howard added. "At the press conference, we present a quick fix for the threat. First, the North American Union as a way to have unified control over the whole continent on matters of security, beginning with control of the roads by controlling the issuance of driver's licenses. We can sell that as an anti-terrorism tool and as a way to fight the importation of drugs and illegals. We also sell it as the way to greater economic security for Americans. We can open the roads, relying on Mexico and Canada to regulate licenses before the North American Union develops its own regulations as a first step. That would enable us to meet the Together Tomorrow timetable and open the way to the political money tree."

"The other major thing would be to deal with religion. We have to be smart and present it as a way to fight terrorism without disclosing how it would affect any religion other than radical Islam. The amendment to the Hate Crimes Act is an easy sell if we present it as a definition of terrorism and a way to control the hate speech by the Mullahs. The terrorists have made hate and violence a religious act. To encourage terrorism by sermons is the same as running a recruitment campaign for suicide bombers. What we stay away from is talking about the consequences that would overflow to other religions. If we are successful, we can take religion off the public stage as the invisible policeman and stop its interference, allowing people to make their own choices without condemnation. That, after all, is the definition of freedom – the right to do what you want as long as you don't hurt someone else."

"Agreed, but we need to do this quickly. What about the subpoena on the old man?" asked Chairman Crow.

"Simple. Let's use the press conference as an opportunity to mourn the loss of the innocent process server and ask that the old man appears voluntarily. He would look really bad if he refused. It would take some work and we would have to be careful, but I bet we can organize a show before your committee that would be nationally televised and would make the case to the public for controlling all forms of radical religion."

"Sounds to me like a winning formula," the former president added with glee. "How soon can you take this production public?"

"I will schedule it for noon tomorrow. I want to see what comes of the ITN Williams' special before we go public and, by the way, Mr. Former President, tell that Together Tomorrow crowd that they owe me a new television set."

"Done," Cox said laughing. "It will be here in time to watch the show tonight."

"Hold up just a minute, please," said House Majority Whip Eric Besserman, "I have sat here quietly and listened to the discussion. I have been considering the North American Union proposal and the strategy to negate religion as a political force, but there are still some questions no one has bothered to answer. Who or what is behind this Together Tomorrow group and why the 'emergency' push to open the roads in such a hurry?"

"You sound like Strong," Cox angrily responded.

"Perhaps, but these are legitimate questions that someone is going to ask and I want to know before I support this effort. Where is the money coming from?"

"Together Tomorrow is a PAC organized by two naturalized Saudis," Cox responded. "I don't know or care where the money comes from, but assume it is tied to Saudi princes or relations tied to the ruling family. I don't know for sure."

"Why would the Saudi's want to put money into opening the roads to Mexico and why now?" asked Besserman.

"I don't know why, but their money follows their interests so it has to be for their own purposes. I understand they own some trucking companies in the States and in Mexico. What difference does it make if it doesn't hurt us? This is politics and we all have supported efforts we considered foolish to keep some group or money source on board. It is the nature of the beast," Cox answered.

"What about the timing issue? What's the hurry?" Besserman continued.

"I don't understand the timing issue either," Cox responded. "All I know is that if we don't have at least the open roads piece in place by Memorial Day, the money goes away. Look, Eric, you have a tough race coming up and you need their support."

"I just don't know about this one," Besserman responded. "I may have to step aside and let someone else carry it. I am not comfortable right now. For me, it doesn't pass the smell test and I don't like the backdoor attack on religion. I know it's not popular, but religion is a real part of my life and I am kind of partial to having a standard out there beyond any of us as the guide."

The long silence was finally broken by Majority Leader Howard. "Eric, think about it. This could be a problem for you. It could cost you your position in the leadership."

"I will think about it," he answered. "You can have my resignation as majority whip any time," and with that, he left and the mood turned somber.

ENDNOTES

1. Footnotes are included which reference from where in the Bible a statement, concept or example is drawn to provide the reader with an avenue to further study the ideas and theology presented in the book.

2. John 14:1-3

3. 2 Corinthians 4:4; 1 Corinthians 2:14

4. 2 Corinthians 4:6

5. 2 Corinthians 1:21-22

6. Genesis 2:1-7

7. Matthew 4:3

8. Matthew 26:41; 1 Thessalonians 3:5

9. Galatians 5:19-21

10. Luke 22:31-32

11. Matthew 4:1-17, Hebrews 4:14-16

12. Matthew 5:21-22 and 27-28

13. 1 Corinthians 10:13

14. Galatians 5:22-23

15. 1 Samuel 15:2-3

16. Psalm 139:7-8

17. Revelation 1:17-18, Job 2:6

18. 1 Timothy 2:3-4

19. Acts 9:1-20

20. 2 Samuel 11:1- 12:23

21. Genesis 12:1-8

22. Genesis 17:5

23. Deuteronomy 7:6

24. John 11:47-53

25. Revelation 12:7-9, 12

26. Matthew 17:14-18

27. Ephesians 6:12

28. Mark 5:1-13

29. John 16:8

30. John 6:44

31. Galatians 5:19-21; Revelation 21:8

32. James 1:5-8

33. 2 Corinthians 4:18, Ephesians 6:12

34. Ephesians 6:12

35. John 3:19-21

36. Matthew 23:1-33

37. 1 Peter 4:17; Revelation 2 and 3

38. Jeremiah 32:35

39. 1 Corinthians 2:14

40. John 8:44

41. Revelation 4:1-2

42. Matthew 13:58

43. Matthew 13:18-19

44. 2 Peter 3:9

45. Luke 23:39-43

46. Ephesians 3:20

47. 2 Peter 3:9

48. Luke 23:40-43

49. John 8:2-11

50. Revelation 20:11-15, Matthew 13:32

51. Revelations 20:6,14

52. 2 Timothy 3:16; 2 Peter 1:21

53. Matthew 3:8

54. 2 Corinthians 12:7-10

55. John 6:44

56. 2 Corinthians 4:3-4

57. John 6:65

58. 2 Kings 6:15-17; Daniel 7 and 8; Luke 9:28-36; Revelation 1, 4-22

59. 2 Kings 6:17

60. Revelation 20:6,14; 21:8

61. John 10:10

62. Revelation 20:10

63. Daniel 10:18-21

64. Hebrews 4:13

65. John 16:13

66. Acts 27:21-26

67. 1 Corinthians 2:14

68. 2 Corinthians 11:14-15

69. Daniel 10:12

70. Daniel 10:13-14

71. Luke 18:1-8

72. Ephesians 6:11-18

73.   Job 1:6-12; 2:1-6

74.   Job 42:10

75.   Job 42:7-8

76.   Luke 4:5-7

77.   Isaiah 14:12-17; Ezekiel 28:11-17; Revelation 12:7-9;

78.   Ephesians 6:17; Hebrews 12:12

79.   Daniel 10:11-14

80.   Daniel 10:12-14

81.   John 3:18

82.   Luke 19:41-44

83.   Isaiah 14:12-17; Ezekiel 28:11-17; Revelation 12:7-9

84.   Matthew 25:41

85.   Ephesians 1:7

86.   Genesis 9:12-13

87.   1 John 4:8

88.   Luke 9:1-6; 10:17-20

89.   Matthew 8:29

90.   Matthew 28:18

91.   Matthew 6:13

92.   James 4:7

93.   Matthew 7:1-5

94.   John 10:27-30

95.   2 Peter 3:9

96.   Acts 8:1-3; Acts 9:1-20

97.   Luke 6:8

98.   Matthew 27:69-75

99.   John 8:12

100. John 3:19-20

101. John 16:8

102. John 16:13

103. John 6:44, 65

104. Acts 4:24

105. Matthew 5:9

106. Matthew 7:1-2

107. 1 John 4:8

108. Luke 13:1-5

109. Matthew 6:13

110. James 1:5

111. Acts 4:24-28

112. Deuteronomy 1:42-45

113. Revelation 12:7-9; Isaiah 14:12-17; Ezekiel 28:11-17

114. Ezekiel 22:30-31;

115. Matthew 27:3-5

116. Acts 19:23-31

117. Revelation 1:17-18

118. Matthew 18:20

119. Revelation 13

120. Ezekiel 18:31-32; 33:11

121. Matthew 14:15-21

122. Matthew 8:16; Mark 1:39

123. Luke 8:26-33

124. James 4:7

125. 2 Corinthians 4:3-4

126. Matthew 16:13-15; John 16:13

127. John 14:26

128. Romans 8:9; 1 Corinthians 3:16; 2 Corinthians 1:21-22; 1 John 4:13

129. Luke 9:23

130. John 8:12

131. 1 Timothy 2:4

132. 2 Peter 3:9

133. Luke 19:41-44

134. Matthew 23:13-15

135. 1 Corinthians 16:22

136. Matthew 23:15

137. Galatians 1:8

138. John 3:3

139. John 3:3

140. Ezekiel 36:26-27

141. 2 Corinthians 5:17

142. Luke 23:42

143. Luke 23:40-43

144. Jeremiah 29:13

145. Matthew 7:7

146. Romans 8:16

147. Job 1:10

148. Deuteronorny 28:15; Isaiah 63:10

149. Romans 10:9-10

150. Daniel 9:20-23

151. Luke 1:19

152. Luke 2:15-17

153. 2 Corinthians 5:17

154. John 3:3,5

155. 2 Chronicles 20:12

156. The Tet Offensive was a series of surprise attacks by rebel forces sponsored by

North Vietnam and North Vietnamese forces, on scores of cities, towns, and hamlets simultaneously throughout South Vietnam beginning in January of 1968. It was the turning point in the Vietnam War as the American public came to believe that the war was lost and demanded that it be ended and President Johnson not be reelected. Later that year he declined to run and the emphasis shifted to a negotiated peace to end the war.

157. John 3:20

158. John 15:7

159. 2 Corinthians 4:18; Ephesians 6:12

160. Matthew 28:18; John 13:3; John 19:11; Ephesians 3:20

161. Acts 27:23-26, 30-32

162. Luke 1:8-17, 26-37

163. Matthew 26:41

164. Luke 19:41-44

165. Hebrews 12:1

166. Matthew 17:1-8

167. Judges 13:1

168. Deuteronomy 28:15-68

169. Genesis 41:1-36

170. Genesis 30:19-21

171. Acts 16:31; 2 Corinthians 4:5

172. Acts 3:15; Acts 4:12

173. Isaiah 53:5-6; Revelation 5:8-10

174. Matthew 4:17

175. Hebrews 8:10-12; Ezekiel 36:26-27

176. John 14:15, 21 & 23

177. Romans 10:9

178. Matthew 6:9-13

179. Revelation 2:23

180. Matthew 5:9-13

181. Revelation 12:7-9

182. John 11:41-42

183. "Slay them wherever ye find them and drive them out of the places whence they drove you out, for persecution is worse than slaughter" (Sura 2:191); "O Prophet! Make war on the unbelievers and the hypocrites. Be harsh with them. Their ultimate abode is hell, a hapless journey's end" (Sura 9:73); Ye who believe! Murder those of the disbelievers" (different translation of Sura 9:123).

184. Mark 11:15-17

185. Matthew 21:33-44

186. Luke 19:41-44